THE NEW YORKERS

SARAH CRICHTON BOOKS   *Farrar, Straus and Giroux* ■ *New York*

The New Yorkers

CATHLEEN SCHINE

WITH DRAWINGS BY LEANNE SHAPTON

Sarah Crichton Books
Farrar, Straus and Giroux
19 Union Square West, New York 10003

Library of Congress Cataloging-in-Publication Data
Schine, Cathleen.
    The New Yorkers / Cathleen Schine.—1st ed.
        p.   cm.
    "Sarah Crichton Books."
    ISBN-13: 978-0-374-22183-6 (hardcover : alk. paper)
    ISBN-10: 0-374-22183-9 (hardcover : alk. paper)
    1. Dog walking—Fiction.   2. Manhattan (New York, N.Y.)—Fiction.
I. Title.

PS3569.C497N49   2007
813'.54—dc22

                                                        2006032711

Designed by Abby Kagan

www.fsgbooks.com

1   3   5   7   9   10   8   6   4   2

This book is dedicated

to the memory of

Buster

who in eighteen months taught me more about the city

than I had discovered in thirty years

and to

Janet

who loved him

too

contents

	Prologue	*3*
one	*"I live here! I live here!"*	*5*
two	*"Everything looks different today"*	*17*
three	*À Deux*	*29*
four	*"George! Wake up!"*	*47*
five	*A Gentleman*	*59*
six	*"The Flowers That Bloom in the Spring"*	*71*
seven	*The Chick Magnet*	*81*
eight	*"Do you ever buy flowers?"*	*91*
nine	*Heat*	*103*

CONTENTS

ten	*This Is Longing*	*117*
eleven	*A Blind Date*	*125*
twelve	*"Someone who would be right for you"*	*139*
thirteen	*"No regrets!"*	*149*
fourteen	*Was She in Love?*	*171*
fifteen	*"Just for a little while"*	*183*
sixteen	*The Happy Couple*	*193*
seventeen	*"It's urgent!"*	*199*
eighteen	*"Just my luck"*	*211*
nineteen	*"He bites"*	*221*
twenty	*"But what I really meant was love"*	*227*
twenty-one	*"We have to talk"*	*241*
twenty-two	*The Spinster*	*251*
twenty-three	*He Had Come for the Dogs*	*261*
twenty-four	*Thanksgiving*	*269*
twenty-five	*"I don't just mean the dog"*	*281*
	Epilogue	*289*

THE NEW YORKERS

Prologue

It's been some years since I lived on the street that figures in this story. It was never one of New York City's fashionable blocks. There are no mansions there, no narrow houses of historical importance, no plaques attesting to former residents of consequence. It was not even a particularly beautiful block. The apartment buildings, though old, were architecturally indifferent. Commercial ventures existed side by side with the street's residents. The brownstones that lined the street were mostly broken up into apartments, and most of those apartments were rentals. It was in this way, the way of the rent-controlled apartment, that the street had largely escaped the sweep of gentrification taking place all around it. Struggling musicians and actors and secretaries and window washers could still afford to live there, and they still did, some of them growing successful, some simply growing old. A government-subsidized senior residence that held AA meetings every Thursday night added to the slightly raffish nature of the place, as did the two churches in the doorway of each of which could be found its nightly resident homeless person: an enormous but orderly bearded man at the Lutheran church, a disoriented woman on the steps of the Catholic church. A bar at one end contributed to a sparse but constant supply of beer bottles on the sidewalk. The street's proximity to Central Park made it a favorite with professional dog walkers who could hardly be expected to keep track of the waste of the seven or eight dogs pulling them forward. And so the street, not distinguished by great beauty to begin with, was not terribly clean either. And yet, it was the loveliest street I have ever lived on. And the most interesting.

one

"I live here! I live here!"

We'll begin our story with Jody. She had lived on the block in her studio apartment since college, a luxurious accommodation at the time, certainly when compared to the dorm room she was leaving. After twenty years, the one room no longer struck her as luxurious, but the morning light was still lovely, the stabilized rent remained artificially low, and the large room with its beautiful bay window, high ceiling, and molding in the shape of twisted rope continued to be her home.

In the back of the room there was a step up into a doll-size kitchen, and behind that another step led to the bathroom. Jody had recently painted the apartment herself—a soft yellow color called Nigerian Peony. The moldings and the ceiling, of which she was particularly proud, were white and glossy. Whenever the room glowed in the sunlight from the big bay window, Jody congratulated herself on the serenity of her well-ordered existence, reassured that the weekends spent atop a tall ladder had been worth the effort. She kept the ladder in the linen closet with her expensive and carefully folded sheets. Jody was frugal in general, buying her clothes at reasonably priced chain stores, but sheets were in an entirely different category. Sheets were sacrificial objects offered with fear and humility to the gods of the night. Each night, Jody stretched out beneath the smooth Egyptian cotton not as a sybarite, but as a penitent, a pilgrim, a seeker, and what she sought was sleep.

In the middle of the night on which our story begins, as in the middle of most nights, Jody lay in bed and worried. She was a cheerful person by day, almost to the point of officiousness, but at night she suffered. The fragments of her busy life loomed above her like ghosts, like the IRS, like mothers-in-law. She stared into the darkness and faced her faults and her omissions. It was a heavy darkness that surrounded her at these times, both hot and close, the breath of recrimination, and, at the same time, vast, icy, and uncaring. She tried counting, of course, and counting backward, as if she were about to undergo an operation and had just been administered the anesthetic. She tried singing, sometimes the tune of a piece she was practicing, sometimes Gilbert and Sullivan songs, a staple of her household growing up, to which she knew all the lyrics. Sometimes she would have the impulse to sing the most melodic bits loud and clear, letting her voice ring out in the dark bedroom. But she would stop herself. Even if no one was beside her, and it was usually the case that no one was beside her, the sound of her voice among the demons of her sleeplessness was jarring and ridiculous.

She would tell people at school the next day that she hadn't slept a wink. This was one of the few compensations for her insomnia: the other teachers nodded not with sympathy, exactly, but with understanding and, most important, with respect. They, too, had known sleepless nights, but they had eventually come to admit that Jody was the most sleepless of them all. It conveyed upon her a certain status that she had come almost to treasure.

Jody always smiled as she described her battle to fall asleep. Her habitual and sincere modesty fell away and she became positively smug. Perhaps she would have behaved differently if she had looked as sleepless as she was. But Jody's eyes were clear and bright and no dark circles swelled beneath them. With her short blonde hair, and dressed in crisp ironed blouses and tight-fitting pants, she was pretty in an open, sunny way. She smelled fresh and clean and moved with a soft, invigorated energy. The children loved her, she worked hard, and people were grateful to her. They turned to her when they needed assistance or counsel on the job, and though she was only thirty-nine years old and looked younger, she was referred to affectionately as "Good Old Jody."

Her colleagues respected her and they were friendly to her, but not one of them was her friend. Jody sometimes wondered if this was her fault. But then, who else's fault could it be? It's not the mailman's fault, she would remind herself. It's not the vice principal's fault. It's not even the Republicans' fault. Wherein, then, did her own fault lie? This was a mystery to Jody, one she pondered at night in bed.

Naturally, she had gotten herself a dog. She originally set out to get a cat, thinking that as she seemed to be moving headlong into eccentric spinsterhood, she should begin collecting some of its accoutrements. But when she arrived at the ASPCA, she saw an elderly dog, an oversize pit bull mix so white it was almost pink, a female, who wagged her tail with such stately pessimism that Jody took the huge beast home. She named the dog Beatrice, though she had sworn not to give her new pet a person's name, thinking it faddish and particularly pathetic for a childless woman. But the dog seemed to her to deserve a real name. Beatrice was not a youngster. The ASPCA had picked her up wandering the streets of the Bronx. Half starved and covered with ticks, she had obviously survived a harsh and difficult existence. Beatrice was a name with inherent dignity. Jody felt the old dog deserved that.

Fattened up and well groomed now, Beatrice was a noble-looking animal with enigmatic blue eyes that constantly sought out Jody's with measured determination. She moved slowly, and though she was not playful, she was amiable and particularly loved strangers, throwing her great weight at them in a joyful greeting, unaware, presumably, that such a welcome might not always be, in fact, welcome. She trusted everyone, which was a testament to her gentle nature, as no one until now had ever earned her trust. But Beatrice seemed to be above the failures of the world, and they far beneath her. She had seen a lot, she seemed to be saying, and so nothing surprised her, nothing frightened her, nothing fazed her. She was lucky to be alive, and she seemed to know it.

Jody turned on the light and looked at Beatrice sprawled on the rug beside the bed. She petted the dog's wide forehead. Beatrice's head was big and boxy, like a child's drawing of a dog's head. She seemed to grin, her mouth and jaw were so wide. Her tongue lolled out like a great pink washcloth. Then Beatrice lifted her square head and licked Jody's hand. Jody scratched the dog's ragged ears and thought, I have become an eccentric music teacher with a dog instead of an eccentric music teacher with a cat. I take brisk walks in the rain with my dog by my side instead of curling up by the electric fire with a cup of tea and my cat on my lap. Although maybe, she thought, as Beatrice heaved her pale bulk onto the bed, there's not all that much difference. And she smiled at her fate. She had gotten Beatrice eight months ago, eight months of blissful, energetic adoration and companionship on both sides. When she was lonely, she would glance at Beatrice. When she needed someone to talk to, she would talk to Beatrice. Jody felt that her life, though hardly complete by customary standards, would do very well.

Then, Jody met Everett and fell in love. This occurred just two days after the sleepless night described above. Jody, after a long week teaching small children to sing in harmony and tap wooden blocks to a 3/4 beat, had set out for a leisurely weekend walk with Beatrice. It was February and the sky was getting lighter each evening, but this particular afternoon it was snowing lightly, and the world was gray. In the park, Beatrice was as excited as a child, pushing her nose along the thin white film on the grass, rolling wildly, her muscular legs kicking the air. Amused and touched, Jody stayed even longer than usual, though it began snowing in earnest and she was wet through by the time they headed home. They waited at a red light at Columbus Avenue in the swirling wind, and it was when the light turned green and they crossed the street that Jody saw Everett. She didn't know his name. But when he smiled at her through the shroud of snow, she thought she had never seen a man so beautiful in all her life. She turned and watched him go into the corner market. He must live nearby, she thought. He's gone out to get milk. She would have stayed and waited and followed him home, but for the cold, the shame of it, and the large pit bull pulling on the leash.

I really am a spinster now, she thought—falling in love with an oblivious handsome stranger in the street. And, as if to prove it, she put on the teakettle as soon as she got home.

Everett hadn't even known it was snowing until he got outside. He pushed open the door and whirling crystals stung his eyes. A bicycle chained to a signpost was topped with pillows of snow, the handlebars, the seat, the curve of the wheels.

Everett was an ordinary-looking man, until he smiled.

Then he became handsome, beautiful even, and showy, like a big, fragrant prize-winning rose. He appeared boyish, a sullen boy but boyish nevertheless, with his somewhat round face and regular features. His hair was brown, neither dark nor light, with just the slightest touch of gray. Only when he smiled and became beautiful did people notice, as if for the first time, that his eyes were a radiant blue, that his cheeks bloomed with the pink of a child though he was fifty years old.

He hadn't smiled much recently. He was feeling down in the dumps, as his mother would have put it. He had worked hard all his life and he continued to work hard, and he was  bored. He frightened the young chemists who worked for him, and he was glad, it was a break in his boredom to watch them duck their heads and mumble their findings, their questions, even their names in tremulous confusion. When a fifty-year-old man is bored, he is said to be having a midlife crisis. Everett's girlfriend, Leslie, had pointed this out to him.

"No," Everett said. "Boredom is simply a failure of imagination."

And as soon as the words came out of his mouth, he realized they were true, that his imagination was failing, and he became not only bored but depressed.

"You need Prozac or something," Leslie said.

But Everett was already taking Prozac.

"Oh," Leslie said. "Well. A trip, then."

"I'm not going anywhere," Everett said. His tone was harsher than he meant it to be. Leslie was just trying to help, after all. But it occurred to him that though he had been dating Leslie for only a month, Leslie was one of the things he was bored with.

"This too shall pass," she said, kissing him on the cheek.

They had been walking down Central Park West. The gray evening had settled around the Museum of Natural History. The blue glow of the planetarium rested easily within the night sky, the bare trees, the nineteenth-century brick. Everett noticed the curious harmony and found it comforting.

"Yes," he'd said.

"Kind of like herpes," Leslie said. "You know? Or shingles."

Everett missed his daughter. The snow would have delighted her when she was a child. Now she would just squint into the wind and try not to slip on her way to the subway, like everybody else. Everett could feel the absence of her little hand in his. Once she left home to go to college, the apartment had become empty, and Everett and his wife, Alison, had looked at each other across their bed as if across a vast, weary wasteland. Their daughter had been baffled and furious when they divorced. She wanted to be able to come home to the home she'd always had. She didn't understand that she had taken that home away with her, forever.

Everett realized that he had not been a particularly attentive father, and so his desolation came as a surprise. He had enjoyed Emily, certainly, observed her, as if she were one of a colony of ants in a glass-sided ant farm, and gloried in her, too. She was always so busy, had so many projects and worries and schemes and demands. She was so noisy. Now his life was quiet, muffled, like the snowy street.

He stood on the corner waiting for the light to change. When it did, the blur of red becoming a blur of green, a peppy little woman and a giant dog appeared, apparitions in the silver storm. The dog stared at him through its narrow slit eyes. They walked toward each other. The dog was so white its pink skin showed through. It looked like an enormous lab rat. With slit blue eyes. Everett thought how cold the dog must be in the stinging snow. As they passed each other, the pink beast wagged her tail and pushed her face against his thigh, leaving a thin trail of slobber.

"Beatrice!" said the woman.

Everett wondered why dogs liked him. He certainly did not return the sentiment.

"It's nothing," he said, for the woman seemed truly upset. She was small and wide-eyed, rather pretty in a hurried, breathless sort of way, he thought. He forced himself to put his gloved hand on the dog's head. "It's nothing," he said again, and he smiled, first at Beatrice, the dog, then at the woman.

"Oh!" she said. She looked at him intently.

Everett walked on. What was the etiquette for a chance trail of dog slobber in a violent snowstorm? He had done his best.

He pushed through the heavy plastic curtains that protected the oranges and strawberries and apples and tulips from the cold, snowy wind and made his way into the Korean grocery. He didn't know if they were really Koreans. He supposed the ones who spoke Spanish to each other were not. He bought milk and went home, his shoes wet and white with the new, brief purity of snow. He passed the gay man who ran the corner restaurant struggling along the slippery sidewalk carrying his dogs, one under each arm. He nodded, but the man, whose name was Jimmy, he thought, or something like that, did not seem to notice him, and he felt a little let down.

When he saw the flashing red light glowing and haloed in the winter storm, he stood on the sidewalk and waited as a stretcher was wheeled awkwardly through the drifts and into the back of an ambulance. He congratulated himself on not staring at the figure bundled in blankets, respectful of someone else's tragedy. But then, in a sudden, irrational panic, he called out, "I live here! I live here!" A policeman took his arm and said, "There's been an accident. Apartment 4F." Everett thought: 4F. The disgruntled elderly man downstairs. He always carried an umbrella. Everett waited for the elevator. He noticed two cans of Fancy Feast cat food on the console in the lobby. Tenants often displayed things there that they didn't want but apparently could not bear to throw away. It enraged Everett: Was this the Salvation Army? He lived on the fifth floor but got off on the fourth and stood in front of the door of the man who always carried an umbrella.

"He's dead," a neighbor said excitedly. She was standing, in orange fuzzy slippers, with other neighbors in their Sunday afternoon disarray, as well as several police officers, outside apartment 4F. "I don't even know his name," she said. She grabbed Everett's arm. "He killed himself," she said softly.

"I don't know his name, either," Everett said after an awkward silence, and he felt guilty, as if that were why the man had killed himself. He imagined the man stretched out in the ambulance, his long face covered, his umbrella beside him.

"What about the dog?" the neighbor in fuzzy slippers was now saying, still clinging to Everett but addressing a policeman. Everett looked with distaste at her footwear, at her generally disheveled outfit of sweatshirt and exercise tights. It occurred to him that he knew none of his neighbors' names, though he had lived here for two years. He stepped away from her.

"Should we call the ASPCA or something?" this nameless person was asking.

"There's no dog here," one of the police officers said.

"A little puppy," the woman insisted. "He got it last week."

Why, Everett wondered, would a man get a puppy and then kill himself? And he went home to put away his quart of milk, almost invigorated and considerably less bored than when he had gone out.

The storm raged for twenty-four hours, then settled into a gentle billow of fat, wet flakes, then stopped altogether as the temperature dropped to three degrees. Small dogs ran up the sides of cars buried in drifts to pee triumphantly at the crest of these mountains. Streets were silent and impassable. It was too cold for children and their sleds. At five that evening, Jody took Beatrice to the park. The old dog, in a thick pink cable-knit sweater, bounded through the snow as Jody struggled to keep up. Branches creaked, glassy, coated with ice. The air was still and cold as death, then alive with blasts of bitter, angry wind. The pathways in Central Park had been sprinkled with sand, already ground into the filthy ice. Jody watched each step in order not to slip. She had wrapped a scarf around her head and it covered her nose and mouth. She breathed the heat of her own breath. Her hood blocked her vision, like the blinders on a carriage horse.

She closed her eyes against the stinging cold, then immediately opened them again in order to keep her balance. The streetlights led her through the looming dark. Like Hansel and Gretel's crumbs, she thought, one after the other, yellow pools of light. They stopped at the top of the stairs of the Bethesda Fountain, and she looked down at the frozen lake. The ice lay undisturbed, smooth and dark. I am alone here, Jody thought. She felt a surge of joy. In New York City, in the middle of Manhattan, she was alone. It didn't seem possible, but no matter which way she turned, she saw nothing but snow and ice and bare trees against the stark, black sky. There was no one else. Not even a squirrel. Jody's voice was muffled inside of her scarf. Beatrice looked up at her. Jody pulled her scarf away and breathed in the freezing air.

"We are alone," she said again.

When she turned onto her street a few minutes later, she was aglow with her solitude. Even the cross-country skier coming up the street could not dampen her sense of freedom and boundless melancholia.

The snow remained deep and the weather numb with cold for the next week. Jody envied the people next door, two men and a large number of small children, who could just let their two cairn terriers out into the yard. Her bathroom window faced the back, and she could look down and see the dogs, bounding like porpoises through the deep drifts. She had planned to see a movie with the art teacher, Franny, a wild-haired woman of fifty who believed in the healing power of crystals. But the weather was too uninviting, and Franny had announced her determination to smoke a joint and watch videos in the safety and comfort of her own apartment.

In front of Jody's building, a furrow ran between two snowbanks where the sidewalk had been. Paths of frozen footsteps turned off, leading to doorways slick with ice. Jody followed Beatrice, who was again wearing her pink sweater, which Jody had knitted for her. She admired the dog's odd bowlegged gait and wondered which path led to the man who had smiled. She hadn't seen him since the day of the blizzard.

Beatrice squatted daintily in front of the Lutheran church, leaving behind a deep, saturated yellow hole. Jody looked at the punctured snow. What would the parishioners say? She used her foot to cover it with fresh snow and skulked back toward her building.

two

"Everything looks different today"

When it finally came, the thaw was sudden. The snow vanished and left behind it expanses of sodden filth, oceanic puddles at every corner, rivers of debris. Beneath the white winter blanket it was revealed that treasures had been buried. Banana peels, french fries, and take-out menus, liberated at last, floated gaily in the gutters. Dog shit that had been deposited high atop the snowbanks now melted on the wet sidewalk.

Jody, when she took Beatrice out, stood eyeing a rushing gutter stream, seeking the safest place to ford it, when a man, who had come up beside her, said, "Colorful, isn't it?"

"It's like little dead bodies bobbing to the surface," Jody said.

The man let out a snort of laughter, then leaped across the water, leaving Jody stunned and silent as she recognized the man she had been searching for, the man who had smiled. She watched him, helplessly, as he hailed a taxi and disappeared.

"Colorful, isn't it?" she repeated to herself, pleased with the phrase.

That Saturday afternoon, as she sat looking out her window, Jody saw the man again. She had taken up knitting as a joke almost, thinking it fit her spinster life, but, to her surprise, she had found that she liked the gentle monotony of it and that she was extremely good at it. She had been waiting, sitting in her window seat for some time, the knitting needles clicking softly but with an almost ferocious speed. Perhaps I will make him, whoever he is, a scarf, she thought, looking down at the ball of pale blue wool she had been planning for another sweater for Beatrice, wondering if it would work for a man's scarf. Then she looked up to see him turn into a building across the street. Now, at last, the man with the smile had a home.

For the next few weeks, Jody walked Beatrice on the side of the street where she now knew Everett lived. She liked especially to stand near his building and have a nice chat with Heidi, a fellow dog walker. Heidi was in her eighties, a survivor of the Holocaust unexpectedly and unaccountably bursting with the liveliness and surprise of true optimism. She had recently lost a tooth in a fall, which could not be fixed until the following month, and she had therefore been trying, with limited success, not to smile. Her dog, a fat pug named Hobart, sat at her feet making soft gurgling noises. She walked him around the block four times a day, rain or shine. Even in the snow, Heidi and Hobart navigated the icy ravines of the sidewalk. She had once had a pit bull, and so she loved Beatrice. She needed someone to talk to, and so she loved Jody. She was interesting, brimming with stories—of the war, of Israel after the war, of visiting her old house in her old town in Germany just five years ago, of a divorced husband and a devoted son in New Jersey, of parents lost in the Holocaust, and a family of wild ducks that lived in her childhood backyard—and so Jody loved her.

On the first sunny morning in weeks, during Jody's February vacation, she walked down the steps with Beatrice and stood on the sidewalk admiring the brilliant clear sky. She saw Heidi and her little dog, who was swaddled in an argyle sweater, coming slowly up the street, and she walked toward them.

"Everything looks different today," she said.

"Saturated with color," Heidi said.

Another elderly woman, small and brightly dressed, waved to them as she rushed past. "*Muchacho, muchacho,*" she called to Hobart, who did not even turn in her direction.

Heidi was wearing pants and a beautifully cut wool jacket, and even in her heavy waterproof boots she managed to look, as always, European and elegant. "You look so elegant," Jody said, and Heidi could not repress a gap-toothed smile.

Everett walked by at that moment, and Jody, caught in Heidi's grateful gaze, could just see him from the corner of her eye. She turned away from Heidi, rather rudely she realized, hoping to catch Everett's eye, but he had already passed.

It was 8:10 on a Tuesday morning, and the cars parked on the downtown side of the street had all been moved and double-parked on the uptown side because of alternate-side-of-the-street parking. Jody had enjoyed watching this ritual when she first moved to New York. It was a quiet, graceful, synchronized street dance. When 10:15 arrived, the owners would return to their cars and guide them back to the empty spaces waiting on the south side of the street. Then the drivers would sit in their cars, waiting until 10:30 to quit the dance floor. When Heidi finished her story about the wild ducks, one of Jody's favorites, Jody led Beatrice into the street and they walked along the line of double-parked cars past a lime green Prius and an ancient Volkswagen bus covered with unfortunate, droll bumper stickers. Jody was heading toward a wide, sandy pothole near the Korean market where Beatrice sometimes would scratch and circle and take a dump. Before reaching the pothole, Beatrice stopped by a white SUV, squatted, and began to pee.

Jody was looking off into the distance, partly out of politeness to Beatrice, partly from sheer abstraction, when a thunderous noise brought her attention back.

"Get your goddamn mutt away from my car!"

A woman was screaming from the white SUV, her hand out the window banging against the car door. Jody was standing close to the car, almost leaning on it, but the huge side mirror and the reflection on the tinted windshield had hidden the driver from her. The banging fist was level with her face. She was momentarily terrified.

"Get outta here!" the woman screamed.

Jody backed up, pulling Beatrice with her. The woman, who had a weirdly orange face, shook a finger at them.

"I'll be watching you two," said the woman.

Jody was a little shaky as she walked away from the SUV. The woman had startled her, certainly, but, more than that, she had offended Jody's sense of place. She turned around suddenly and said, in the general direction of the SUV, "We live here, too." But she said it softly, and felt confused immediately afterward, as if they did not live there, too, at all.

Everett felt sulky about having to go to the lab at all that morning. He looked at the brisk blue February sky. What good did it do him? He would spend the glorious day in his inglorious lab. He stopped at the Korean market to buy a muffin. Then, almost without thinking, he found himself buying some tulips, too. This is ridiculous, he thought in some confusion, heading for the subway with the bright yellow flowers. He could put them on his desk, he supposed, perplexing his colleagues, putting them off balance. There might be some pleasure in that. Then he saw that little blonde woman, with her big white dog, standing on the sidewalk looking oddly forlorn, almost lost. There was something about this woman standing in the sunlight looking so abandoned that touched him and he walked toward her.

"Beatrice!" he said to the woman, her name coming suddenly into his head.

The dog wagged its tail.

"You look so gloomy," he said.

"I'm sorry," the woman said, looking even gloomier.

"No, what I meant was, that I bought these flowers. I didn't know why, but when I saw you there, I realized . . ."

Good God, Everett thought, pausing in his little speech. Am I really going to deliver this line? I realized I had bought them for you?

"I realized . . ." He paused again. "Well, here, Beatrice," he said, handing her the flowers and hurrying away.

"Thank you," she called after him. "But . . ."

He turned and waved and went to work with his muffin, reflecting on his impulsive act with a rather solemn pride.

Jody put her flowers in a vase. She no longer looked gloomy or lost. She had seen him and spoken to him, and he had spoken to her and given her flowers, even if he did think her name was Beatrice.

The days passed and the stems of the tulips looped downward and the yellow petals floated onto the table and Jody went to school each morning and taught music to small, distracted children. She came home each afternoon and practiced her violin. Some evenings, she played with a small chamber group. Occasionally, she filled in for a friend in the orchestra pit of a Broadway musical. The scarf she was knitting for the man whose name she did not know was finished, and she had begun a complicated pattern for a cable-knit sweater in a deeper blue that she hoped would complement his eyes. This occupied Jody during the long sleepless nights when Beatrice would lie on the rug beside the bed, her back legs stretched out behind her, her front paws stretched out before her, a pinkish white Superman with a long skinny tail. The man never needed to know about his blue sweater, of course. She reassured herself that the sweater could just as easily be for her father, though he would have little use for it in Florida.

February turned into March in this uneventful way. Late one windy night, Everett finished the report he was writing. He was surprised by the hour. He had no sense of time anymore. Sometimes he worked until three without realizing it. His apartment was no longer connected to anything, he thought bitterly, not even time. He checked his e-mail, hoping for a note from Emily. There was nothing but a political chain letter from Alison, his ex-wife. She sent him petitions or requests for contributions almost daily. It was practically the only contact between them now that Emily was in college. There were financial matters and arrangements for holidays, of course. But otherwise the person with whom he had spent his entire adult life until two years ago was a stranger. A sudden stranger, he thought, liking the sound of that. She occupied in his heart and his thoughts and his memory the kind of position and space that his cousin Richard did. Best friends as children. Drifted apart as teenagers. Strangers ever since. Everett missed Richard as he thought of this. They had ridden their bicycles and listened to the Doors and made stop-action movies with Richard's eight-millimeter camera of themselves driving a nonexistent car down the street where Everett lived. They swam at the beach and went fishing. They crushed ants and sat for hours in stupefied boredom in front of the TV. Everett felt old and almost frightened that he had worked until one in the morning without noticing. Soon he would be one of those people who barely slept at all, a lonely old man who went to bed at 2:00 a.m. and woke three hours later, not sleeping again until the next day after dinner in front of the TV.

The e-mail from Alison alerted him to the pending appointment to the FDA Reproductive Health Drugs Advisory Committee of a doctor who had written a book called *As Jesus Cared for Women: Restoring Women Then and Now* and who refused to prescribe contraceptives and told women who were suffering from PMS to read the Bible. Recipients were to sign, and every twenty-fifth person was to forward an e-mail of protest to the White House.

Everett detested chain letters. He detested politics. Worse was a political chain letter, and worse yet was an uninformed political chain letter. The dread doctor, who really was an outrage, had been appointed and confirmed years ago.

"Dear Alison," Everett wrote back. "The deed is long done. Your petition is spam. Warmly, Everett."

He immediately wished he had not responded at all. What a bitter old man he was becoming. Alison was getting married again, and surely her new husband would not become a bitter, lonely old man dozing in front of a blaring postprandial TV. He would become a harassed old man dragged on Smithsonian walking tours of the wine country of Chile. Everett had never met the man Alison was going to marry, but Emily had told him that Bernie was a lawyer. Bernie the attorney, Everett had said, and Emily had sneered, half in disgust, half in amusement.

He sent a note to Emily. He breathed the air in his living room and felt it to be airless air. He opened the window, letting the cold wash over him. He saw that woman with her big white dog walking below him. Suddenly, almost without realizing it, Everett called to her. She looked up, startled, then smiled.

"Hold on!" Everett shouted, and dashed out the door, leaving the weight of his empty apartment temporarily behind him. He had been proud of himself for giving her tulips, thinking perhaps he was not so old, after all, so hidebound and predictable. His ex-wife could remarry, but he could spontaneously present a woman with flowers. He had thought of the tulips often, remembering the blur of vivid color as he handed them to Jody. What he had done—buying flowers for no reason and pressing them on a stranger—fascinated him. When he had looked down at her from his window just now and recognized her, her existence was both delightful and impersonal for him, like the box of geraniums growing through the wrought-iron guards of the church window in the summer or the cat sleeping pressed against the glass at the ground-floor apartment on the corner or the bright red wall of the second-floor apartment across the street, for Everett had thought far less of Jody than he had of his own remarkable behavior.

Jody had seen him standing in the window before he called down to her. She had idly wondered if he was looking for her, as she so often sat at her window looking for him. Of course he was doing no such thing, she knew, but there was no harm in a little dreaming. She had thought for a moment of waving up at him, but when it came to it, she did not dare.

Now, Jody walked beside him on Central Park West. She could hardly believe it. Beatrice had leaped up when she saw him, her massive paws on his shoulders, looking him in the eye and licking him in the ear, whining with excitement.

Everett, pushing the big dog off him, wondered if the price for companionship at 2:00 a.m. was perhaps a little high. Dogs to him were inconveniences. The very word was used in phrases that were exclusively negative: someone dogged your steps or there were dog days on which you were dog tired. Old books were dog-eared. You lay down with dogs and woke up with fleas, after which you went to the dogs.

"How long have you lived on the block?" Jody asked him after he had introduced himself.

"A little over two years. Since my divorce. I have a daughter who lives with me sometimes. Right now she's away at college. The house feels so empty."

"Is that why you're up wandering the streets?"

"I guess it is. What's your excuse?"

"Restless? I don't know. I never sleep very well."

Everett then learned that she was a violinist and a music teacher at the Trumbo School, one of the more progressive of the good Manhattan private schools. He hadn't wanted Emily to go there. The children did not wear uniforms and ran wild, as he recalled. Children, Everett thought. Children and animals. This was the company Jody kept. He disliked animals, and the only child he could stand was his own, who was not even a child anymore. But Jody seemed a decent sort. She was so chipper, so cute in a blonde girl-next-door sort of way. And she was an awfully good sport to take a walk with a neighbor at 2:00 a.m.—a weird neighbor who gave her flowers and hollered at her from the fifth floor. It was a miracle she didn't think he was stalking her.

"I wonder if my father missed me when I left home," she was saying. "I certainly didn't miss him."

"You didn't?" Everett didn't like the sound of that.

"No. But I miss him now."

Everett tried to remember missing his parents when he was in college. He couldn't.

"He lives in Florida. Both my parents live in Florida," Jody said. "Together," she added hastily.

They walked past the museum, then turned back and walked home on Columbus.

"My wife's getting married," he said.

She smiled.

"That is an odd sentence, isn't it? Ex-wife, of course," he said.

"Is that good or bad? Or a little of both?"

"If she stops sending me political chain letters, it will be wholly good."

Jody nodded in sympathy, and Everett wondered why he was confiding, as much as he ever confided, in this stranger at this strange hour. The dog plodded between them and the night was quiet enough for him to be able to distinguish the noises of the street. A radio from a passing car. The frenzied yapping of what sounded like several small dogs behind brownstone walls. The beep of a car door being unlocked. The clatter of the lid of a metal trash can as a man with a ponytail deposited his garbage.

"Funny time to take out your garbage," Everett said.

"Funny time to be out noticing people taking out their garbage," said Jody.

Everett frowned. "He should cut his hair, at any rate," he said.

Jody just laughed, and Everett, who had seen the absurd man and his night-owl garbage as an easy conversational foil, was silent and put out.

"Ponytails on bald men are the worst, don't you think?" Jody said.

Everett, mollified, agreed and left his new friend at her door.

Jody lay in bed, furious and anguished at her unpredictable and unruly social skills. She had spent weeks dreaming of Everett and his beautiful smile, and tonight he had called to her from above, from the very heavens. He had confided in her, looked to her for sympathy. And how had she received his confidences? With the same breezy, casual manner she received everything. She might as well have been at school. "The cu-

cumbers in the salad bar are always so dry," another teacher might remark. "Ah, well," she would respond with a cheerful smile, "no drier than the radishes." Had she offered Everett the sympathy he obviously craved? No. She had told him she didn't miss her father when she went to college, the very last thing he wanted to hear. She had teased him for his priggish response to the man with the unfortunate ponytail and late-night garbage. She had revealed herself to be the unromantic, unyielding, unlovable spinster she was. When he said his wife was getting married, she had laughed at him. Laughed at him! It was unbelievable. He would never call to her from his window again. He had descended, like a god, in the cold night, and she had chuckled. Gods were not accustomed to chuckles at their expense. Gods did not have much sense of humor at all.

"Why would I be interested in a man with no sense of humor?" she said aloud.

Beatrice, who was stretched out beside her, lifted her head.

"The world is full of mystery, Beatrice," Jody said, and the dog closed her eyes, reassured.

three

À Deux

I think it's time to turn our attention to George, though he does not yet live on the block. George, now twenty-eight years old, had been a child prodigy. No one knew it. Except George. He hadn't been sure in exactly what field he was a child prodigy, but the elusive nature of his gift had neither eased his burden nor dampened his determination.

He was gawky as a little boy, thin, shy, adorned with toy men, their legs and arms bursting from his pockets. He was conscious of his dress, insisting on picking out his clothes and putting them on without assistance, and so appeared to the adult world as messy and mismatched. George's status as a child prodigy was a secret, and his secret was safe with him.

He grew up to become a handsome young man, in a pale, romantic, unhealthy, dark-haired way. Though he continued to wear mismatched clothes, he had acquired a certain facility in his choices, which transformed what had looked like simple poor judgment into what now looked like style. His pockets no longer bulged, for they were filled with nothing more than a few crumpled receipts, an expired MetroCard, perhaps, and a worn wallet he'd gotten for his college graduation. He was employed as a waiter at this time, but his secret still sometimes came upon him, like the tingling of a foot that has fallen asleep.

George had one sister whose name was Polly, a sister who from their earliest days had looked up to George in a protective fashion. He was her older brother and was of course stronger by virtue of size alone. His eight years had been worldly to her six, and he'd excluded her from his room and from his games, thereby winning her unbounded devotion. But Polly, though just a little sister, had a sharp eye. She adored George, and so she watched George, and what she saw made her childish heart expand not only with love but with tender, exasperated bossiness. George needed her. If only he knew how much. She felt a great responsibility for him, as she did for much of the world around her.

She had been a hearty-looking child, pink cheeked, loud and demanding, but shrinking inside. Sometimes, even when she was small, she would wonder at the sound of her own voice. It seemed to boom with authority, while she huddled behind it. Her brother turned to her in time of need. Even her parents would ask her advice and defer to her judgment. She had been conscious of this great burden for as long as she could remember. She was, to her confusion, powerful, and it had taken years to become used to her own manner. Now, of course, she took advantage of it, as if it were a fabulous figure, something she had neither earned nor deserved and could not therefore take any credit for, but something expedient nevertheless. Polly had learned to make her way in the world as if she knew she could. There was this inconvenience, of course: if everyone around you listens to what you recommend, you might begin to do the same. Polly, let it be admitted here at the outset, was as impulsive as she was imperious. But what she lacked in analytical depth or patient reasoning she more than made up for in generosity and breathless enthusiasm.

On the day of the February snowstorm, Polly was walking up a dark, narrow flight of steep stairs in an equally dark and narrow building, the Lower East Side tenement that was then the home of her brother. She went up one flight of stairs, then the next flight of stairs, then another. It was a five-story building, and George lived on the top floor. Polly was small and fit and prided herself on the speed of her ascent. She pretended she was in a race, and she was winning.

A boy she had gone out with had once noted that her head was large for her body and that many powerful people had big heads, like Bill Clinton. He meant it as a compliment, but she hated him after that, for it was true. She had looked at herself in the mirror and seen a Polly doll with a bobble head. Still, she sometimes reminded herself, *Bill Clinton* . . .

The great bulk of the Sunday *Times* was cupped in her hand and pressed against her waist, heavy and slippery. The smell of ammonia from George's downstairs neighbor's cat box stung her eyes. There was a sticker on the woman's door alerting the fire department to the cats in case of emergency. It said she had six. Polly knocked on George's door.

"It's me," she said.

When the door opened, and her brother stood before her smiling, winter light poured out into the hallway. Despite the smell of the cats and despite the misery that had brought her there, Polly felt the warmth and blinked in the brightness of George and the light and thought, Is it possible not to be happy? Then she remembered that it was and leaned her head on George's shoulder.

"Men are pigs," he said. He took the paper from her.

"No," she said. "That can't be the answer."

"No?"

She shrugged and sat down on the couch. Anyway, what was wrong with pigs? They were smart. And they made bacon. George's TV was on with no sound. A travel show? There were aerial views of a coastline. He took the bag she was still holding. Bagels and smoked salmon and cream cheese. He brought her a cup of coffee. He was an attentive brother in that way, making her comfortable, bringing her gifts.

"I'm sad," she said.

George looked puzzled, patted her, then told her a funny story about the restaurant where he worked, for he was not an attentive brother in this other way: on the rare occasion when she allowed herself to express any worry or exhibit any weakness, George immediately changed the subject. Once in a while, like this morning, Polly declared her unhappiness just to test him.

His story was actually an old joke about a man who pretends he's blind in order to get the bartender to allow him to bring his Chihuahua into the bar with him.

"I never saw a Chihuahua Seeing Eye dog," says the bartender, who, in George's rendering, was a guy named Keith.

"What?" says the man-pretending-to-be-blind. "They gave me a *Chihuahua*?"

"You never fail to fail me," Polly said genially.

"Look," George whispered, pointing at the wall, awestruck, as if they were in the forest. As if what they saw were a fox. But it wasn't a fox. It was a cockroach. A white cockroach, pale and scuttling. "Albino."

Polly was momentarily mesmerized by the albino cockroach. She meant to stand up and smash it with the newspaper. But the strangeness of the chalky insect whisking itself across the chalky wall distracted her from her own movements. She meant to get up and kill the cockroach, but she sat and stared as it vanished behind the TV.

"Unbelievable," George said. He was grinning.

Polly and George had been thrown together from a very young age. Their parents divorced when George was five and Polly three, and they had traveled back and forth between the two houses à deux, as Polly liked to think of it, like ballet dancers. For as long as she could remember, George had been her partner in this dance, the constant in her life. She could not imagine a week going by without seeing him, or a day without speaking to him on the phone. Whether they had met up earlier in the week or not, they almost always got together on the weekend. Sometimes they met for brunch with other friends. Sometimes George stopped by her apartment at 4:00 or 5:00 a.m. after a late night, and she'd wake up in the morning to find him curled in her armchair like a skinny stray dog, and she would make him eggs. And once in a while, like this morning, she trekked to his horrible apartment on the Lower East Side and brought him bagels and lox. She adored him.

"That was the most revolting thing I've ever seen, ever. I'm never coming here again," she said.

George did not reply. His mouth was now full. He had the urge to speak, his sentences sticky with cream cheese and half-chewed bagel, if only to annoy Polly. He raised his eyebrows at her, parted his lips.

"Don't," she said.

The winter light was silver, wavy with the window's interference, a weak, uneven, rectangular patch within which his sister sat, superior as a cat. But she is superior, he thought. She was dressed in her version of casual clothes, which were related to his clothes tangentially, the way, say, chimpanzees and humans are related. She wore jeans, but where did they come from? A magazine? They were perfect, the warp and the weave of them, the denim dye at just the right pitch, the fit knowing, almost prescient of what the fashionable fit must be. Her sweater was finely knit, luxurious. George reached out and patted her soft shoulder. She leaned her cheek against his arm.

"Oh, George," she said, and he sensed rather than heard a forlorn sigh. He leaped up and began pacing across the small living room, turning almost as soon as he'd taken a step, and then turning again. He hated it when she was sad. It struck him as a kind of betrayal.

"What's the matter?" Polly said. But she knew.

"Let's go to the movies," said George.

"I have no place to live," Polly said as she put on her coat.

"Stay here with me."

Polly looked at the place on the wall across which the albino cockroach had recently journeyed. "I don't think so."

George handed her the long scarf she had dropped on his rickety futon sofa. "It is pretty horrible here," he said. "Hey, isn't the wife supposed to get the house?"

Polly ignored the remark. She was not married to Chris, it had been his place for years before she moved in, and she hated the apartment even more than she hated Chris. In fact, at this moment, the apartment seemed to her to be very like Chris: a nondescript one-bedroom in an aloof and shiny tower. That was a perfect description of Chris, surely, though there had been a time when she'd liked his blandness, when she had viewed that quality not as blandness at all but as dependability. When she had moved into the building whipped by the wind off the Hudson River, it had seemed to Polly to be leaning away from mighty Manhattan toward the similar towers across the water in New Jersey. It was so isolated from its own city that the building management provided a shuttle bus to take residents to the nearest subway stop.

"You can stay here tonight, anyway," George said. "On the futon."

Polly shuddered.

"I have a week," she said. Chris had gone cross-country skiing, a trip she had planned to take with him, but she would now use the time to find an apartment.

They walked down the stairs and into the snow, which had billowed from a smattering of bright windy flecks, when Polly had arrived an hour ago, into a vast, dense, whirling cloud. My boyfriend is breaking up with me, she thought. *Has* broken up with me, she corrected herself. Has dumped me. In addition to which, I will never find an apartment in a week. I'll have to live with my brother and his albino insects. She looked down at her feet on the snowy sidewalk. Her boots would be ruined.

As George and Polly struggled through the snow downtown, Simon sat comfortably in a leather armchair, his feet stretched out on a leather ottoman, the only two pieces of furniture in his tiny living room. Simon did live on our block and had moved there eighteen years before, fresh from graduate school, though few would have described Simon as fresh, even then. He had been an elderly young man, enjoying his solitude in, if at all possible, his bathrobe. He worked with people, but he had no affinity for them and privately referred to himself not as a social worker but as an asocial worker. Now, at forty-six, he still lived in his ground-floor one-bedroom apartment at number 232, a tall, somber brownstone on the south side of the street. Simon relished his weekends, and on this Sunday he had, as usual, read the paper in a thorough though leisurely fashion, finished a pot of coffee, dozed off for an hour as he often did after drinking coffee, and was staring out his window at the small, snow-covered garden beyond. Every weekday morning at 7:45 precisely, Simon could be seen strolling toward the Seventy-second Street subway stop, then home again somewhere between four and seven, depending on the scheduling of his appointments. He labored as an asocial social worker in the far-off fields of Riverdale and carried a briefcase swollen with files pertaining to those whom he thought of as the unfortunate, the unhappy, and the unkempt. The only change in Simon's routine came in the autumn, when he would suddenly, and completely, disappear. This happened every year, for as long as anyone would have remembered, had anyone been paying attention. But Simon was just one of the many figures hurrying along the sidewalk, and his neighbors, also hurrying along the sidewalk, were hardly obliged to keep track of every pedestrian swinging a briefcase. Still, the doormen to whom he nodded each morning, the elegantly dressed black man in the wheelchair who called out a courteous good morning from his customary spot on the sidewalk, the teenage boy stationed beside the flowers at the Korean grocery store to discourage shoplifters—all would sense something odd about their mornings once the summer was over; then they would shrug and toss it up to a change in the weather, a new snap in the air. And, indeed, Simon's absence correlated exactly to the turning of the leaves. Come November, Simon closed up his files, abandoned his briefcase, and turned the unfortunate,

unhappy, and unkempt over to his colleagues. November was fox-hunting season, and in November, Simon was to be found in shining black boots, a black coat, and a black velvet hat atop an enormous bay gelding in the rolling hills of the Virginia countryside.

For the rest of the year, he lived alone on the ground floor of the brownstone that faced the beautiful garden. He did not himself have access to the garden—that privilege was limited to the family on the two floors above him, one member of which gave repetitive and resonant piano lessons for a living. Still, each spring he could look out his windows and see daffodils covered with the last unexpected snowstorm. He could see the four slender white trunks of the birch trees and the yellow warbler among the new tender green leaves, and then the gray August grass and gray August leaves, so still against the gray August sky. All his friends left the city for at least part of August. They escaped to Cape Cod or Maine or sometimes Paris or Venice. But Simon stayed, waiting patiently for fall. He sometimes thought of moving from his small, dark, damp apartment. Only two things kept him there. The garden, which he knew so well now after so many years. And the rent. Simon's apartment was rent-controlled. Hunting was an expensive sport. Simon was there to stay, and, each autumn, to leave.

He was tall and almost lumbering, and he had the crumpled face of a man who has just climbed out of bed. This endeared him to most people before he even opened his mouth, which was fortunate, for he did not speak often, and did not speak particularly well. His voice was low and indistinct, causing people to lean in to hear him. He was a good listener, though. He was intelligent and disciplined with regard to his work, but outside of that setting, Simon was extremely shy. It was, therefore, just as well that he was such a self-sufficient man. On this snowy day, he had enjoyed sitting quietly by himself in his armchair, but by two o'clock, hunger intervened. There was nothing to eat in the house, for he never ate at home, preferring to sit at a bar in a restaurant reading a novel. But what restaurant would be open on such a day as this? He put on his coat and boots and grabbed a copy of *The American Senator*, pulled on an absurd knit hat that his aunt had sent him for Christmas, and stepped out into the storm. Simon always dressed with great care, but at the last minute he sometimes lost concentration. In his colorful floppy cap he shuffled along the sidewalk, what little of it that was clear, behind a narrow woman in a long mink coat whom he recognized by her fur as someone he'd seen on the street before, though he did not know her.

The woman in mink lived across the street from Simon's brownstone in a large apartment in a small apartment building, and had done so for all the years of her married life, which now numbered over forty. She was a thin, nervous person with a perpetual tan of an alarming hue not usually observed in nature and particularly unlikely in a snowstorm. She was older than she looked, but that was only because she looked no particular age at all. Some people seem to be well preserved. Doris seemed to be, simply, preserved. People did not like Doris, generally, and Doris, for her part, did not care. She was a guidance counselor at an exclusive boys' school, one where the children did wear uniforms, and she viewed all the world as if it were a spoiled and recalcitrant adolescent, full of menace and hormones, an orb of incivility and underachievement. This, the world, was her burden. And though she resented the weight of it, she did not shirk from the duty. She went about the business of guiding and counseling and of life in general with a grim superiority coupled with an almost hysterical sense of urgent pessimism. She was now headed for the restaurant on the corner to buy some soup to take home. At least, she hoped for soup, but she assumed, too, that she would be disappointed. For that was how the world was—disappointing. As hard as you tried to help it, the world let you down. She marched forward on an inhospitable day when she could easily have opened a can of Progresso lentil soup for lunch. She chose to support her local restaurant, to bring home two large containers of split pea, her favorite and the special soup every Sunday, which day it happened to be, storm or no storm, and yet she was quite sure the restaurant would be closed, opening in time only for Monday's escarole soup, a bitter, thin affair that was her husband's unaccountable favorite but that she judged inedible. Well, she would certainly not go out again tomorrow for it. Not in this weather. Harvey would have to go himself. She was only human.

To Doris's surprise, the Go Go Grill was open, and the proprietor sat at his usual table with his usual glass of wine as if there were no storm of any kind outside. He greeted her with the same warmth he always showed, the warmth he showed all of his customers with such evenhandedness that no one could complain, yet no one was entirely satisfied, either. It was one reason people came to the restaurant—the hope that this time they would be distinguished by some special mark of favor.

"I'm surprised you're open," Doris said, and she sounded let down, which was, in fact, the case. She had been expecting to have her hopes of split pea dashed, and that expectation had not been met.

"I have nothing else to do," said Jamie. His two cairn terriers lay at his feet, asleep. He welcomed dogs to the restaurant, against city regulations, and had, for five years, paid the occasional fine and gotten away with it. His relaxed attitude toward those things that, Doris knew, were the ever antagonistic forces of the world—the weather, the government, his very customers—was, for Doris, a concern and an irritant. Jamie never seemed to be doing anything at all, and yet the restaurant was always full. Storms raged, dogs dozed, and there was always food to give to people and waiters to serve it. Dishes got washed and fish got filleted. There were pots, and there was pasta to put in them.

Jamie turned to say hello to the tall man in the garish knit hat who had followed Doris into the restaurant. Doris did not like it when people turned away from her. Jamie, she told herself with the comfortable, familiar warmth of her own disapproval, was a selfish and entitled man, not unlike the boy who'd been sent to her office on Thursday. Nathan Ehrenwerth. She would have to speak to the parents again. The mother could barely remember her own name. Margaret Nathan, Doris thought with distaste. Perhaps that's why they named the boy

Nathan—a mnemonic device for the absentminded mother. How the woman had written a book—several books, wasn't it?—Doris could not fathom. No wonder the boy was so unfocused. The father, on the other hand—Edward Ehrenwerth, a charming Englishman. Beautifully spoken. Doris could not imagine what this articulate, highly educated man made of his son, an abstracted monosyllabic underachiever with eyebrows that met in the middle, untied sneakers, and an iPod hanging from the droopy waistline of his pants. Now, Jamie's eyebrows did not meet in the middle. And he presumably did not cut math, hiding out in the library reading comic books, which was the student's offense. But how Doris would have liked to demand a written apology and a week of community service detentions from Jamie. Naturally, community service would never even occur to such a one as Jamie, unless perhaps he gave a few dollars to an AIDS fund. Gay men were terribly narcissistic, Doris believed. True, Jamie did not appear narcissistic at first glance. At least, he did not dress with the taste one might have expected. Nor was he physically fit in that exaggerated way they usually insisted on being. He actually had a tousled, comfortable appearance. Jamie, she concluded, was altogether unreliable.

She waited for her soup in silence, sitting at the bar.

"Can I treat you to a drink?" Jamie said, coming to sit beside her.

Doris looked at him with suspicion. A drink? In the afternoon?

He patted her hand. "Tea? To warm you up. A cappuccino to thank you for venturing out on such a terrible day?"

She accepted a cup of decaffeinated tea thinking, whether under the influence of the warm beverage or the warm attention I cannot be sure, that poor Jamie, in spite of his faults and predilections, was still a young man with potential. A family man, too, she reminded herself. In the spirit of reconciliation, she asked after his children. She had already learned from earlier conversations and observations on the street that he had five. Two sets of twins—boys age two, another set age five—and a seven-year-old girl. His boyfriend, or partner or spousal equivalent or spouse, for all she knew—they might have gone off to Toronto or even Provincetown, she supposed; it had come to that, hadn't it?—was an investment banker, so they could afford it, certainly, but five children in this day and age? No wonder he looked rumpled, even with their two nannies.

Jamie, who assured Doris that his children were fine—a red flag, Doris thought, if ever there was one—turned to Simon, who still wore his silly hat, though he sat at the bar eating an omelet. "Why don't you move to Virginia and let me have your apartment?" Jamie asked him plaintively.

Simon looked startled. How did Jamie know he went to Virginia? He ate in the restaurant almost every night, but he was not in the habit of discussing his precious vacation month in the hunting fields with anyone. "I guess . . ." Simon stopped. Why, indeed? he wondered. He stared at his food. Beside the omelet, the broccoli rabe glistened in the light from a little votive candle. "I guess I live here," he mumbled.

Although Jamie lived in a large brownstone, just two doors down from Simon, he was constantly on the lookout for vacant apartments. In addition to his five children, he seemed to support a small flock of good-looking ex-boyfriends. He reminded Doris of a duck sometimes, followed everywhere by the long line of his little ducklings. The ex-boyfriends worked in the restaurant as waiters, managers, chefs, and bookkeepers. Some of them had once been young, some still were. They looked dazed and petulant and out of sorts. They were of many nationalities and spoke in many tongues. Jamie had learned a fair amount of Swedish and Russian. His Spanish and German were perfect, his Portuguese passable. Go Go, the name of the restaurant, meant dog in Chinese.

"You should do something with all those languages," Doris said, but when he asked what he should do with them, she couldn't say and took her soup through the howling storm home to Harvey, who had developed the unpleasant habit of watching poker tournaments on television and was far less appreciative of the soup than she felt she had a right to expect.

Simon, too, took soup home with him, which he heated up for his dinner, then packed his briefcase with resignation for the next morning's commute and went to bed having, as always, thoroughly enjoyed his weekend days of rest.

Back in the high-rise she would have to move out of, Polly, undressed and ready for bed, sat in the living room and looked out at the faint sparkle of city lights penetrating the gray of the storm. The apartment was on the twentieth floor and she could see the Empire State Building, its spire red and shedding a glow as rosy as the dawn. Across the street she could just make out a dance class, or was it martial arts, people in white moving, sweeping, across the windows of a studio. I hate it here, she thought. But she was crying and didn't want to leave. I hate Chris, she thought. But she was holding an old shirt of his against her cheek. He had left a half-empty beer bottle on the coffee table, which was typical. She missed him. They had been together for two years, living together for one of them. He was leaving her for a girl he'd met at work. A lawyer, like himself. When Chris and his new girlfriend broke up, Polly thought, they could sue each other for palimony and not have to pay any attorneys' fees. Except they were both real-estate lawyers, so they would both be incompetent and would both lose the case. This thought provided Polly a certain degree of comfort, and she got up and rinsed out the beer bottle and put it in the recycling bin. She kicked the recycling bin, listening to the tinkling clatter with satisfaction.

In spite of the cold and the snow, Polly immediately began calling real-estate brokerages the next morning. She finally found one young man who, having made it into the office, eagerly offered to show her a new listing that afternoon, and she put on her cross country skis and huffed her way up West End Avenue in the winter gloom, crying all the way, to meet him at the appointed time. It had taken her an hour in the frigid darkness to reach her destination, but now, her body sweating with exertion, her face numb with cold, she swished past a person bundled in scarves with a big white dog, and she saw the address on an awning sagging with snow.

The real-estate agent was younger than Polly, which was not reassuring, but the apartment was rent stabilized, which was. He wore a suit and tie beneath the bulk of his parka. They got off on the fourth floor and stood before a door festooned with yellow police tape.

"Don't mind this," the agent said, pulling it aside.

"Okay," Polly said. She was thinking of Chris and her ears rang with a sudden rush of rage and misery. The agent politely handed her a tissue, which she needed but resented. Though she had bravely skied the streets of New York City on the coldest day of the year, this real-estate boy wearing dress shoes in the snow still sensed her helplessness. This was an unusual and unwelcome sensation. She often felt helpless, but it was rare that anyone else could tell. She squared her shoulders.

"Thank you," she said in her big voice. She looked him in the eye.

She watched, gratified, as the real-estate agent lowered his glance deferentially. That was more like it. Then she felt tears rolling down her cheeks again. Turning away, pretending to look at the miserable little indentation the real-estate agent called a galley kitchen, she wiped her eyes and blew her nose with as little noise as possible. Galley kitchen, she thought. That's redundant. A galley is a kitchen. On a boat. Galleylike kitchen was what people ought to call it. Or why not just galley, the rest of the information being implicit, since they were so obviously not on a boat. Or just tiny-kitchen-indentation? She walked behind the real-estate agent and tried to pay attention. The building was nondescript on the outside, though the red bricks had looked quite pretty in the snow, but the apartment itself was shabby and dark, bigger than she really needed, and more than she really ought to pay. She wondered why she had bothered.

The real-estate agent flicked on a harsh overhead light. They stood beneath it, each in a separate puddle of melting snow. "The landlord is a friend of mine," he said.

Polly, hugging her skis and sweating, stared at him, barely comprehending the words and even less the significance. She wanted to go home, but she had no home.

"Well, okay, he's my uncle—that's why I know about it. The, uh, former tenant, just vacated. Left all his furniture. It's a great deal."

"He left his furniture?"

The real-estate agent looked at the floor.

"He kind of died."

"Oh," Polly said.

She looked around her with more interest.

"So don't his relatives want his stuff?"

"Would you?" said the real-estate agent.

The couch was cheap and old and sagging. There was a small bookcase of peeling oak-patterned veneer crammed with yellowing newspapers. The coffee table, of matching chipped oak veneer, had only three of its four legs. In one bedroom, Polly could see a mattress with dirty sheets on the floor. The other was piled high with more old newspapers.

"You don't have to take it furnished," the agent added quickly.

Polly looked out the window of one bedroom. She was on the fourth floor. The top branches of a snow-laden tree spread out before her. In the deep velvet sky a piercing white sliver of moon was shining. The windows across the street were lit with a warm, yellow light.

"When did he die?" she asked.

"Um, the day before . . . yesterday."

"How did he die?"

"Um, he, um, hanged himself."

"He hanged himself here? Two days ago? And you're showing the apartment? Are you crazy?"

The real-estate agent turned red.

"It's my first commission," he whispered.

"Jesus," Polly said, wondering if they were committing a crime just by being there. "I mean, really."

They stood there, the boy real-estate agent staring at the floor, Polly staring out the window. She hoped they could put the yellow tape back up.

"It's rent stabilized," he added.

"Your uncle should be ashamed of himself," Polly said. "God." She watched a parked car spinning its wheels in the snow below, unable to escape its parking space. She heard the whining of the car's engine. The driver got out, slammed the door, and stumbled away. Polly heard the whining again. But now she realized it was coming from inside the apartment.

"Do you hear that?" she said.

The mortified real-estate agent shrugged. "It *is* a really good deal," he said.

Polly followed the sound to a closet. She opened the door and saw there, on a nest of clothes on the floor, a tiny puppy.

"Whoa!" said the real-estate agent.

Polly scooped the puppy into her hand. He mewled.

She turned to the real-estate agent, who had taken out his cell phone.

"Uncle Irv?" he was saying. "You won't believe this . . ."

Polly said, "Tell Uncle Irv I'll take it."

four

"George! Wake up!"

Any one of you reading this who has ever looked for an apartment will have to admit that apartment hunters are not very sensitive to those who came before them. As soon as the real-estate agent opens the door and the strangers march in to open the closets, the old tenants, whether they have moved to South Dakota or are standing anxiously right there in the hallway, become utterly irrelevant. I have stepped over other people's small and perhaps delightful children and noticed only the condition of the carpet on which they played and the insufficient size of the closet where their toys were stashed. I have been on the other side too, invisible to strangers making plans to dismantle my home, callously examining bookshelves with the obvious intention of tearing them down or horrified at the shade of green I had been so proud of. There is little courtesy in the real-estate hunt. The previous life of the apartment is superfluous. But even the most desperate, the most avid apartment seeker might be expected to feel some qualm when the place has come on the market not because of a new job in Memphis or unexpected triplets but because of a suicide that took place in the living room. However low the rent in however tight a market, Polly's decision to take apartment 4F might reasonably be considered indelicate.

What for you or me might be out of the question, however, was inescapable for Polly, and I must admit I like her all the better for it. A puppy had been abandoned, an apartment had been abandoned—a whole life had been thrown aside. While she could do nothing for the life, for the dog she could do a great deal. The dog was there, and it needed her. The apartment was there and, by extension, in Polly's mind, it, too, needed her. Polly heard the cry, and whenever Polly heard a cry, and sometimes even when she did not, Polly answered it.

And so, as soon as the streets were cleared of snow, the dead man's stuff was removed, men in jumpsuits came to clean away the scent of death, and the apartment was smeared in a fresh, dull coat of landlord-white paint and the floors slicked with polyurethane. Polly scoured the bathtub herself, and just two weeks after first seeing the apartment, she rented a U-Haul truck, loaded it with her few things from Chris's apartment, and drove out to IKEA with Geneva, her best friend, where they bought a living room, a bedroom, a set of dishes and glasses and flatware, a pot, two frying pans, and a teakettle.

"One-stop shopping," Polly said to Geneva as they pulled up to her new building. Geneva climbed into the back and began pushing boxes down to Polly, who then had to push each box up the steep wall of the snowbank and down the other side to the narrow, rutted sidewalk path.

On the day Polly was moving in, Jody and Beatrice were walking along the same path. It was slippery and Jody kept her head down, concentrating on each step as Beatrice pulled her along. The dog's long tail waved back and forth, as fast and hard as a whip. Beatrice was so strong, Jody thought proudly. Magnificently strong, like an athlete. Even in her thick pink sweater. Perhaps that was what inspired people to train pit bulls to fight—their beauty and athletic grace.

Jody shook her head. Sometimes her benevolent nature annoyed even herself.

"Excuse me," said a loud voice.

Jody looked up to see a small, pretty young woman in a smart coat with a fur-trimmed hood. She was tugging a cardboard box over the drift of sidewalk snow.

"I'm sorry," Jody said, trying to pull Beatrice to one side. "We're blocking the whole sidewalk."

"No, actually I wanted to ask you if you have a good vet, a vet you like."

Jody thought. Did she like her vet? He was okay. Self-promoting, but kind and up-to-date in his approach. She told the woman the name of her vet and watched as she let the box slide back toward the street and entered the information into a Palm Pilot.

"I just got a puppy," said the girl, who introduced herself as Polly.

What a commanding voice Polly had. Jody felt quite awed. And what beautiful boots. "Congratulations," she said.

Jody thought she heard a querulous, less commanding voice call for help from inside the U-Haul. She turned toward the truck, but as Polly paid no attention, she decided she must have been mistaken. Polly was squatting in the snow, her face against Beatrice's muzzle, which made Jody like her. Beatrice licked the girl's cheek, sniffed her pockets, then stood stoically in the blunt, aching cold.

"I'm moving in," Polly said as she got to her feet. "Today. And there was a puppy in my apartment. I found him in the closet." She unconsciously cupped her hand and held it out, as if showing the puppy to her neighbor.

" 'Out of the closet and into the streets!' " Jody cried out irrelevantly. She had seen a Stonewall documentary on PBS the night before. "Or is he too young to go out on the street?" she added in a more sober tone.

"Is he? I don't know exactly how old he is. My brother took him to the ASPCA and they said he was about six weeks old. And he got a shot. But I don't know what to feed him. I went online, and I called a pet store, and, but if there's a nearby vet, that seemed like a much better idea . . ."

The commanding voice was oddly matched to the uncertain words, creating a voice from a different time—a girl from a thirties movie, a socialite/newspaper-reporter girl. She had a shy smile, too, that somehow added to her unexpected charm. Jody agreed that a nearby vet was a good thing. It was clear to her that young Polly was the kind of girl with whom one wanted, if one possibly could, to agree. Polly seemed both vulnerable and strong. To Jody, who in her vision of herself as a spinster thought she must be considered by others to be hardened rather than strong, and pathetic rather than vulnerable, Polly was something of a marvel.

The voice from the van came distinctly now, more urgent this time.

"Okay, okay," said Polly.

"Good luck with your puppy," Jody said as she and Beatrice squeezed by on the snowy path.

"The man in the apartment hanged himself," Polly called back to her.

Jody stopped. The man in the apartment hanged himself? She had heard something about that on the day of the snowstorm. There had been an ambulance and a crowd of onlookers when she came home from her walk with Beatrice. This girl had moved into the dead man's apartment. She wondered if anyone had died in her own apartment before she moved in all those years ago. The idea had never occurred to her, yet the building was over a hundred years old, and it was quite possible. She looked across the street at her doorway just visible above the snowbanks.

"Gosh!" she said.

But it was none of her business, and Beatrice had begun to shiver. She waved, a signal that the visit was over, and walked off.

And my boyfriend dumped me, too, Polly wanted to yell at the receding figure, as if the two occurrences were related, were comparable. She sighed, then went back to the van to help Geneva, who was freezing and showed no interest in Polly's new neighbor or her big white dog in its pink cable-knit.

"This whole apartment thing is macabre," Geneva told her. "And totally bad karma."

"It's my karma, though."

Her parents had called and forbidden her to take the apartment. "There are so *many* apartments in New York City, Polly."

"But the others don't have abandoned puppies," Polly explained as calmly as she could.

George was upstairs with the puppy, and Polly proudly buzzed her new buzzer beside which her name had been written on a piece of masking tape placed over the dead man's name.

George had been waiting for them in the bare apartment, sitting on the floor fondling the sleeping puppy. It was a soft bundle of a puppy, the color of honey, with white paws and one white ear. He had taken the dog to the ASPCA to see what shots it needed, and the vet told him it was about six weeks old, too young to have been taken from its mother. George had held the puppy against his heart after that as much as possible, wondering if it would be comforted. The buzzer startled both of them.

In the elevator, a middle-aged man looked at George suspiciously.

"My sister is moving into 4F," George said. He extended his hand. "I'm George."

"4F?" The man frowned. "But . . ."

"I know," George said. As the man made no motion to shake his hand, George withdrew it. "Real estate," he said, a halfhearted attempt to defend his sister. "And she found this dog there." He held up the puppy he'd been holding against his waist with his other hand.

"Good God," said the man. "There *was* a dog."

George was beginning to dislike this man.

"My sister's name is Polly," he said, in a last attempt at civility. "There she is." The elevator doors had opened, and they could see Polly, teetering on her high-heeled boots, sliding a large box up and then down the enormous snowdrift toward the building's entrance.

The unfriendly man held the door for Polly and nodded slightly. "5D," he said, and left them.

Polly barely noticed him. She had known none of her neighbors in Chris's building, and anyway she was more interested in the puppy, whom she took from George, and in the lobby of her new building.

"Howdy," she said softly, which is what she had named him.

"Why don't you just name him Hello?" her father had said.

"Look!" Polly said now, gazing over the puppy's head at the lobby's little entrance table. "Party favors!" Someone had put out an obsolete video game and a rolling pin with red handles. She picked up the rolling pin. Perhaps she would bake a pie, or hit someone over the head with it, like a wife in a cartoon. Then she put it back.

"I don't want to be greedy," she said. "On my very first day."

Polly was the copy editor at a shelter magazine, a job she loved and kept, she was sure, because of her high school Latin training. And though the magazine was devoted to interior design, she was far more interested in dependent clauses than in wall coverings or window treatments. When, with the help of George and Geneva, the boxes were unpacked and the furniture assembled, the apartment reflected Polly's prejudice. Bare rather than minimal, the colors drab rather than serene, it had the feel of a clean new dorm room, and Polly was ecstatic.

That night, when George and Geneva had gone, Polly put the sticky take-out containers in the refrigerator and sat on her new sofa in her new apartment. She watched the puppy skitter across the bare wood floor. She watched him pee a foot away from the newspaper she'd put out for him. When she had cleaned up the little puddle, she tossed a squeaking rubber hamburger to him, then watched him bat at a tennis ball with his big paws while she thought of the apartment's previous tenant. It was almost as if he had never really existed at all. Polly felt that she should set up some kind of shrine in his memory. She lit one of her new IKEA candles and put it in the window.

"It was chemical, right?" she said to the puppy. "Sometimes there's just nothing anyone can do." She thought of the huge yellow sign high above Seventy-second Street, painted on the side of a building: DEPRESSION IS A FLAW IN CHEMISTRY, NOT A FLAW IN CHARACTER.

Howdy chewed on her sock with his needlelike baby teeth.

"I'm sure it was a chemical thing," she said again. "Or genetic." But still she felt a vague, familiar sense of responsibility.

"I'll take care of you," she said to the puppy.

If George had still been there, he would have accused her of being grandiose. Mostly, he would have added, things take care of themselves.

"You're the only one who understands me," she said, addressing the puppy. She lay on the floor while Howdy played with her hair, and she brooded. What was Chris doing right

now? Sitting on the couch, checking his fantasy football team on his laptop, the TV on, a beer at hand? The usurper girlfriend would be beside him with her own laptop. It was unfair that Polly had fallen in love with such a shallow man. She told herself, at any rate, that Chris was shallow, and she suspected it was true. But how little that had mattered to her for the years they were together, and, oddly, it mattered even less now that she was separated from him. She had loved him, and she missed him. He could have been as flat as a cardboard cutout, and it would make no difference, especially now that he was out of her reach. Polly let out a little sob. She turned onto her stomach and buried her face in her arms and cried, half expecting the dog to sense her misery and poke his soft muzzle against her tear-stained cheeks to comfort her. She waited, even allowing herself a moan of despair louder than it might otherwise have been, which sounded so sad that she immediately began to sob hysterically in earnest. Howdy played on, oblivious to her need, and Polly, when she was fully cried out, sat up, disgraced, washed her face and consoled herself as best she could with the remains of an egg roll.

Earlier that day, Doris and Simon, preparing to leave the Go Go Grill at the same time, had both stopped for a moment to stare out the restaurant's large window at the truck blocking the street. Doris, already annoyed that the tall man with the silly knit hat had turned up again, did not like the look of the U-Haul truck and its many flat boxes from IKEA, either.

"Young people," she said bitterly. And immigrants, she thought, keeping that to herself. That's who shopped at IKEA, and both young people and immigrants were likely to litter and play loud music on their car radios.

"It must be the suicide apartment," Simon said. He too had seen the ambulance and the stretcher in the snowstorm. "That was fast."

Jamie came up behind them. "I call that unseemly haste on somebody's part."

"He hanged himself," Doris said. "The doorman at 213 told me."

"Two bedrooms," Jamie said, and he shook his head sadly, gesturing with one hand at a few good-looking waiters gathered at a table having their lunch.

"He was an ill-tempered man and the place was as bad as the Collyer brothers, that's what I heard," Doris said.

"I couldn't live there, I'll tell you that. Too ghoulish," said Simon. "And there's no garden . . ." He paused, thoughtfully, then added, "Is there?"

Doris looked at him with pointed disapproval.

"Well . . . ," Simon mumbled, then pushed open the door and disappeared down the street.

"Let's hope they recycle all those boxes," Doris said, nodding her head at the U-Haul, and she too left the restaurant.

Jamie sighed and returned to the table of ex-boyfriends in their black pants and white shirts and poured them, his staff, more wine.

That evening, George tramped over from the subway to Mott Street to work. He had driven a cab at night for a while. But then this job as a waiter had come along through a friend. It was not a very good restaurant, expensive, pretentious, heavy on hipster decor and a blight, in George's eyes, on the once down-and-out area, but it had the advantage of being three blocks from his apartment. Sometimes the work was frantic and overwhelming, a furious rattle of customers and specials and dirty dishes. But then would come lulls, and he would begin daydreaming. He daydreamed at home, too. He knew he should stop daydreaming and use his free time for something productive. Instead, when he was home and not daydreaming, he would play computer games or watch movies or listen to music on his iPod.

His daydreaming moved on to his sister. What should he do about Polly? He was not used to worrying about her. That was her job, worrying. My job is daydreaming, he thought with distaste. He had left Polly sitting on her new sofa, exhausted but mostly unpacked, and seemingly proud of her new apartment. George could not imagine living there himself. What did she need two bedrooms for? She barely had enough furniture for the living room and her own bedroom. The other bedroom was now piled with the few boxes they had not gotten to. And how could anyone move into a place that had so recently been the site of a suicide? He was not superstitious, but it struck him as morbid. And, then, Polly was so obviously unhappy right now. It seemed to him particularly unwholesome for his depressed sister to move in to take the place of a depressed man who had hanged himself. But Polly wouldn't listen to him. Polly never listened to anyone.

George was upset about Polly's breakup with Chris, too. He had for Polly's sake tried to play the whole thing down, but the truth was he liked Chris. Chris was not the most fascinating man on the planet, he was officious at times, and though his work as a junior real-estate lawyer was dreary beyond anything George had ever encountered, he talked about it incessantly. But Chris also liked to party, and George had often joined him. They went to clubs and bars and drank and flirted and danced. Polly frequently came too, but she began to flag and had to go home early most of the time. When George and

Chris tired out, they would settle into a booth at a dive of a bar and drink beer in silence. These were friendly, male, companionable moments. Would George have to give up these late nights with Chris now that Chris and his sister had broken up? Of course he would, George thought bitterly, and at that moment he was sure he felt the loss of Chris fully as much as Polly did.

"What's with you?" asked the restaurant hostess. Her name was Alexandra, she was probably the same age he was, she scolded him at every opportunity, and had twice tried to get him fired. Both times he had talked his way out of unemployment, but only just.

"Nothing," he said. He had been leaning against the bar. He snapped to attention and swiveled his head in a search of diners waiting to order, to be served, to pay.

"Oh, please," she said.

"Why are you always on my case?"

She pointed at a man and woman sitting near the window. "You forgot to put in their order, George." Then she nodded at six gay men laughing boisterously at a round table. "You didn't offer them the next round of drinks, George. That's how we make our money, George."

George felt the color rise to his face. He was angry, and ashamed.

"You spilled the leek puree and . . ."

And I spit in the lamb stew, he thought, but you didn't see that.

"I'm sorry," he said.

Alexandra snorted. "What are you even doing here?" she said.

And George had to wonder, not for the first time, exactly the same thing.

"George! Wake up!"

She hit his head with her pen and stalked off.

George remembered a little girl in second grade who used to chase him across the playground in order to hit him with a pencil, then try to kiss him. He spent the rest of his shift convincing himself that he could sue Alexandra for sexual harassment. At the end of the night, he quit.

five

A Gentleman

For Simon, the thaw, when it finally came, brought to mind the spring, and the spring suggested summer, which meant fall could not be far behind. There are fortunate people in this world who enjoy the moment they live in, who are blessed with perfect temporal pitch, for whom the beautiful, ringing note they are always able to find is right there with them, in the present. Simon was not one of them. For him, the only music was in the month of November and any weekend on which he could afford to go down to Virginia after that. Everything else was just an echo. But he enjoyed the echo, however faint, dreaming of pulling on his boots and feeling beneath him the long rolling strides of the huge horse he rode each season. Simon's college roommate and closest friend had inherited a house and a stable and a life, and each November Simon was invited down to stay in the guest cottage and share that life. After twenty years, it was the only life that really mattered to him.

The boots Simon had on now were waterproof and he stomped up the stairs from the subway and sloshed toward home through the vast puddles. It was not yet six, but the sky was dark. An ambulance and its siren shrieked past, splashing him with cold, black water. It was at times like this that he allowed himself to admit that he hated New York and, not for the first time, he thought of looking for a job in Virginia. As usual, though, at precisely that point in his musings that suggested any real change, Simon's thoughts veered to another subject. He might not be entirely happy in his ways, but he was set in them. So now, noticing that a big white dog beside him had also been splattered with mud, he turned his attention in that direction.

"You're going to need a bath," he said to the dog. "Me too." He found it easier to talk to dogs than to their owners, and he continued looking down at the animal. But the owner, a rather attractive woman, had become flustered and pulled a package of Kleenex from her bag. "Here," she said, handing him a tissue. "Will this help? Look at your nice coat. I hope at least whoever was in that ambulance was *critically* ill." Then she realized what she had said and started to laugh. Simon, who had accepted the Kleenex out of politeness, although he knew it would shred and be useless, worse than useless, the minute he rubbed it against his camel hair overcoat, was trying to keep the dog from pawing the parts of his coat that had escaped the mud.

"Beatrice," the woman said, rather sharply, and the dog stopped and sat with such a forlorn look on its face that Simon wished he had let it plant its filthy feet on his coat, which he would have to get cleaned anyway. He petted the dog.

"Poor Beatrice," he said. "Don't look so sad." And Beatrice obeyed, jumping up on him, her paws on his chest. She licked his chin as her owner tugged at the leash.

When Beatrice finally returned to earth, Simon spent some

time calming the owner, who seemed quite beside herself with shame.

"I'm so sorry," the woman kept saying. "She doesn't realize how big she is . . . She's very sweet . . . I'm so sorry . . . I hope she didn't scare you . . ."

Simon soothed the woman by squatting down to allow Beatrice to kiss his face, just to show the woman and the dog there were no hard feelings.

"You're such a gentleman," the owner said.

Simon liked the sound of that. He had always tried to be exactly that, a gentleman, and, to his own complete surprise, he invited the woman, whose name he learned was Jody, into the Go Go for a drink.

Though the Go Go Grill stands on the southwest corner of our block, its door a few steps from where they had been talking, Jody had never set foot inside.

"I've never been in here," Jody said. "Funny, isn't it? I live two doors down. 236."

"I'm 232!" Simon said, as if that meant something, as if their doors, lined up on the south side of the street, bound the two of them together. "You can bring the dog," he said, waving his hand at the restaurant. "At least, the owner always has his there."

Jody was standing close to him, her face tilted up as she strained to hear the undercurrent that was his voice. "Some places let us sit at a table on a patio in the summer," she said. "But not that often. Beatrice scares people." She spoke loudly, as if he were hard of hearing

Simon moved back, just a fraction of an inch, said Beatrice did not scare him, and they sat at the bar and had several companionable drinks and a plate of fried calamari while Beatrice slept on the floor beneath them.

The restaurant was small, the bar running the length of one wall. Tables against a banquette upholstered in a fashionable brown lined the other wall, and there were seven or eight small tables in the middle. It was a pretty room, simple and rather spare, the only color from oversize red lampshades that hung from the ceiling. Jody knew it was the only really good restaurant in the immediate neighborhood, and she wondered why she had never found her way inside. She ordered white wine, reflexively, and when Simon asked for bourbon, she realized that was what she would really have liked. She said nothing, however, accepting her wine and sipping it in what she hoped was a demure but sophisticated manner.

What a nice man, she thought, then wondered what it would be like to sit beside Everett. She hadn't seen him since their late-night walk, though she made sure always to walk the dog on his side of the street. If the taxi had splashed him instead of Simon, would he have invited her for a drink?

"Yes, of course," she said when she registered what Simon had just asked: Could he have the last piece of calamari?

She wondered if the two men knew each other. Perhaps they were friends. That idea caused her to smile at Simon, who blushed and drank an entire glass of water while Jody sipped her wine and gazed absently out the window.

Simon watched a waiter fill his glass.

"Thank you," he said.

The waiter did not seem to hear him, but he was used to that. Simon leaned down and stroked the sleeping dog. Beatrice thumped her tail loudly on the wood floor, and Jody turned away from the window and faced him again. She has shined her countenance on me, Simon thought. He wondered if they would see each other again, have dinner sometime, or brunch on Sunday. It might be awkward bumping into her on the street if they did not. He thought he would call her. She was easy company, he realized. Perhaps because she was somewhat inattentive. He ordered more wine, a bottle this time, and asked for another glass. He was feeling expansive.

By the time Doris and her husband, Harvey, arrived at 6:15, in time for the pretheater prix fixe, Simon was a little tipsy. Still he recognized the woman with the unearthly tan and the mink coat. He nodded to her, and she nodded back, unsmiling. I live in a community, Simon thought. A neighborhood. He started humming the song from *Mister Rogers' Neighborhood* without realizing it.

"Yeah," Jody said softly. "It's so sad he died."

Then through the window she saw Everett and a girl who looked so much like him she had to be his daughter.

"There's a neighbor," she said.

Simon glanced out the window at their receding figures. "Really?" he said. "You know them?"

"Well, no," Jody admitted, feeling absurd now. How could she explain he had called to her from the sky and given her a burst of yellow tulips? "I mean, not really."

Then she noticed, sitting alone in a corner of the restaurant, the girl who had stopped her on the snowy street to ask about a vet, the girl who had moved into the suicide apartment. She wanted to point her out to Simon as yet another neighbor, to tell him that she had taken the dead man's apartment, but her identification of Everett had left her embarrassed and shy. She watched as a young man, a very pale young man with black hair and an oddly pleasing getup of mismatched pinstriped jacket and pants, joined the girl at her table.

Polly, while she had been waiting for George, did not recognize Jody or even notice her. She had been too busy thinking about George and her plan to have him move in with her. The apartment was too expensive for her and it was too big. The idea of a real roommate made her angry at Chris and at the world in general. But George? He was her brother. And he needed her.

"You'll have a bedroom and bathroom," she had told him. "It's ridiculous for me to live in such a big place all alone."

He'd been helping her unpack several cases of books that had lingered in the second, unnecessary bedroom. He had stared at her, stunned. George had often said to himself that he would do anything for Polly. And he had an idea of himself as someone who helped others generally. He liked opening doors for people, for example, or giving up his seat on a bus, or helping someone across the ice. He imagined himself, sometimes, as an anonymous Good Samaritan, a kind of superhero of small, meaningless, random gestures of moderate goodwill. But moving in with his sister? To the Upper West Side with its strollers and upscale markets? Would that be a gesture of goodwill or of the absence of any will at all? Either way, it seemed vastly too large a gesture for George. He was arranging all of Polly's books alphabetically, as requested. Wasn't that enough?

"You have got to be kidding," George said.

Polly had not been kidding, and as she waited for George to join her at the restaurant, she was thinking of ways to reopen the discussion when she was distracted by an argument between the restaurant's owner and the bartender.

"You're fired," the owner said, obviously exasperated. He then appeared to repeat this information in what sounded like Portuguese. The bartender was outraged, at least he banged his fist on the bar and headed out. At the door, though, he hesitated, calling back plaintively. Jamie gave him a withering look after which the bartender, finally, skulked off.

Polly thoughtfully watched him go. George's decision to quit his job as a waiter, if it could be called a decision, and Polly did not think it could, seemed to be more distressing to her than to George. She had tried to get used to having an older brother who had no direction whatsoever. She knew he had some secret store of self-confidence that she could not understand, the way the doubter cannot understand the true believer, but his serenity was unbearable. He had not even mentioned his unemployment to their parents, though that was less serenity than a wise aversion to cross-continental censure. But it left Polly feeling that, as was so often the case, she alone must take responsibility for her brother. He was drifting. She did not like the idea of drifting, having some half-conscious notion that drifting inevitably led to crashing or even catapulting. "Drifting." The word made her think of rivers, and rivers made her think of steep rocky falls. Polly never drifted. She crept forward, perhaps, but, as she told herself, the important word there was "forward." George was different, floating indifferently, it seemed to Polly, and she was sure it was time to step in and pull him back to dry land. When she witnessed the bartender storming out, she saw her chance.

"George," she whispered when he came in, all thought of his moving in with her banished by this more urgent opportunity, "the bartender just quit. Can you tend bar?"

"Here?"

"Does it matter? Can you or can't you?"

George shrugged in a way she had over the years come to hate.

"You can," Polly decided and gave him strict instructions as to his supposed bartending experience.

"Now go talk to him," she said, and George twisted himself out of his chair and obeyed.

He did not need to exaggerate his experience or his abilities too much, as it turned out.

"Do you have a place to live?" was the only question Jamie asked.

"What? Well, yes."

"You're hired."

"I am?"

Jamie went on to explain in a peevish voice that he knew the rest of his staff far too well, that they all depended on him far too much, that he had his own children at home, he couldn't have a restaurant run by children, that none of them bothered to learn English, that there was a limit, after all, that loyalty was one thing, and no one could claim he wasn't loyal, but that no one would put up with what he put with and anything George didn't know he, Jamie, would teach him as long as he could start that night.

"If he comes back," Jamie said, glaring at the door through which the previous bartender had slunk, "he can wash dishes."

Jody watched the transaction, fascinated. The owner of the restaurant was clearly one of the men whose large backyard was visible from her bathroom window. She recognized the two dogs that followed at his heels as he led the boy in the pinstripes behind the bar. The girl Jody had recognized came and sat at the bar across from the pinstripe boy, looking extremely pleased with herself. If only Mister Rogers would come in and don his old cardigan, Jody thought, enjoying the familiar faces and, equally, the fact that she didn't know them well enough to have to speak to them. She wondered how the puppy was doing, but she avoided the girl as she and Simon left. One new neighborly interaction was enough for her for one night. Simon paid the bill over her protestation and then walked her home. It had almost been a date, she realized when she got upstairs—an old-fashioned date. She thought what a pleasant man he was, then sat down by the window to wait for Everett and his daughter to pass by on their way home from wherever they had gone.

They, Everett and Emily, had gone to dinner at a Japanese restaurant on Seventy-second Street. They ordered a platter of sushi for two that arrived on such a long tray, hanging a foot off the table on both ends, that Emily looked around the room self-consciously when it arrived.

"Leslie said she was sorry she couldn't join us," Everett said.

Emily gave him a quick, involuntary, savage look, then ducked her head, obviously trying to hide it.

"Right," she said.

Everett knew she didn't like his girlfriend Leslie. Why should she? Even he didn't like Leslie all that much. Why had he even mentioned Leslie, who had not, as a matter of fact, expressed sorrow at not being able to join them, perhaps because he had not invited her?

"Look, I have a right to have a life, honey."

"I'm not stopping you. I didn't say a word."

But that was the problem. She hadn't said a word.

"Never mind," he said, and they moved on to the more comfortable topic of what Emily would need to purchase for her summer trip to Italy.

By the time they passed beneath Jody's window, they were arm in arm, and Jody smiled down at them, her knitting needles clicking in the quiet night.

As the weeks went on and the days were less gray and the late March wind more vibrant, Polly watched George at his new job with a sense of satisfaction and growing confidence in her other scheme of having George move in with her. Polly was an enthusiast, and her latest enthusiasm was George. She would take him under her wing, which meant into her apartment. She loved her apartment. She loved George. George needed a protector. She needed a roommate. According to Polly's personal mathematical theories, it all added up. She had bided her time and laid her plans. Often, when George left work late, he would end up sleeping at her apartment anyway, and she encouraged this, ordering a bed for the second bedroom, suggesting he leave clothes there. She even bought him an electric toothbrush. But the greatest inducement, she knew, was Howdy.

Howdy had grown quite large, but he was still not allowed to set fat white paw to pavement. Not until he reached the age of four months, when he would get the last of his shots, could he be walked on the street or in the park. He had finally learned to wait in his plastic crate with its fleece blanket until he was taken to the bathroom corner of special blue-backed pads. Polly had bought them at the pet store (though they looked exactly like the pads her grandmother had to lie on in the hospital when she had her hip replaced), and there he would dutifully pee. He had even learned, when loose in the apartment, to return to that bathroom corner of blue pads to pee. This had not been easy, though it had perhaps been easier for Howdy than for Polly. He had cried in his crate the first week of nights Polly locked him up in it, and when he cried, Polly cried and called George and woke him up. This happened for ten nights, ten sleepless nights during which Polly had to listen to heartbreaking yelps and George had to listen to her desperate voice, ten mornings when Polly had to rise at 5:00 to take Howdy to the crumpled, ignored blue pads, then put him back in his kennel, then take him out again ten minutes later, and ten minutes after that, until finally he lifted his leg. Polly listened to the pitiful yelps and whimpers, pulled the dog out of the crate and maneuvered him back in, over and over again, until just as she was about to rebel against the books she had read and the articles she had downloaded and allow the puppy free rein of the apartment to pee where he would, Howdy seemed to get the hang of it, began to use the pads on a regular schedule and plopped down on his blanket when the wire door was clicked shut, there relaxing immediately into sleep. And so the puppy was crate trained and paper trained and Polly stopped crying and calling George in the middle of the night. But a puppy cannot be left alone all day, and Polly had convinced George to spend part of every afternoon there with the puppy, letting him out to pee on his pad and playing with him while Polly was at work. Between his new job and his dog sitting, George spent most of his time on the block, and Polly saw no reason not to formalize this arrangement. Each time she brought it up, however, George merely laughed. She reminded herself that he had to be handled delicately sometimes. He could be so stubborn. Look at the way he dressed. It made no sense to anyone but him, but to him it made perfect, imperative sense, and so there was no talking him out if it. She would have to tread gently.

In the meantime, she had other, equally important ideas for her brother. One of these was Geneva. Of all of Polly's friends, Geneva was her best friend, and it had gradually become Polly's hope that this best friend might become her brother's best friend, too. Polly looked at her brother sometimes, at his weird clothes and his ostentatious absence of ambition, and what she saw before her was a vast, compelling expanse, a prairie of waving grass awaiting her sharp, deep plow.

six

"The Flowers That Bloom in the Spring"

The spring rain was dreary enough, going on and on, day after day, but the constant discussion of it was what disgusted Everett. Every drugstore clerk, every elevator operator, every colleague, and every human being he spoke to on the phone, no matter what part of the country he or she was actually in, mentioned the torrential rains.

"Yes," Everett would answer. "It's raining."

But, however much he disliked talking about the weather, he was not immune to its trials. He hated the fussy rigmarole of opening and closing his large umbrella. He hated the low, slate sky. He hated his wet shoes and damp socks. Taxis and buses splashed him. People scowled at him and he scowled back. It was in this mood, of oppressive weather and exasperation, that he decided finally to break up with Leslie. They had already agreed to "see other people," whatever that meant to her. To him it meant they were too polite to break up suddenly, and that the term "break up" sounded ridiculous for someone his age, as did "girlfriend" and "boyfriend." Nevertheless, break up is what he finally had to do.

"I never made you happy," she said, her mouth quivering.

"Yes, yes, of course you did. You're wonderful," he replied. "Wonderful. But . . ."

"No one can make you happy, though," she added, and she stood up dramatically. Everett watched helplessly as the table wobbled and her wineglass toppled to the floor, spilling its contents, an excellent Gavi, on his pants.

Leslie took one last look at him and his wet pants before sweeping out of the restaurant. "I knew I should have ordered red," she said.

It was on the way home from this encounter, on the eighth day of rain, that Everett saw Jody and Beatrice. He'd paid for dinner, which was not at all bad, he would definitely go there again, and realized as he walked out into the suddenly heavier than ever rain that he had left his umbrella in the taxi on the way downtown. Furious, he waited for almost twenty minutes until an empty cab came by. When he got in he was somewhat appeased to see that an earlier passenger had left behind an umbrella. It was a good omen, he thought, though he did not believe in omens.

He got out of the cab just as Jody and Beatrice were passing by his front door. Both were wearing bright yellow slickers, like two curiously shaped schoolchildren. Everett hesitated for a moment, wondering if Jody would see him. He was tired after his "breakup" with his "girlfriend." And he was wet. But then she did see him and smiled in such an easy, friendly way that he relaxed.

As soon as they began talking, Everett opened his newly found umbrella, feeling almost smug, as if it had been provided for this very moment by his own foresight, only to find it was lined in a shocking pink pattern with green frog faces scattered across it. But he could hardly close it up again without bringing more attention to it, and he and Jody stood together talking beneath the pink dome for almost an hour. Then Everett said good night, petted the dog's wet head, and went upstairs where he immediately washed his hands. Jody had smoked a cigarette beneath the umbrella, which had surprised him. She did not smell of stale cigarette smoke, as so many smokers did. She seemed so wholesome. And intelligent: she liked Gilbert and Sullivan, as he did.

He made himself a martini, telling himself he had earned it by finally ending his straggling relationship with Leslie. He listened to the ice cubes jingling in the shaker. He'd taken off his wet shoes, as well as his socks, but he was still in his damp suit. He took the glass into the bathroom, peeled off his clothes, and lay them across the edge of the tub. Then he put on light blue pajamas, washed and ironed at the dry cleaners, sat on the edge of his bed, and turned on the news. Then he missed his daughter. It had become an activity, missing Emily. Not a feeling anymore, but a physical act that required time and space.

He finished his drink and looked at the olives. Emily had always eaten the olives from his martinis. The apartment was quiet and feeble without her, as big as a house, as useless as someone else's house. Her absence echoed in his ears as he huddled on the edge of the bed staring at the TV. The rest of the apartment, beyond this corner of his bed, was absurd. He didn't need it. He didn't belong in it. Everett told himself that this bizarre melancholy made no sense. His daughter was not even gone, not really—she was in college. She came home for vacations. She slept in her bed, left the bathroom light on, banged the refrigerator door. Everett felt suddenly, as if it were happening at that moment, the pull of Emily's tiny rubber boot as it finally came off her two-year-old foot.

She was scrupulous about splitting her time between her parents, and Everett resented the days she spent with her mother. He never had when she was growing up, nor in the first year he and Alison had separated. It was only now, when there were so few of those days to go around.

Perhaps Alison and I should remarry each other, he thought. That would double my share.

But the thought of marriage to his ex-wife was not appealing. Children who left the bathroom light on were one thing. A wife quite another. With the exception of his daughter, who could do no wrong in his eyes, Everett was an intolerant man. He had never encouraged Leslie to spend the night. She had intruded on his solitude, on his loneliness.

Emily called that night. She had lost her cell phone and didn't want him to worry when he couldn't get in touch with her.

"That's very considerate of you," he said. He smiled. He waited. He knew what came next.

"Um . . ."

He still waited, still smiling. Even the requests for money were precious to him.

Of course he always told her about financial responsibility, about the importance of budgeting her money, of planning ahead, of the novel idea of putting something aside for  emergencies, and of course he gave her the extra money she needed for skiing, books, shoes, pillows, parking tickets, library fines, whatever it happened to be that week, that month, that day. She had been an entitled, cranky teenager. She was no longer cranky. She was ashamed of being entitled. These were improvements, and Everett noted them with satisfaction.

As he brushed his teeth, he thought about Jody. He should have invited her up for a drink. He would have, too, if she hadn't had that big, wet dog in its ridiculous raincoat. But they had arranged to meet at the Go Go for dinner the next night. Presumably she would leave the dog at home. He went to bed feeling guilty about Leslie. I'm a heel, he thought. But he slept the sleep of the innocent.

Jody, on the other hand, was wide awake. She held her violin in her hand, silently fingering a difficult passage of Sibelius over and over, using an imaginary bow. When she tired of that, she sat on the window seat in the bay window with her knitting. She had seen the look of surprise when she'd lit a cigarette. Why had she bothered? She had only recently begun to smoke again, and she didn't really smoke much. Why had she chosen that moment?

"Oh, so what?" she said out loud.

But she found that it mattered to her. She had spent so little time with Everett that each moment, each expression on his face, stayed with her. She thought about what she would wear tomorrow. She had noticed his hands on the stem of that bizarre umbrella. It was then she had lit the cigarette, nervously. Beautiful hands. A beautiful man. Perhaps the umbrella was his daughter's. He was a bit stiff in his manner, but he was so confident. No one but a confident man could walk around with a pink-lined umbrella with froggies. Confidence like that was so much like strength. It often wasn't strength, she knew that, but she found it reassuring nevertheless. And she was going to have dinner with him, she, Jody, the self-styled spinster. She got up and put her knitting in its basket, then went to the bookcase where the phone books were. She looked up his name. Seeing it there on the tissue-thin paper excited her. She turned off the lights, got into bed, and listened to the dog snore until the morning light came through her tall windows and the golden-yellow walls glowed in the dawn. The rain had stopped. She woke Beatrice up then and walked with her to the boat lake in Central Park and watched the water ripple in the wind.

George had spent the night at Polly's, as he sometimes did when he worked late. But he had forgotten to pull the shade down, and the unaccustomed morning light woke him up much earlier than he would have liked. He got up and went to the window to rectify the situation as Jody and Beatrice were making their way home from the park. George recognized Jody as one of the customers from the restaurant, or rather he recognized the dog. He had trouble remembering faces, which made his job as a bartender a little harder. But he was carrying it off. And he didn't mind it. It was temporary, after all. Someday he would do . . . something.

He went back to sleep until noon, when he took Howdy out of his crate and let him pee on a pad. Then he threw a toy to the puppy and watched him tear it to pieces. George ran around the room and let the puppy chase him, lifting his foot now and then, Howdy dangling from his sock by the teeth. He watched Howdy groom himself. The puppy always started with his left paw, licking it, sometimes passing it over his ear like a cat. He wondered if dogs could be left-handed.

When Polly came home after work, George was still there. It was too much trouble to go all the way home just to turn around and come back again.

"Do you think dogs can be left-handed?" he said.

"They don't have hands," Polly said in her annoying copyeditor voice. She then immediately began harassing him about moving in with her. "Look at you. You're here. You might just as well give in. You live here already."

"Just enjoy your privacy, Polly. Privacy is nice."

"No. I'll spiral into a postbreakup depression." She said it like a threat or a boast, her bottom lip pushed out in a pout, then added, "I'm doing this for you."

George sighed. It was difficult for him not to do what Polly needed him to in order for her to think she was doing something for him. He held the puppy in his lap, bringing Howdy up to face him, back paws on George's thighs, front paws limp as puppet arms. Howdy lunged, licking him and squealing. George thought of living in Polly's apartment. It was an appalling thought. He thought of living in Howdy's apartment. That was far more tempting. Howdy would be there every night as he went to sleep, every morning when he woke up. He had taught Howdy how to sit already, to lie down, to wait while George went into another room and then to come when he called him.

Polly said, "Your lease for that squalid piece-of-shit apartment is almost up anyway . . ."

"Polly, shut up about this."

This had been going on for weeks. George sometimes wondered if living with Polly would be better than arguing with Polly.

"You shut up," Polly said.

George thought about his squalid piece-of-shit apartment. The roaches were getting bolder and bolder. The shower did not drain.

"It is really far from the restaurant," he said to himself, but he must have said it out loud, for Polly walked over to him, took the dog from his lap, said, "So that's settled, then," and sat down with Howdy, clicking on the TV.

George looked at his sister, still in her office clothes. The decision had been made, he had not been the one to make it, he was not even sure how he knew it was finally settled, whatever Polly chose to say, but settled it somehow was. He felt relieved. He hated arguing. He hated decisions. Both difficulties had been vanquished by this simple expedient of giving in. Nevertheless, it was humiliating and he felt compelled to say, "But, Polly, you know how I like to walk around naked."

Polly frowned.

George, feeling a little better, went to the refrigerator and got himself a beer. There was always beer in Polly's refrigerator, another salve. And milk and bread and goat cheese and yogurt. There were olives, too, and apples and a box of Petit Écolier cookies. There was an unopened bag of blue potato chips on the counter.

Then Polly, still frowning, said, "No, you don't."

"Well, I did once have a roommate who walked around naked," he answered, sitting beside her, happy now with his beer, the bag of blue potato chips, and the box of cookies on his lap. "Sometimes he sat on the kitchen counter naked."

But Polly, triumphant, did not rise to the bait.

That night, while George served drinks and Polly sat at the bar watching her brother with a sharp but benignant eye, Jody was shown to a table where Everett sat waiting. He stood up when she approached, which she found quaint and touching, though his expression was tense—that of a punctual person who has been kept waiting. Jody involuntarily checked her watch. She was less than five minutes late, not even enough to apologize.

"With aspect stern and gloomy stride . . ." she sang, not meaning to at all.

Everett smiled his sudden, glorious smile. "*The Mikado*," he said. "Well, I hope this dinner is not 'a dreadful fate . . .'"

Jody sat down, relieved, but chastising herself at the same time. Behave yourself, Jody, she told herself. What is the matter with you? Do not insult, do not tease the man you want to impress. He had overlooked the tease, not even seemed to notice it this time, accepting the Gilbert and Sullivan lyrics as a bond between them rather than as a comment on his own growling demeanor. But her luck might not hold. She had considered bringing Beatrice with her to dinner, seeing how fond of Everett the dog seemed to be, and vice versa, she noted to herself, remembering the gentle pat on the wet head the night before, but now she was glad she hadn't. Tonight, handling herself would be more than enough trouble.

She had some difficulty not breaking out into a rendition of "The Flowers That Bloom in the Spring" when Everett paid the check. It was something her father did every time he took out his wallet to pay, tossing the bills or credit card gaily on the table. But she was able to limit her outburst to a simple "Tra la!" which Everett did not seem to mind, and she retired to her sleepless bed that night in a restless but contented mood.

After leaving her at her door, Everett stood in his lobby waiting for the elevator. The weirdos in his building had left a doll stroller and a battered paperback mystery called *Return to Sender* by Violet Shawn Dunston on the console. Why anyone would bother putting out a ragged old mystery he didn't know. And who on earth would want a used doll stroller? A used doll, he supposed. He suddenly missed his old building, his doorman, and his elevator man. He had lived there since graduate school with a series of roommates, then with Alison, when the building had gone co-op and the two of them had bought at the ridiculously low insider's price. Now the apartment, all three beautiful bedrooms, had been sold, the proceeds divided between them. They each had come away with a nice profit, but there was more to life than money, he thought, the banality of the sentiment making the loss of his co-op even more depressing. Everett missed the place. And he suddenly missed being married, too. It was unnatural, a man his age living alone.

By the time he got upstairs, unlocked his own door, and gazed upon the quiet, orderly apartment that was waiting for him, he felt quite a bit better. He got into bed and read through a glossy booklet of real-estate properties that had been sent to him, then checked the real-estate ads in the paper, as he did every night. He wasn't going to rent forever, that much he knew. He thought about Jody. What was her apartment like? he wondered. He liked her. She was funny in a hidden, sardonic way. This worked well with her jolly exterior manner. And she had not mentioned the end of the torrential rain once. Everett looked through the rest of the newspaper, but he had read as much as he wanted to that morning. He turned off the light, wishing as he did so that he had picked up the Violet Shawn Dunston mystery from the table in the lobby, whoever Violet Shawn Dunston might be.

seven

The Chick Magnet

Has it ever occurred to you that bossiness is a kind of generosity? A need to share what the gods have miraculously bestowed? I think that may have been the case with Polly. That and her youth. She was, after all, only twenty-six years old. She felt lucky every morning, astonished at the blue of the sky or the gray, such a lovely gray. For the first few months in New York City, when she had come here for college, Polly would look around her and cry out, "taxis!" not trying to hail one, just marveling that they were there. This excitement with the world, this joy, this cry of "taxis!" may have been why the breakup with Chris hit her so hard.

Polly believed that the world was full of promise. If she sometimes got confused and thought that it was she who had made the promise, who had unwittingly committed herself to straightening all that was crooked in the world around her, we shouldn't blame her. It was as if she had heard her own big grown-up voice spreading the word. And like a child, she obeyed. If, like a child, she didn't really examine the word in question, we must remember that Polly also spent a full week's paycheck on hand-press stationery and sometimes didn't wear a bra to work. She was young, and when her decisions came back and thumbed their noses at her, she was always surprised, though she was never defeated.

Her decision to live with George full-time, for example, turned out to include one of those impertinent surprises, for Polly, in such proximity to her brother, was of necessity introduced to George's habits of dating, and had he really sat naked on the kitchen counter, she could not have been more disgusted.

At first she had noticed only George's domestic habits, which were not nearly as bad as she had feared. George had limited his mess to his own quarters, and she could have had no complaints on that score anyway, as she was messy herself, except for her closets, which were impeccably neat and organized. In the kitchen, George did the best he could, leaving the freezer open only now and then, turning off the lights more often than not, and emptying the garbage whenever instructed. His job as a bartender was enough to pay his share of the rent. He was genial, almost solicitous, and he was wonderful with the dog. Wonderful, wonderful . . . walking him, feeding him, playing Frisbee and tug-of-war, teaching him to sit. Wonderful, yes, but as with so many wonderful things, it was this wonderful attention to the dog that turned out to be the problem for Polly.

Although Howdy was barred from walking the streets of New York, he was expected by the books and the downloaded articles to meet people on the street, hear noises on the street, see cars and bicycles and strollers and umbrellas and Rollerblades and fire engines on the street. This socialization was to be accomplished by putting the puppy into a Snugli-like sling made especially for dogs, and then parading up and down

Columbus Avenue with Howdy's head beneath one's chin and his furry legs and enormous paws dangling in all directions. This duty often fell to George. George was home during the day, so it made sense, but Polly was grateful nevertheless, for her brother was always good-natured about it, and extremely diligent. Howdy, as a result, was a very friendly, well-adjusted dog, afraid of no person or animal, of whatever size or shape or age or temperament, calm before the approach of screaming sirens, roaring mufflers, radios, helicopters, marching bands, political rallies, crashing thunder, shrieking baby twins, or deafening jackhammers. Polly was proud of her puppy and, in the protective and doting manner she had taken on since childhood, she was proud of her brother, as if he were a puppy himself.

But George was not a puppy, as Polly had to admit to herself. He was a man in his late twenties with no apparent idea of settling down anywhere or at anything, and at the same time that she basked in the success of George with Howdy, Polly could not help but notice that George seemed to have a different girlfriend almost every week. She did not have much contact with them, as the brother's and sister's living arrangements were extremely private. Because the apartment had once been two apartments, it still had two front doors, one of them opening directly into George's room. This room, formerly a studio apartment, was large and bright, with its own bathroom. The only time Polly bumped into one of the girlfriends was in the cubbyhole kitchen. There she would frequently find a scantily clad girl making coffee in the morning, and they would smile and make friends. But sooner or later, usually sooner, the friendly girl would be replaced by a new friendly girl.

Polly objected on behalf of all single women. She resented George's promiscuity at the same time that she was envious of it. She sympathized with the exes, whether they had tired of George or George had tired of them. Did they sit at home and mourn their lost love and dashed hopes as she did? She told herself they were not really girlfriends at all, that they had not lived with George for a year, shared every thought with him, lived life as a couple, secretly thought of marriage, as she had with Chris. Even so, when she met a new girlfriend, she wanted to warn her. This is how it starts, she wanted to say. And then, it ends.

But what if this was the start of something that didn't end? What if this time it took? Wouldn't that be a good thing, rather than a bad thing? Surely not every relationship ended up in tatters. The girl would be so happy. George would be so happy. Or would he? In this way, a looping, infinite way, Polly busied herself worrying about George. He was so unsettled generally. He had been drifting so stubbornly for the six years he'd been out of college. Worse, Polly also became attached to each of the girls and missed them when they were gone. She and her brother were constantly bumping into spurned lovers. When she walked with him, he sometimes pulled his hood low over his eyes, or shrank down inside his collar until one of the ex-girlfriends, if they could ever have even been called girlfriends, had passed.

"Don't shit where you eat," she said to him.

But George only shrugged.

"I know you don't pick up all these gorgeous girls at the restaurant." She knew this because she was usually there herself, with him, hanging out as he mixed drinks and poured beers.

"Polly, do I bother you about your love life?"

"No, but I don't have a love life."

George immediately began to make jokes and steer the conversation away from Polly's bleak romantic prospects and his own triumphs.

Polly knew she was jealous, George knew she was jealous, and they both knew to ignore the jealousy until it could be shed and left behind, like a snake's dry, useless skin in the sand. Still, sitting at home with Howdy on her lap, Polly sometimes tried to imagine where George was. She suspected he met up with Chris now and then, but she was afraid to ask him in case it was true. That would be very disloyal, and she didn't want to think of George as disloyal. She depended on George. He was funny and cheerful in a detached, morose sort of way, and he softened her loneliness.

For Polly found she was very lonely. The other editors she worked with at the magazine seemed okay, but they were older than she was and talked about their children's tuitions, while she was still trying to pay off her college loans. She spent hours on the phone with Geneva, and when Polly wasn't sitting at the Go Go bar facing George, she would meet Geneva at a proper downtown bar, though Polly did not have the heart even to flirt with anyone and tended to talk too much about Chris. She was afraid, too, whenever she went out with friends, that she would bump into Chris. There were several of her friends from college who lived in the city, and they would get together for someone's birthday, for dinner, for drinks. Sometimes they played pool. Sometimes they went to the movies. In the days before the breakup, Polly had been the one to find the new restaurant, to try the new drink, to herd her friends to the new movie. She had her own pool cue in a leather case. But now the pool cue was in the closet, she hated to leave the neighborhood, she drank whatever was around, and she preferred television to movies. Polly was sore and alone, and George, her brother, was the one who most soothed that agitated, empty feeling. Socializing was work, weary and laborious, and if George could have carried her in his papoose to do it, she would have joined the dog there gladly. Papoose, she thought. Webster's defines "papoose" as a Native American child, not the sling used to carry it. Well, too bad. She was off duty, and papoose it was, and George was the one wearing it.

No matter how imperious Polly was toward him, George was still her big brother, the same one who had helped her

pack her little suitcase when they moved back and forth together from the custody of one parent to the other, two times
a week, every week, as Polly demanded obeisance with her
loud voice and clung to his hand. Now she sat in the living
room wishing he were there. For someone with no real life, he
seemed to be incredibly busy. The living room of the apartment had two windows that faced what the real-estate agent
had described as a courtyard but that anyone else would have
called an air shaft. At the bottom of the air shaft, which Polly
could see from her windows, there were piled many bags of
garbage as well as several old stoves, mattresses, doors, broken
lamps, three-legged chairs, a grimy mauve sofa, and a colorful
plastic jungle gym twisted into a shape no child could possibly
climb. The air shaft, Polly realized soon after moving in, recog-
nizing the bookcase and the coffee table of the man who had
killed himself in the apartment, was used as a Dumpster. She
had immediately gotten bamboo shades to block the sight of
the garbage. But shades also blocked the light, and now that it
was spring, she liked to pull them up and open the windows,
letting in the narrow sliver of sun that appeared for an hour or
two each morning. She did this for Howdy, who lay contentedly in any wan city splash of light he could find. When the
windows were open, the sounds from the other apartments
fronting the air shaft were clear and distinct. The children
across the way whined. The couple upstairs bickered. And the
two singers, a soprano and a tenor, in two different apartments,
sang. They both gave voice lessons, and the scales of their
pupils sometimes battled each other in the air shaft. On this
night, only one voice could be heard, the soprano, accompa-
nied by a piano. Polly put the radio on to drown out the endless repetition. Howdy softly licked her hand. She watched
Howdy's eyes closing and thought about her roommate. What
was next on her George Agenda? She wondered whom he
was going out with now and resolved again that George and

Geneva, though neither had shown the slightest interest in each other as of yet, were meant to fall deeply in love, requiring just the smallest bit of assistance, which she was determined to provide.

While Polly was plotting his romantic future, George was riding his bicycle along the Hudson River toward Battery Park. He rode at night, after work. He never told Polly of these excursions. She would have worried, making his life a living hell, and her own, too. Funny, living with your sister. He wanted so much to make her happy, but, finally, he was the one man in the world who absolutely could not do that. That she needed a man he did not doubt. She had become obsessed with the dog, which he understood. He was attached to the puppy, too, thinking about him, about the expression of his dark eyes, the way his head cocked in a questioning tilt, the silky golden coat, the way he lapped water from his bowl . . . George laughed. It was like being in love. He thought much more about Howdy than he did about the girls he was dating. Date? Stupid word. Fuck was more like it. No. That was unfair to himself. He started every encounter full of hope. The girl he was seeing now, Sarah, had seemed perfect. She had been on her way home from a Farrelly brothers movie when he met her, and she had been carrying a copy of the collected poems of W. H. Auden, his favorite poet, that she'd bought at Barnes & Noble before the film. She stopped and petted the puppy squirming in the papoose, her face close to George's, and his heart seemed to stop, she was so beautiful. High and low, kind and stunning. What else could he ask? Why wasn't he in love with her? What was wrong with him?

It never occurred to George that there was anything wrong with the girls he failed to fall in love with. He was honest enough, and vain enough, to take the responsibility wholly on his own shoulders. He was rarely the one who did the actual breaking up. They just somehow knew and then drifted away.

He felt as if he were an open window. They wafted in, then out, leaving behind a flutter of the curtains. I am a gaping, empty window, he thought, almost enjoying his self-pity now  that it came with such a nice image. He imagined the feel of the soft breeze, the caress of the curtains against his face in the soft sunlight. But, no, the curtain couldn't graze his face. He wasn't looking out the window, he was the window.

At least he was trying. Polly, on the other hand, thought of excuses not to go out. Sometimes she hung out with her friends watching *Friends*, which struck him as particularly, nauseatingly sad. She sat around at the Go Go when he was there. He dragged her out to play pool now and then, or to a bar. But she never spoke to anyone. He wondered why it mattered so much to him, but it did matter. Polly's happiness had always mattered. She was his competent, bossy little sister and until now all he had to do to make her happy was allow her to tell him what to do. He was content with that, and good at it, too. Polly took care of things. Polly had always laid out the rules, and George, as well as their mother and father (reeling with both guilt and anger), had tried, with limited success, to follow them. When the parents transgressed, when their father bought George an air gun that their mother had forbidden, when their mother refused to let the children attend a paternal uncle's wedding on one of her custody days, when malice and competitiveness toward each other overcame the parents' logic and love for their children, it was Polly who straightened them all out. She was busy and loud and stubborn, and George had been grateful, leaving affairs of the world in her hands and retreating comfortably into his own quiet, dreamy realm. But now, with the wind against his face, the stars bright above the Hudson River, he coasted past the skeletal hulls of piers that undulated like roller coasters into the dark water, and he decided he would, he must, find Polly a boyfriend.

It was just a week later, one evening in April, when the days were drawing out and the air was fragrant and moist and warm, that Polly discovered the secret of George's success with the neighborhood female population. She had walked home from work through the park because it was such a beautiful day. The daffodils, thousands of them, were bright and fresh, and they flashed in the sun, still wet from that morning's shower. Forsythia was spilling over the park's stone overpasses. The smell of the moist earth brought tears of joy to Polly's eyes. Spring! It was back! Trees were as yet bare of leaves, but birds had come from somewhere on their way to somewhere else and were singing from the branches. Polly walked home with other men and women in their office suits and office shoes, all of them seduced by the fragrant spring, swinging their briefcases gaily.

Polly bought some bread at a bakery on Columbus, clutching the warm loaf to her breast, feeling privileged to live in a world in which fresh bread also existed, then made her way up the few blocks to her street. It was there, at a bench outside of a café on the corner one street below their own, that she saw George. He sat with Howdy dangling from the sling in front of him. Howdy was glowing and fluffy in the soft waning light. George smiled and cooed at the dog, kissing the silky top of Howdy's head, and Howdy twisted and squirmed in order to lick George's cheek. Polly stopped, her heart bursting with pride and love. She had never seen anything so sweet, she thought, and then noticed that she was not the only one admiring the couple. Two exquisite girls with large leather bags and expensive sunglasses stopped to stare and chat in French-accented baby talk. When they moved on, another girl, a dark-haired young woman with a pale, offhand beauty not unlike

George's, also stopped and petted the dog. As Polly stood on the other side of the street and watched, this new girl sat beside George on the bench. Polly walked on quickly and went home.

"You use the dog to pick up girls?" she said when George and Howdy came home.

"He's totally a chick magnet," George said. "It's unbelievable."

"You use Howdy, who's already had to witness the suicide of his owner, to 'pick up chicks'?"

Polly spent sleepless nights sometimes thinking about the former occupant of the apartment. What had he been like? Why had he been so unhappy? She hoped the little puppy had given him a moment of pleasure and warmth before he died. Then she would get angry at him for leaving the puppy alone and locked in a closet. Then she would apologize to the soul of the dead man, who obviously had been agonizingly sad. Then she would wonder what he looked like and where he was buried and what his parents had been like. Then she would turn on the TV and watch old movies, her mind a murky pond of resentment, embarrassment, and anguish for the stranger who hanged himself in her apartment. His apartment, she would correct herself, sometimes turning on a light at this point.

Now Polly pulled Howdy out of the sling and held him in her arms.

"You're disgusting," she said to George.

George just laughed, and Polly was more determined than ever that George should settle down with a proper girlfriend and that that proper girlfriend should be Geneva.

eight

"Do you ever buy flowers?"

It was at about this time that Polly started smoking again. She didn't smoke a lot. It was forbidden in the office, forbidden in restaurants, forbidden even in bars. She was so used to going outside for a cigarette that even when she was home, where smoking was allowed, by her, she always went outside and leaned against the brick wall of the building, watching the comings and goings of her neighbors. Jamie snapped at his unusually tall boyfriend as they wrestled a bunch of kids out of a minivan. A heavy old woman in a black dress crept slowly by, curled over a cane, muttering in Italian. Three or four young couples emerged from the Malaysian restaurant, laughing, leaning on one another. Polly had seen the woman with the big white pit bull a few times and had thanked her for the name of the vet and discovered the dog's name was Beatrice, and as she stood outside on that soft spring evening smoking and trying to decide how to get George and Geneva into the same room without being too

obvious and yet being obvious enough so that they would notice each other, Beatrice and her owner came sauntering down
the street. The woman smiled at Polly in a friendly way. She
was dressed in a short-sleeved Oxford shirt neatly tucked in,
Polly noted, but she still managed to look if not stylish, then
crisp and attractive.

"When will I meet this puppy?" the woman said. "The vir-
tual puppy?"

"Just go to the café one block down any afternoon," Polly
said. "My brother hangs out there with him trying to pick up
girls."

"Really? Using the puppy as bait? That's creative."

"George is nothing if not creative. Of course he doesn't
actually create anything you could name . . ."

Polly was feeling bitter and though a corner of her consciousness held the knowledge that trashing her brother to a
relative stranger was perhaps unseemly, she couldn't stop herself. She offered a cigarette to her listener, who surprised her
by accepting.

"Really? Nobody smokes anymore."

"I just started again," the woman said.

"Really? Me, too," Polly said, and she continued complaining about George for several minutes until she felt the door
move behind her and stepped aside. A middle-aged man and a
girl of about eighteen came out of the building. Beatrice
lunged for the man, pushing her nose into the palm of his
hand.

"Hi there, Beatrice," said Everett to the dog. "I remember you."

"She sure remembers you," said the girl.

"Yes, she does," said Jody. She looked at Everett, who
immediately averted his eyes, then seemed to pull himself
together and introduced Emily and Jody to each other.

"And I'm Polly," Polly said.

Jody smiled at the "and." As if Polly were the part that made it all complete, she thought. So much assurance in someone so young. It was amazing.

"I live in 4F," Polly continued.

"Ah," Everett said, raising an eyebrow.

"Yeah," Polly said. "That apartment."

"Well . . . ," Everett said.

There was a pause.

"Polly has a puppy," Jody said quickly, then realized that, as the puppy was not there with them, this information was irrelevant. And why, she wondered, does my one contribution to this stilted conversation sound like baby talk? Polly has a puppy! Polly has a puppy! She hadn't seen Everett in weeks. She hadn't heard from him. And this was all she could manage? Of course, he was not doing much better.

"How are you?" she asked. "How have you been?"

"Oh . . ." He shrugged. "Okay. Busy . . ."

Jody realized she had put him on the spot, which she had not intended to do. Or had she?

"Dad?" Emily said. "We're kind of late."

And Everett and Emily walked off toward Broadway.

Jody hopelessly watched them leave, then turned slowly back to Polly.

"It's funny that I knew your dog's name but not yours," Polly said. "I just thought of you as Beatrice's mom."

Jody disliked it when people re-
ferred to themselves as if they were
their dogs' parents. She found Polly
a bit jejune for her taste, which was
not Polly's fault, she had to admit.
Polly was after all only a girl: she
was supposed to be jejune. And
there was something Jody found
appealing about her in spite of that,

the way she found her students appealing. Polly seemed tender and exposed, yet triumphant and irresistible, a kind of vulnerable juggernaut, Jody thought, in a way that she associated with cheerful, noisy young children.

Jody walked home slowly, wondering what had come over Everett. It was not that she had expected him to fall head over heels in love with her. But they had had such a lovely dinner. She thought surely they would get together again. And she had certainly expected a warmer welcome in the event of a chance encounter like tonight's. Perhaps he was embarrassed in front of his daughter. He was extremely attached to Emily, Jody knew that. That must be it. Emily was home, and Everett was self-conscious and preoccupied. She heartily wished Emily would go back to college where she belonged.

Jody was right about Everett and Emily. The minute his daughter walked in the door, he forgot all about Jody. Seeing his neighbor there with her dog on his doorstep had surprised him, and he had been self-conscious and awkward. Worse, he realized, he had been cold, even rude to Jody. She was a perfectly nice person and didn't deserve that. He felt ashamed as he walked away with Emily, an uneasy feeling. Everett kicked a bottle on the sidewalk. It bounced off the curb and shattered.

"Dad!" Emily said.

On the other hand, was he obligated to Jody in some way just because they had a shared a delightful dinner together? He thought not. Single women were so demanding, he told himself—so needy. He stood up a little straighter. What right had she to make him feel guilty? And by the time he had settled himself beside Emily in the subway, he was almost angry at Jody, which was a great relief.

Polly asked Jody how she knew Everett, but Jody didn't seem interested in talking about him and wandered off down the street, the dog stopping to pee beside the tire of a large white SUV. Polly had noticed the greeting Everett received from the big white dog. She had seen Everett smile at his daughter, as well, a big bounteous smile. She had seen his beautiful blue eyes.

Dogs never greeted Chris like that, she thought. Chris disliked dogs. And dogs, instinctively it seemed, disliked Chris. That should have told me something, Polly thought. That should have shown me something, and I'll show him. She repeated this combination and found it invigorating. The two sentences seemed linked not just by their verb, but morally, psychologically, logically, philosophically, spiritually . . . That should have shown me, and I'll show him.

After what seemed to her to be sufficient time for two people to eat their dinner, Polly brought Howdy down to the lobby to play ball. She wasn't sure why the lobby seemed suddenly an ideal place to play with the dog, but she was sure that it did. She asked Howdy out loud in the earnest high-pitched voice so common to dog owners addressing their dogs why they had never thought of playing there before. In reply, Howdy ran back and forth across the long lobby, chasing the tennis ball and bringing it back, sliding clumsily and vigorously on the polished marble floor, until Everett and Emily appeared. Then Howdy ran to Everett, dropped the ball at his feet, looked appealingly up at his face, and was, to Polly's mind, the best, most obedient dog in all the world.

"Okay," Everett said to no one in particular. "Two dogs in one night."

"You've got the power," said Emily, in a singsong voice. "The power of voodoo."

"Who do?" Everett said blandly, but dutifully. He was tired. He wanted to get home.

"You do!" Polly said, suddenly remembering the bit from a Cary Grant movie.

Everett was not a terribly nice man. Those who worked for

him would have attested to that. He was bored and he was, therefore, irritable and exacting and cold and not well liked. But though he was not what you would consider nice, he was not a bad man, either. And it was his fortune, perhaps he would have said misfortune, that dogs, small children, and women loved him. The sight of this woman, so young she was practically a child, and her dog, both so obviously taken with him, did not surprise Everett. But it did not please him, either. She was interfering with his precious Emily time. And she had addressed him with an unseemly authority. She was talking now as if she were a perfectly assured and sophisticated adult. She was only a few years older than Emily. Her confidence disturbed him. It looked ridiculous on her, he thought, like an eleven-year-old boy with a cigarette in his mouth. What was she doing hanging around in the lobby, anyway? If he had been living in his old apartment on West End Avenue, with its great square lobby and its uniformed doorman, this would not have been possible. Divorce was inconvenient in so many ways.

"Well, good night," he said abruptly, taking the stairs so that he would not have to wait for the elevator with the girl and her puppy. Emily stopped kissing and fondling the puppy in order to follow, and soon they were home watching reruns of *Seinfeld*, which Everett had never liked. But he was with Emily, and Emily was happy, laughing and alerting him to each line she thought was funny, and so he was happy, too.

Polly also went to bed happy. George was at work under the watchful eye of Jamie, who forbid his employees to flirt with patrons, perhaps because most of his employees were his ex-boyfriends, and so Polly did not have to worry about what inappropriate stranger George might be dating that night. When she began to feel sad about Chris, she reminded herself that he was a contemptible being rejected by the canine world. And Everett, though abrupt and distant, was nevertheless an interesting new curiosity. Perhaps best of all, Howdy, the dog who had been waiting in the closet just for her, was in her bed, his head flopped on her pillow, his breath soft and even against her own.

By May, the park was a rich green, the grass like the rolling lawn of an estate in an English novel, the branches a canopy of lush young leaves. Instead of heading directly home from the subway after work, Simon began to go there to sit on a bench, his briefcase between his feet, watching the other office workers and their briefcases, the children and their nannies, the dogs and their people, the elderly and their companions, the teenagers and their cigarettes. Sometimes he strolled along the bridle path hoping to see one of the nags rented out from the stable uptown. When he passed a pile of horse manure, he stopped reverently, breathing in his memories.

He often passed the woman with the dog, Jody and Beatrice. He found their names amusing, the woman with a man's name, the dog with a woman's name. On one of these evenings, he ended up going with Jody and Beatrice for a drink at the Mexican restaurant that was the first of the places on Columbus to put tables and chairs outside.

"Do you ever buy flowers?" Jody asked as they walked by the blooms in plastic buckets at the corner market.

"Well, no," Simon said, a little surprised at the question. Did she expect him to buy her a bouquet? "It seems so silly, really. They just die, don't they?"

Jody nodded her head in agreement. "Yes," she said. "But then so do vegetables."

To which Simon replied, "I don't buy those, either."

A week later, they had dinner there together. And a week later another dinner. It was so easy, Simon thought. He had never been much good at dating. The attention required to actually single out one person to be interested in, then to pursue that person, to speak to her, call her, dream up activities to share with her—it was far more than he could access. But this! All he had to do was sit on the bench, and if Jody and the pit bull came by, and if Jody was free that night, then Simon had a date. If not, he had gone to no trouble. He had made no plans that could be dashed. He told himself that this casual, spontaneous arrangement was ideal. He told himself this as he sat on the bench, not moving, forcing himself to turn neither left nor right, not allowing himself to search for a small energetic woman and a large white dog.

One night, a beautiful evening when Simon had perched longer than usual on the edge of the bench, Polly, unable to resist the lure of the park, had decided to walk home. It was cool and breezy and the sun was still shining when she started, but soon enough the sky darkened and the breeze grew stronger and Polly knew from the agitated heaviness of the air that it was going to rain. She hurried now, as did everyone around her. This was not what she had calculated. She was worried, for this was a special evening, a strategic evening that was to feature an event she had plotted and anticipated for weeks. Operation George and Geneva. Tonight was the night she was going to put it all into action.

Polly's plan was simple. She had mulled it over and worked out many different scenarios, but finally she came back to the easiest and most obvious solution. She would simply arrange to meet Geneva at the café where George and Howdy hung out, and, voilà! If George could use Howdy for bait, so could Polly. George and Geneva would see each other, they would be drawn to each other . . . and her work would be done. Polly put a large degree of faith in fate, once she had decided exactly what it was that fate would deliver.

Hurrying through the windy park, she prayed the rain would wait until she had brought her brother and her friend together. Then, let it pour if it must, she thought: George would become irresistibly solicitous, stripping off his own jacket, his shirt, even, to keep Geneva dry. Polly's heart beat faster, in part from delight at this possible romantic development, in part because she was now almost running.

When she noticed the man with the briefcase on the bench, it was because he sat up so straight. He was so still, oddly motionless, surrounded by the leaves whipping in the wind and the people rushing for cover. Then she saw Jody and her dog coming toward him from the other direction. Polly reached the statuelike man just as they did, and she knew she had to stop to say a quick hello, after which she could say she had to go meet someone, surely, and slip off to her matchmaker's duties.

"It's going to pour!" she said, the bellow of her own voice startling her as it still so often did. The man looked a little startled, too. Polly felt sorry for him. It's only me, she wanted to say.

"Polly, this is Simon," Jody said. "He lives on our block."

Jody was so light and delicate, Polly thought. Why can't I do that? It's not that complicated. You don't need a Ph.D., as her grandmother would have said. What would be the light and delicate thing for her to say in this situation? It's lovely to meet you. No. Bland. Hi, there, neighbor. No. Too corny. What a pleasure to meet a new neighbor . . . Honestly, she had never said anything like that in her life. She didn't have to. She would just bark out a hello and hold out her hand and people deferred to her, were respectful toward her, afraid of her or, very occasionally, put off by her.

"You're waiting so patiently," she said, still searching for something charming to say and realizing immediately that she had failed. Then she made it worse. "For the rain?"

"Sort of," Simon said, looking embarrassed. Polly thought he was good-looking. What is the opposite of slick? she wondered. He seemed to her to be the opposite of slick. His hair was rumpled and so, somehow, was his expression. And yet he was dressed impeccably. What beautiful suede shoes he had. They would be ruined in the rain. Beautifully dressed, she thought, her eye running again from his rumpled head to his suede toes. Except his socks, she noticed. They did not quite match.

Big drops began to spatter on the leaves, then on the pavement, then on the three people gathered around the bench beneath the tree. Simon stood up and the three of them ran, Beatrice loping beside them, out of the park, across Central Park West, and under the canopy of the nearest building.

Doris looked down at them from the high perch of her white SUV. She recognized the woman and the dog who had pissed on her car and was filled with rage. She was already furious at the filthy rain, which was leaving charcoal streaks on the polished white paint of her vehicle. She was furious that she could not find a parking space. Of course she should have taken the train to see her sister in Bedford. But equally of course she could not have done so. What was the point of having this behemoth automobile in New York, spending hours of her day waiting for parking spaces, if she couldn't use it to drive to visit her sister? She cursed her sister, the rain, and the woman and her white dog. She opened the window and shook her fist at them as they huddled under the canopy.

"I'm watching you," she cried, her voice trembling with fury.

Lightning crackled and thunder crashed and Jody could not hear what the woman with the orange face said, but she saw her, small and eerie in her tall, tanklike car, as sharp as a falcon on a ledge.

"I think that woman is following me," she said.

"What am I going to do?" Polly said. "I can't stand here waiting. I have a date."

Simon noticed that Polly had on a very pretty dress and he was sorry she had a date. He had been wondering if she, too, might come visit him on his bench some evening.

"A date?" Jody said. She knew Polly had recently been dumped by her boyfriend. What a plucky little thing she was. "Good for you."

"No, not for me. For my brother."

She left Jody and Simon and plunged into the rain, running as if that would somehow keep her dry. How was it that puddles, huge puddles, formed so quickly? She splashed toward the café, her hair streaming, her dress clinging to her. It's only water, she reminded herself. She stood at a red light, pounded by rain. She'd read that in Sweden they had recently outlawed the little man wearing a bowler hat on the "Walk" and "Don't Walk" lights and changed him to a bareheaded gender-neutral stick figure. She wished she had a bowler hat.

When she reached the café, naturally there was no George and no Howdy. Who would sit at an outdoor café in a thunderstorm? Polly stood beneath the awning, waiting for Geneva, cursing her luck, when Geneva called her cell phone and said it was too crummy out, she was going home to have a bath and a bowl of cereal for dinner and go to bed. Polly remarked to herself that the two lovers were extremely uncooperative and unromantic and went home herself where she, too, had a bath as well as some leftover pizza. George did not come home that night at all, as far as she knew.

Doris did finally find a parking space, although she would have to move the car the next morning. She resented her sister for this, as for so many things. Natalie had married well, divorced better, and remarried best of all. She had never worked a day in her life—for pay. But she did work grueling hours on the boards of charities and as a docent at the Met. There was something admirable about this, Doris knew, but was there nothing admirable about going to an office, day after day, to be underpaid? No, there was not, and Doris, in protest, walked especially slowly, majestically across the street, her umbrella held high, not even looking at the impatient truck driver who honked his horn to hurry her progress.

Jody waited until the rain lessened to take Beatrice home. There would be no sitting outside at the Mexican restaurant tonight. She thought she noticed that Simon was disappointed and considered how lonely he must be to want the company of a spinster schoolteacher and her pit-bull mix. Spinster schoolteacher, she said to herself again. She liked referring to herself, privately, in this way. It produced a little frisson of something—not pleasure, exactly, and not pain, but the satisfaction of scratching a hard-to-reach itch. It's true she had gone to dinner once more with Everett, when his daughter's spring break was over, and now she had done the same with Simon. Was that dating? Did that return her to being single instead of being a spinster? She wasn't sure that suited her. Single. It sounded so unfinished. Spinster, on the other hand, had some teleological heft.

"Good night," she said to Simon, who walked her home. "You're very gallant, aren't you?"

She went upstairs with Beatrice, thinking about Everett. Perhaps she would invite him to the performance of *The Mikado* next month. Yes, that might do nicely.

Simon continued on to the Go Go Grill in a relatively good humor. He did not have a date, but he was gallant. And, perhaps best of all, he was both gallant and able to eat his dinner in effortless silence.

nine

Heat

A New York street in summer
is best seen in early morning, if at all. Our street was no different. The summer heat on some days was so bad you could
almost hear it. The cans of garbage, labeled with the address
of the building they belonged to, overflowed with the trash of
passersby. Enormous black garbage bags, piled like unloved
corpses, seemed to absorb the sun's heat during the day and
send it back into the humid air at night, along with the faint
stench of old take-out meals. But early in the morning, when
the sun is just coming up, there is a pause on New York City
streets, a freshness and a gentle climate, an expectant stillness.

It was only the beginning of June, but Simon had begun to
wake up even earlier than usual in order to take a walk while it
was still possible to bear the heat. There is a particular smell in
New York on a summer morning when the doormen and su-
pers are out in front of their buildings spraying the sidewalks
with hoses. The black trash bags have been collected by noisy,

groaning sanitation trucks, and the smell of garbage, hot and dense and vegetative, has been washed away. Instead, the water, evaporating from the sidewalk, has a damp, city, mineral smell. The sky was bright and white on the morning in question, a Saturday, and Simon, passing the Korean market, breathed in the scent of roses and freesia and ripe nectarines. He ambled past the bustle of shopkeepers raising the gates in front of their stores, and deliverymen unloading boxes of broccoli and strawberries in front of the supermarket, and waiters putting out plastic tables and chairs to create sidewalk cafés. When he reached Central Park, he entered into the quiet, which always happened so suddenly, as if he had closed a door behind him. He strolled through the sultry smells of grass and leaves, through the deep shade, then made his way slowly back home. He knew enough not to leave the city even for a day in the summer. If he'd gone to the Hamptons or upstate or to the Jersey Shore or to Connecticut, he would have come back and found a city shabby and enervated, deserted by anyone who could afford to get out, a sad, steaming maze of filthy concrete. As it was, the city was vibrant and rich and full of life. He could see it all. You just needed perspective. The perspective of no perspective.

When he got home, disappointed but not surprised that he had not bumped into Jody, he had his coffee in his big leather armchair, read the paper, and settled in for his nap. But he found he could not sleep. He took his saddle down from the high shelf in the closet and laid it tenderly across the back of his chair and polished it with a big sea sponge scented and lathered with saddle soap.

He had missed Jody by just a few minutes. She, too, liked to sneak out before the heat could find her, which is how she thought of it. The other people walking their dogs would greet them and stop to visit, and though Jody didn't know most of their names, she found these anonymous encounters curiously intimate. The man with the shaky old blind Bernese mountain dog was worried about his son getting into a good college. The cellist with her beagle whose belly was more or less distended depending on what cabinet he had gotten into the night before told Jody about a new recording by Les Arts Florissants. The handsome young man from the Netherlands with the new keeshond puppy beamed with pride and unexpected joy as he related his dog's triumphant house-training. The exquisitely turned out Parisian widow with her small, bizarrely shaped three-legged mutt discussed the stock market. The ponytailed guy with a Russian wolfhound, a greyhound, and a saluki, leading all three on their leashes from his bicycle, waved hello, while his daughter, in a child seat behind him, ate a Pop-Tart with slow concentration. Jody's mornings were full of stories and advice and revelations from the elderly man with his elderly bichon, the athletic young couple with their breathless pug, and of course Jamie with his two cairns nipping at his pant legs.

On this morning, Jody greeted the caretaker of the little redbrick church as he spread coffee grounds on the square of dirt surrounding the church's ginkgo tree; petted Sofie, a neighbor's elderly tufted terrier with sad eyes and long balletic legs; then continued on, enjoying the wan, white light. She wondered why the base of the church's tree was so bare. A doctrinal decision, perhaps? The heat was overwhelming but still fresh, and all along the street were flowers that had been planted carefully around the bases of other trees. Jody let Beatrice linger at the fire hydrant, then at the green poles holding the NO PARKING signs. She admired the part of the sidewalk that was slate and wondered what time the homeless man got up, for she had never seen him on the church steps in the morning. In this way, she and Beatrice walked slowly to the park, where Jody took off the dog's leash, and they headed north, past the lake and over to a little cove and rocky spit. In the spring, the bird-watchers there had eyed them with suspicion and distaste, but now there was no one around but the two of them and the white clouds overhead.

Jody had spent a particularly sleepless night. She'd practiced a piece she was doing with an informal quartet that met every few months, then she read a little, then turned off the light, then began her night of worrying. One of her credit cards was maxed out. She was a mediocre musician. She really had to call her parents. She should not have bought the Pratesi duvet cover. She took too many cabs. She was untalented, impecunious, and would die impoverished. She tried to reassure herself with the observation that when she was old and impoverished she would be covered by both Medicaid and the Pratesi duvet cover, which was supposed to last a lifetime, but before she had succeeded in convincing herself, she moved on to worry about Beatrice. Was the old dog happy living in a city? Was she getting enough exercise? Should Jody hire a dog walker for her when she was at school? But she couldn't afford that because she had selfishly spent all her money on sheets. What would happen to Beatrice when Jody died? What would happen to Jody when Beatrice died? How petty to worry about a dog when there was so much human suffering in the world. And so she worried about Sudan. Sudan worry then led to political rage and she was forced to get up and make a cup of chamomile tea and read a little, but that brought home to her what a sad, lonely spinster she had accidentally become, and she got back into bed to worry about the reemergence of polio in Africa. And when she would next bump into Everett.

It turned out to be that very morning that her opportunity came, although not, perhaps, just as she would have liked it. The heat was more profound now, almost soothing, swaddling Jody in its extremity, and she was walking home from the park in a dreamy, enervated state when she saw Polly and George come out of their building with their fluffy golden puppy on a leash.

"Look!" Polly called out to her. "It's Howdy's first day out!"

Instantly obedient to Polly's loud, deep voice, Jody did look, then crossed the street to pay homage to the dog's introduction to the street. Howdy jumped on her hysterically, a whirl of excited confusion and goodwill. Beatrice pushed herself between them and the two dogs began the ritual sniffing and circling.

Then, as Jody praised the eyes and ears and nose and coat and tail of the puppy, and Polly beamed and agreed, and George looked both pleased and embarrassed at the same time, the door opened and Everett appeared.

"Hi!" Polly said, almost blocking his way. "Look at Howdy!"

Jody noticed that at the sound of Polly's demand in her decisive voice—"Look at Howdy!"—all of them, like her, even George, obediently snapped their heads to look at Howdy. Howdy, in turn, snapped his head to look at Polly.

Everett appeared to have no idea why he was looking at the puppy, but he made a polite sound. He smiled at Jody, and she felt the blood rise to her face.

"How's your daughter?" she said, Emily always being a safe conversational gambit with Everett.

"Great, great . . . Spending the summer in Italy," he added politely to Polly and George. Then, as if perhaps he had made Emily appear less than serious, he coughed and said, "Studying."

"When you're young it's okay to be feckless in Italy, I suppose," Jody said. What? Feckless? Who talks like that? And who emphasizes how old they are?

"I spent a summer in Italy," Polly said. "In Florence."

Polly stood on the sidewalk in her pretty pastel summer dress, like the girls in that short story, Jody thought, suddenly uncomfortable in her own khaki pants and bright green polo shirt. In the sunlight, Polly looked so young, her pale skin flushed from the heat, her eyes big and excited. Jody watched how she moved, so compact and powerful. So young, so young, so young. Usually she admired Polly's loud, youthful, innocent force. But for some reason this same quality rankled her now, as if Polly were speaking noisily at a concert, drowning out the music.

"Emily's in Florence!" Everett said. He addressed this to Polly. Jody saw this, and she did not like it.

"*You* certainly didn't study," George said to Polly.

"Shut up," she said. "I wish I could go back. Are you going to visit her?" she asked Everett, her skirt swirling gaily as she turned from her brother to the older man. "God, to get out of the hot, muggy city!"

Florence is a hot, muggy city, too, Jody wanted to say. And it's crawling with American students. Like Emily. And you, Polly, not all that long ago. But she was silent, noticing how Everett was looking at Polly.

"Go in the fall," George said. "Less crowded with American students."

Jody decided she liked George.

"Well, that would kind of defeat the purpose, wouldn't it, young man?" Everett said to George.

George raised an eyebrow. It must have been the "young man," Jody thought.

"Huh," George said, turning his back on Everett, kneeling to pet the dog.

Jody felt sad and weary and garish in her green shirt as she waited unhappily for George and Polly to continue their dog walk. Only then could the concert Polly had disturbed with her noisy voice resume; only then would Jody be able to chat with Everett. Why were they hanging around, anyway? Why didn't they walk the damn dog, now that the dog could walk?

She was planning to ask Everett about a real concert, one Polly couldn't spoil. The *Mikado* performance was the following week. She had already bought the tickets. She would offer him Gilbert and Sullivan and in return she would hear his voice and feel his smile turned exclusively toward her. But, after a good ten minutes, the brother and sister showed no signs of moving on, whereas Beatrice had begun tugging at her leash.

Jody waited a little longer, increasingly disgruntled, as Polly flirted outrageously with Everett ("Obviously I'm going to have to take you to Florence myself," Polly was saying with a musical laugh), and George sneered, then Jody finally mumbled a goodbye, hoping but failing to catch Everett's eye.

"I doubt that Emily would appreciate her father following her around the world," he was saying to Polly.

As Jody walked away, she heard the sound of Polly's mighty voice behind her. "No? *I* would. You could take me out to a really good dinner . . . I mean, if I were her."

Polly had been gazing appreciatively at Everett and his startling blue eyes as she spoke, but she stopped talking now, suddenly confused, as if she'd woken up and found herself in a strange forest. "Or not," she said.

Later, Polly sat in her bedroom and ran the conversation through her head. She decided that she was the biggest idiot of the bunch, rambling on about a girl she did not know, giddy and inappropriately girlish herself. George was a close second in the idiot derby. And he'd been a malignant idiot, too, clearly disapproving. Disapproving of . . . what?

Everett.

How did George even know about it? She only just this minute knew about it herself.

Everett?

Everett was so old and rather dull, really. At least, she had always thought so before, if she had even thought about him, which she really hadn't. But when he smiled today (at Jody, it was true, still . . .), Polly had seen that smile for a second time, and again, it was as if Everett were a completely different man. His eyes had blazed and his face had lifted. He had looked young and absolutely beautiful. Everett.

She sat up in bed, confused and embarrassed. She suddenly remembered the touch of his hand as he patted Howdy and it brushed against hers. Oh, brother, she thought.

Brother, indeed. There were downsides to intimacy. George understood too much. And he had been rude and embarrassing today with Everett. Everett had come out the best of the group, she decided, going through the conversation again. He was merely a little pompous. Maybe he was just shy. She imagined going out to dinner with him, to a proper restaurant, then to the ballet. Was it ballet season? She didn't like the ballet all that much, but the picture seemed right for this fantasy. They had to go somewhere, and they weren't going to go to a beer pong tournament, for example, something that Chris might have thought an appropriate night of entertainment.

Sometimes it is awkward to be happy. You get used to a certain jaundiced hue, and the change is jarring, unsettling. For a moment, as she thought of Chris, Polly, so sad for so long, was almost angry, as if Everett had been pursuing her, importuning her, harassing her. Leave me alone, she thought. I love Chris who loves someone else. Everybody knows that.

Then she remembered Everett's smile and Chris's last words to her—"I'll never forget, um, everything . . ."—and she decided that she didn't care how pompous Everett was or was not. Polly may have behaved like a silly girl today, George like an annoying brother, but Everett had behaved like a man. As for Jody, Polly forgot that she had even been present.

But Jody had been there, and she could not forget the scene, either. She took Beatrice to the drugstore and picked up some moisturizer. She got an iced coffee and sat on a bench at the café to drink it. She watched the people walking by as they eyed Beatrice suspiciously. Polly is just a girl, she said to herself. But she felt old and worn and angry at herself. Beatrice put her head on Jody's knee and looked up at her. Jody petted her wide forehead.

"Can we join you?"

It was George and the puppy. They sat down before Jody could answer. Beatrice lay down and the puppy began to walk on her belly, making his way up to her head until she stood up and gently let him slide to the ground.

"You trained him to the leash incredibly fast," Jody said.

George smiled. "I've got nothing else to do."

"Are you a feckless young man?" she said.

He caught the reference and laughed. "That guy is a stiff," he said.

"You think so?"

He shrugged. "Anyway, yeah, I am a feckless young man."

"What is it you don't do?" Jody asked.

"That is the question. If I knew, I would."

That night, riding his bike by the river, thinking of the meeting with Everett that afternoon, George made a decision. As the reader may have noticed, decisions were not really to George's taste. What use was there in this unnecessary step? He preferred to do what had to be done when it appeared before him as absolutely unavoidable. Why think about it beforehand? Decisions, he had explained in many late-night conversations with many inebriated friends, were redundant. Fetishistic, even. Yet here he was, worrying, planning, deciding. But what choice did he have? His sister was about to behave like an ass. He could see it, he could feel it, he could smell it. He had to do something to protect her from her own idiocy.

He shot through the humid night air breathing in the slight, salty breeze off the river. There were no stars visible, just the distant lights of the buildings downtown and across the water. He could see traffic lights in New Jersey changing, on a hill, all at once, a string of red blinking into a string of green.

He would demand that Polly begin walking the dog. That was George's decision, and it would involve a sacrifice from him, for he had enjoyed the feel of the dog on the other end of the leash, sensing a new communication between them. And so many people had stopped to pet the puppy. George was ridiculously proud of the dog. On those rare occasions when someone had passed by without acknowledging Howdy, George was almost as disappointed as Howdy was. Still, he had seen Polly flirting with Everett, that truculent, self-satisfied, utterly inappropriate senior citizen. It hardly seemed possible to George that Polly would be interested in him. But he knew what he had seen, he knew Polly, he knew how stubborn she could be, how impulsive when she was angry or hurt, and he knew he would have to help her escape her own perversity.

"You just want me to get out and meet people," Polly said when he told her the next day that she should take over walking the dog. "Believe me, George, gorgeous guys are not going to be stopping me on the street to pet Howdy. Why don't I just wear a sandwich board instead?"

She did begin walking the puppy a couple of times a day, though. She found it was a perfect time to fantasize about Everett. Howdy gamboled through the park and Polly imagined strolling, hand in hand, with her new lover, Everett, the mature and brilliant lawyer or doctor or whatever he was.

There was, in these weeks, a soft, fresh, ecstatic cloud of scent, surely the scent of spring itself: the Linden trees, the glorious, generous Linden trees. How can anyone fail to fall in love when the Linden trees flower? Polly and Howdy would wander along the lake past ducks and yellow irises and bright, verdant algae and she would replay the conversation with Everett about Florence, recalling the slight touch of his hand again and again until it began to seem to her that Everett had put his hand on the dog's head on purpose just to feel her own hand against it.

She bumped into Everett a few times over the next few weeks, once while taking out the garbage when she was in her pajamas, which was excruciating, the other times in the elevator, but he was closest to her when she took her long walks alone with her dog.

One night, before she went to bed, Polly stood with Howdy in front of her building, vaguely hoping to see Everett. Howdy wagged his tail at the neighbors passing by. He had two favorites: one a young man who was covered with tattoos and the other the caretaker of the church, who was thin and gray and praised the dog in a gentle Irish brogue, but neither was around that night.

"Poor Howdy," she said. "Where is our church friend?"

"Don't you meet anyone normal?" asked George, who had tagged along, probably to make sure she didn't smoke, Polly thought.

"I'm not looking for guys, George."

"Obviously."

He took the leash and, letting Howdy sniff the tires of a silver Porsche Boxster parked in front of their building, bent down to check out the interior. It was magnificent, and he was imagining himself inside, behind the wheel, when he heard the sound of Polly's robust voice greeting someone, then complaining about Chris. George found this sort of thing, which Polly did all the time, ineffably depressing. Where is your sense of privacy? he thought.

Then George had a happy thought. Did this constant harping on poor old Chris mean that Polly was not really interested in truly old Everett? Was it possible that George had misinterpreted the signs? The idea of his sister involved with a man who called George "young man," who made George feel as though he were being interviewed for a job he didn't even want, who was too gray, too joyless, too *old* for his vulnerable little sister with her noisy, brave affect, this idea continued to molder in the dark recesses of his consciousness. Could he, please God, be wrong?

He stood up and saw Polly talking to a slender woman of a certain age whose hair was brilliantly red and whose heels were alarmingly high. For a fleeting moment, George wondered what a retired streetwalker was doing with a key to their building, then recognized her as the French widow who lived on the seventh floor.

"When you are face with the troubles, you face the troubles," she was saying in a heavy accent. "My husband die and I want to die and instead I dance." She suggested Polly take tango lessons as she had done.

George smirked at the idea of Polly at tango school and watched as the woman advanced down the street with a brisk *clack-clack* of her heels.

"Shut up, George," Polly said, seeing his face. "She's in competitions all over the world."

"Hey, do the cha-cha, for all I care. Anything to get you out and about."

"I'm out," she said, pouting. "I'm about."

George shook his head. "All you ever do is walk the dog."

"But that's what you wanted. If I'm satisfied, why aren't you?"

She was satisfied, she realized as she said it. She could fantasize about Everett and hang out with her neighbors and their dogs. It was a quiet, undemanding life full of interesting new behavior and street etiquette. Introductions: dogs pose frozen and forbidding or with paws outstretched and back end up with tail wagging or by lopsided jumping or simple sniffing. Follow-up: owners initiate enthusiastic but ritualized verbal

exchanges. "So cute . . . May I pet . . . ?" Dogs continue sniffing. Owners chat.

For Polly this was preferable by far to the conventional, embarrassing social exchanges people were so often called upon to
endure in the other parts of their lives. George, however, kept
insisting that she had to meet a "fellah," as their mother would
have put it.

"You've got to get over Chris," he said.

"I am over Chris."

"Right. So what is your problem, then?"

"Can't a person take some time off?"

George looked thoughtful. Then he said, "It's that old guy,
isn't it?"

Polly did not like this description of Everett and so she
didn't answer, but they understood each other.

"He could be Dad," George said.

Then they both burst out laughing at the idea of their father, an aggressive, red-faced lawyer, being anything at all like
the dark, dour Everett.

"You could be his daughter, anyway," George said. "And I
bet he wishes you were."

"You're a prig," Polly said. "*And* a perv," she added for good
measure.

Though George might disapprove, though he saw only a
squalid mix of rebound and Lolita, though he did not understand, and Polly did not herself understand, she did know that
Everett fascinated her. He was utterly foreign, like another language with another alphabet, or a new cuisine based on horse
meat. She had to keep herself from studying him, examining
him, testing him out. Everett might be ordinary, something she
was quite willing to admit, but her interest in him was not
ordinary, and it was her interest in him that thrilled her, as
though it were a crime. There was no reason she shouldn't take

an interest in someone a little more mature than the unreliable and irresponsible Chris, or so she told herself. In addition there was the challenge that Everett offered, as if he were one of her projects to be rescued. Rescued from his own ill-natured gravity.

Polly saw Everett the next morning. She was leaving some mail addressed to the dead man on the table in the lobby. It had been put in her mailbox, and she had mistakenly taken it upstairs with the rest of her mail the night before.

"Don't you mind?" Everett said, seeing the name on the letter.

"I think about him a lot."

"I never spoke to him. I'm sorry about that now. Well, truthfully, I'm not sorry, but I feel I ought to be sorry."

"I'm not as sorry as I should be, either," she said. "Because I'm so glad I got the apartment. Also, what kind of a man leaves behind a helpless puppy?"

"A desperate one," Everett said, rather severely, she thought. She didn't like being patronized. But then he added, "He always carried an umbrella," and looked so sad that Polly felt better and asked if he was on his way to the subway. He was, and Polly joined him, almost giddy. He went down the subway stairs to the uptown train and she went down the stairs to the downtown train. Across the platform, she saw him looking gloomy and distinguished, and she told herself that George might understand too much and might talk about her going out and meeting guys all he wanted to, but he couldn't force her to date an appropriate young man. This was America! The land of opportunity! This was New York City, the city that never slept. Polly pushed her way enthusiastically into the crowded subway car, suffused with the buoyancy of hope.

ten

This Is Longing

Doris had a shortened schedule in the summer. Really, she thought, she should have the summer off the way the teachers did. But there were tests to interpret and admissions to influence, and she went to school three days a week, just enough to keep her from being able to rent a house upstate and get away.

"You could bunch the days," Harvey said. "Wednesday, Thursday, Friday. Then we could leave Saturday morning when there's no traffic and come back Tuesday night."

But because Harvey was retired and did not go to work at all, Doris felt his advice was wrong on the face of it.

"Anyway, we can't afford it," she said.

For they could not afford what she wanted, which would be large and have a pool and landscaped grounds with a rolling view. They could not, in other words, afford a house she could invite her sister to.

"We could get a little cottage," Harvey said.

"A little cottage!" said Doris, full of disdain. "Don't be ridiculous."

"I could stay there full-time and you could commute in your big gas-guzzling ecology-trashing truck."

"Natalie invited us for a weekend," she said, Natalie being that sister for whom dinner in a cottage would have been ridiculous.

"Well, that solves our problem, doesn't it?" Harvey said. "Our summer plans are complete."

"Retirement is making you petulant, Harvey," she said. "You need to do something with yourself."

Harvey agreed and obediently turned on the ball game.

With such a husband, can anyone blame Doris for her ill temper and general bad nature? But then, with such a wife, can anyone blame Harvey? And yet they were happy together and had been for many years. Doris sat beside Harvey on the couch, leaned her head on his shoulder, and watched the Mets lose to the Atlanta Braves, as she had so many times before.

"I saw that wild white hound again today," she said. "And that negligent woman who walks him."

"Does he growl?"

"He must. It's in their blood. They're bred to violence."

"A white pit bull? I've never seen it."

"You never leave the house."

"And with good reason! Wild dogs all over the street!"

"I have my eye on that dog," Doris said. "Just one misstep and watch out!"

"What will you do?" Harvey asked. "Hold the dog back a year? Not renew his contract for the ninth grade? Insist on a math tutor?"

"The dog urinates on the street."

"As long as you don't urinate on the street, Doris, darling, I am not worried."

While Doris and Harvey enjoyed the summer days in their own fashion, Simon was enjoying his summer more than he had in many years. The chance meetings with Jody were less and less left to chance. Simon purposely planted himself on his park bench almost every evening, waiting for Jody and Beatrice to appear along the dusty path.

It was not as though he had forgotten the call of the coming autumn, however. After a humid but leisurely dinner with Jody and Beatrice on one of these evenings, Simon, opening the door of his apartment, was stopped in his tracks by the beauty of his glossy black boots in the summer evening's low sun. He had taken them out to be polished that morning, and they rose, two gleaming monuments, from the bare floor toward the incandescent window. He had yet to mention to Jody his passion for fox hunting. It was a private passion, so private and so passionate he was almost ashamed of it. And what if she turned out to be someone who thought the sport was cruel? There were such people. There were many such people. Jody was so devoted to that dog. Suppose she thought of foxes as relatives of dogs and so disapproved of Simon and stopped having dinner with him?

But he suspected, when he allowed himself to, that Jody cared no more about foxes than she did about him. During the dinners they had shared, Jody was polite, even friendly, and chatted confidentially about her students, their impossible parents, the unbearable administration. Simon knew she was from Ohio, that she sometimes played in orchestras of Broadway shows, that she was in a quartet that sometimes played in churches. He knew all this, but at the same time he knew nothing. Jody was so pleasant, so undemanding, that she sometimes seemed to vanish behind her own smile. She told Simon far more about herself than he ever revealed to her, yet she was as much a stranger as when they first met. She seemed to accept his presence without seeking it. He, in the meanwhile, had begun going to the bench in the park as if there were a standing appointment, and when she didn't show up, as she frequently did not, he continued on to his solitary dinners with less and less pleasure.

Simon was right about Jody. She noticed him sitting on the bench, but not in the way he hoped. She saw that he turned up more and more often. She did enjoy going out to dinner with him. She was pleased when he asked for her phone number. She assumed he must be lonely, like her, and that, like her, he was glad of a little company. But mostly what she noticed was that Simon, who was so easy to find and so ready to while away a summer evening, was not Everett.

Everett was not easy to find at this time. He had begun to spend most evenings alone in his living room missing his daughter and enjoying the spare sophisticated furnishings of his apartment. He had realized after he and Alison split up and he moved into his own place that he loved order, that he was neat, that he was, and he liked this description best, a minimalist. He had lived with clutter and decorative excess for so long that he really had lost any sense of his own preferences. Not only had Alison collected things, but so many of the things she collected also turned out to be things that held other things she collected. Baskets, for instance. There had been hundreds of baskets in their apartment, it seemed to Everett, each one of them spilling over with African trade beads or Appalachian dolls.

Everett leaned back in his Eames lounge chair. There were no baskets in his apartment. The paper was neatly folded on the Saarinen table beside him. He would finish the op-ed page and then he would throw the wrinkly paper away. Nothing was wrinkly in his house except his Noguchi lamp. His drink rested on a coaster. His feet rested on the Eames ottoman. Yes, he thought, the house is empty without Emily, but how free of clutter is that emptiness!

He had thought of calling Jody a couple of times, but he was always so tired from work and he was not sure he could manage a conversation, much less a courtship. He liked being alone. It was one of the things he had learned about himself. He was an emotional minimalist, too, he decided.

Then he thought of Polly, the attractive and formidable girl from downstairs. He wondered if his suspicion could possibly be correct. She seemed, inexplicably, to have developed a crush on him. Good God. He must be mistaken. Though, really, why not? He wasn't dead quite yet.

He had certainly not encouraged her. No one could accuse him of that. He barely spoke to her. And that lanky, droopy brother of hers. Anyway, why would anyone want to accuse him of anything? Here his mind involuntarily turned back to Jody. But she had nothing to do with it, he told himself. As for Polly, yes, he was older than she was, but it was not as though he were her boss or her teacher. Polly was of age. He repeated this to himself. But though Polly was of age, Everett had to admit that she was of the age of a kid.

There were plenty of men his age who would jump at a chance to become involved with a pretty young thing like Polly. Everett wondered if he was one of them. He was too enervated to follow up on a friendship with a perfectly nice woman of a suitable age. Why was he even thinking about the possibility of a relationship with a young girl? It would be twice as much work. And he had mixed feelings about kids to begin with. Kids were sparkling and fresh, but they were also foolish and demanding. And kids could be dangerous. They didn't know the rules. They were even dangerous to them-selves—so easily hurt. The idea, suddenly overwhelming, of Emily being hurt made him anxious, almost sick to his stom-ach. He reminded himself that Polly wasn't as young as Emily. Quite. Anyway, how often did a surly middle-aged man have a lovely girl throw herself at him? She seemed such a sturdy soul, and so puissant, with her loud, clear voice. Her interest in him seemed almost a command. Still, he decided, he should have nothing to do with her. She was, there was no getting around it, too young. Years and years and decades too young. It's as obvious as the nose on your face, he told himself, peering into the bathroom mirror and noting with some satisfaction that though he had some fine lines around his eyes when he smiled, lines that were practically invisible when he wasn't wearing his reading glasses, his skin was still remarkably youthful looking.

On that same evening, a soft, light-filled summer evening, Jody sat on a hill admiring Beatrice and the rich green grass dappled in the shade of an ancient oak tree. Beatrice was sprawled on her back, her legs flopped on either side, her rosy tongue draped from her mouth like a skirt on the grass. Her eyes were closed. All was remarkably still. A man at the bottom of the hill moved in the slow motion of tai chi. A toddler sat proudly on a big, bright red ball. A robin stood motionless. Jody lay back on the grass. It had been cut recently and the mown-lawn smell reminded her of home. The home where she'd grown up, so far away, the house sold long ago, her parents off now in a white stucco condo on a Florida golf course. I have to call them, Jody thought. Then she thought about Simon. He had become so persistent, as persistent as a suitor, phoning her at work, waiting for her at various points on her dog-walking route; but once he caught up with her, he seemed distracted, perhaps even bored. No, not bored. Worried, as if he were already apprehensive about where and when they would have their next meeting. Simon seemed always to be in a kind of geographical distress, she thought, like someone who was lost, someone trying to get his bearings. And yet he was the most composed of men, beautifully dressed and graceful in his movements, though he was such a tall man. He spoke so quietly, in that self-deprecating mumble, that it required her to lean in close to him, yet as close as she got in the hushed conversation, the distance remained. Sometimes, when she tilted her face to his in order to hear what he was saying, Jody wondered what it would be like to kiss him. He had dark, thick eyelashes that surrounded his eyes like eyeliner. Once as they sat at the little table at the Mexican restaurant, she had put her hand beneath his chin and lifted his face, looking into his eyes. She thought he would kiss her then, or that she would kiss him, when suddenly a picture of Everett crossed her mind, and she sat back in her chair.

"One of my neighbors has asked me not to practice after nine o'clock," she had said to cover the awkwardness she felt.

"Fair, I suppose," Simon had mumbled, "though hardly flattering."

Jody lay on the grass now, her eyes closed, Beatrice's leash resting in her hand, and she thought of Everett again. This is longing, she realized.

This feeling of hopelessness and hope, this summer scent, the memory of Everett calling to her from his window, the curve of his neck as he leaned from his window, the song of a distant bird.

What kind of bird?

I will never know.

Suddenly, the sunlight flashed across her eyelids, the ground beneath her shook, and the air expanded with a long, resonant boom.

Jody opened her eyes and saw the tree, the tall venerable oak with its leaves and dappled summer shade tipping, falling, spilling, capsizing like a ship, sinking in the air, settling itself with a billowing crash onto the grass.

The tai chi man stood openmouthed. The baby on the red ball bounced excitedly. Beatrice and Jody got to their feet. The branches were still trembling. A huge hole of rich brown earth stood where the roots of the old tree had torn themselves free.

"Oh my God," Jody said, kneeling to comfort the trembling dog.

The tree was all wrong, lying there on the ground. It had missed Jody and Beatrice by about ten feet. It was so tall, its trunk hulking, endless on the grass. When Jody and Beatrice came by the next day, the Parks Department had sawed the tree and hauled it away and filled in the hole. Only a few wood chips remained.

eleven

A Blind Date

July turned into August amid thunder and lightning and drops of rain as big as grapes. It rained for three days, off and on, and when the storms passed, instead of the fresh cool aftermath everyone had a right to expect, the air was heavier and hotter than it had been before. George hadn't minded the weather. He spent the days with Howdy, taking long walks in the rain, like a man in a personal ad.

On one of these rainy days George was sitting at his computer listlessly poking around Craigslist for jobs when the dog, sitting intently beside him, put his paw on George's knee.

"Shake?" he'd said, absentmindedly taking the dog's paw. "Good Howdy." The dog looked into George's eyes then with what could only be described as worship. "Good Howdy," George said again, more interested now, and Howdy wagged his tail, bounded around the room, and returned, expectantly. "Shake?" George said. Howdy enthusiastically repeated the gesture, and George's days had been full ever since.

That afternoon, when George took Howdy out, he saw in front of them a girl struggling with an unruly rottweiler mix. The rottweiler jumped and tugged and the girl, who George instantly ascertained to be, as he put it to himself, a hot tamale, was dragged unhappily behind. George's midlevel chivalry allied itself to his benignly predatory instincts and he was helpless not to interfere. He and Howdy caught up, and under the guise of admiring the enormous rottweiler, George calmed the dog and got her owner's name and phone number.

The dog, glinting black in the sun, saw a Rollerblader and lunged forward.

George stood quietly and firmly until the dog stopped pulling and turned back to look at him.

"Good girl," he said then.

The rottweiler seemed to like that and marched back to them.

"Are you a dog trainer?" the girl asked.

George laughed. "Why not?" he said.

George had not let up on his campaign to distract Polly from her unfathomable interest in Everett. But he wasn't the only one trying to steer Polly into the world of dating that summer. Geneva, Polly noticed, was constantly after her, too, and sometimes did manage to drag her out to a party or a bar. Once there, Polly would stand by the alcohol and think how lovely it would be if a guy would just come up to them the way people came up to Howdy. "Oh my God, she is sooo beautiful," he would say to Geneva, then he would ask if he could pet Polly. Geneva would say, "Well, she's a little shy, though you wouldn't know it from her bark, would you, Polly girl?" And Polly would laugh her big laugh and say no, and the man would laugh appreciatively and ask her age, from which Geneva might shave off a year or tack one on, depending on the age of the guy, and Polly would lie on her back and have her belly rubbed.

"I'll never meet anyone who's interested in me, and I'll definitely never find anyone I'm interested in," Polly said, wondering what Everett was doing. Did he go to parties? She wondered what kind of music would be played at a party attended by Everett. The Beatles? Classical? No. Jazz. Definitely jazz. Polly hated jazz, but she had always known she was wrong to do so and was sure she could learn to appreciate it with a little effort.

"You have to try," Geneva said.

"What?" Polly asked. "Try to like jazz?"

"What? No. Who cares if you like jazz? You have to *try* to *meet men*."

Geneva was tall and blonde and thin and pretty and hadn't had a date in eight months, which perplexed both of them. Even if I wanted to meet someone, Polly thought, which I don't, how am I supposed to find someone if the tall and blonde Geneva can't?

"I feel stubby and disgruntled," Polly said.

"That's pathetic. Get over it." Geneva worked for NPR, and she now insisted on teaching Polly how to do an interview and, more important, how to give one. "Here's the trick—if you don't want to talk about what they're talking about, you just steer the conversation to what you do want to talk about."

"Howdy?"

"You really don't want to meet anyone new, do you?"

"No. I told you I don't."

"I didn't think you meant it."

"Well, I didn't." Polly said. She wished she home. Maybe she'd see Everett in the elevator. She had been next to him in the elevator that morning and had smelled his aftershave. His hair was still wet from the shower. They had reached for the "L" button at the same time. His hand had touched hers, just as it had when they petted the dog. He touched me, she'd told herself. He wanted to touch me. She had looked down at the cracked linoleum on the floor of the elevator, suddenly conscious of how small the elevator was, how near the two of them stood in its warm, close air. Everett coughed. Neither of them spoke. They exchanged not even a glance, each hurrying off in a different direction.

"At least I didn't realize that I do," she said to Geneva now. "Mean it," she added.

Geneva stared at her, then looked around the room, the Queens living room of a boy they knew from college who was in a band. "Still in a band," was how he put it. Someone was vomiting into a wastebasket in the corner.

"Maybe I should get a dog, too," Geneva said, grimacing.

But a dog for Geneva was not part of Polly's plan. George was, and she was more determined than ever to bring him and Geneva together. She finally got her chance when George suggested Polly go on a date with one of his friends.

Polly saw the advantage in this idea at once.

"I will," she said, to George's surprise. "I will, on one condition. I'll go out with one of your lame friends if I can bring Geneva, and you have to come, too, so she won't be a third wheel."

No one likes to be fixed up on a blind date. There is something too much like pathos in a blind date. Luckily, neither Geneva nor George knew they were being fixed up on a blind date. For one thing, they had already met each other so many times before that there was nothing "blind" about it. And, then, they saw themselves more as chaperones than as participants, which effectively eliminated the "date" part. In their eyes, it was Polly, not either of them, who was the victim. They, naturally, preferred it that way. Though they had taken great pains to effect just this thing, they nevertheless, unconsciously, felt toward Polly the pity, the slight contempt even, associated with blind dates. Poor Polly.

But Poor Polly was oblivious to their pity and their contempt. Her blind date, she knew, was no more than a sham blind date, a ploy, a plot to bring together the two people she liked best in the world. Far from the embarrassed resignation of a girl about to descend to the desperation of a blind date, Polly experienced a surge of pride. She was sacrificing herself in order to correct an unaccountable error. She was putting Fate and Eros back on track, hooking them up.

The night that Polly's long-delayed plan for George and Geneva was finally to be put into action, it was exceptionally muggy, with just the occasional puff of hot air that could be called a breeze. George was in a good mood. He had taught Hector and Tillie, Jamie's elderly cairn terriers, to roll their ball back and forth to each other, pushing it with their noses. Jamie had given him a raise.

Polly wished she had not worn such high heels, for George insisted on going to a club near his old apartment on the Lower East Side, and the walk from the subway stop was long, the sidewalks bulging and cracked, the streets dropping precipitously into potholes left over from the winter before. They had decided to have dinner at a Vietnamese restaurant first, and that was where they were meeting Geneva and Ben, George's friend from college who had been deemed "perfect" for Polly.

"He's funny," George said.

Polly shrugged.

"He has a real job. He works for a production company."

"George, it's a date," she said. "A blind date."

"I'm reassuring you."

"I don't need to know his SAT scores," she said ungraciously.

"Okay."

"Is he cute?" Polly said finally, when George was still silent.

"Not my type."

But he was cute. Polly saw that the minute they entered the restaurant. He was about as cute as they come, and he was engaged in an animated conversation with Geneva.

"Fuck," Polly said softly.

"Fuck," George said, simultaneously.

For it was clear even from that distance that the blind date was already racing successfully ahead, though it was racing in completely the wrong direction.

"He *is* cute," Polly said.

"Cute as a button," George said, and they joined the happy couple for dinner.

It's all very well for me, Polly thought, as she now did not have to interact with a strange boy, and it was all very well for Geneva, who had not had a proper date in ages, but what about poor George? George would now be forced to continue his flitting from flower to flower like a crazed bee. George was hopeless and men were foolish, spineless creatures who did not do what she told them to. This led her to contemplate Chris. She wondered if, had she been sitting at the table across from Chris instead of her brother, she would be any happier. An unlikely scenario. Chris had never liked Geneva, and for that reason Polly had usually had to see her on a girls'-night-out basis. Why was it I liked Chris, again? she wondered. Just before they'd broken up, Chris had begun working out almost every day and stopped in front of any mirror he walked past to admire himself. That should have tipped her off. She wondered what Everett looked like without his shirt. What if he was one of those flabby men with gray chest hair she saw running in the park? She shuddered. But wasn't it superficial to care about such things, as superficial and narcissistic as Chris posing before the mirror? She remembered her first date with Chris, a hot summer evening like this one, a cheap Italian restaurant, a pitcher of margaritas at the noisy rotunda overlooking the boat basin on Seventy-ninth Street, a lazy walk down West End Avenue to the high-rise apartment that would become her home. She could remember the first touch and the first sight and the first scent of the body that became so familiar and so much a part of her. Then Chris had taken that body away, as if it were not a part of her at all, pumping it up, doting on its new image in the mirror, bestowing it, finally, on someone else.

Polly decided to drink too much, and did. By the time they got to the club George wanted to go to, she was reeling. If she had to be out on the town, she might as well stagger, she thought. She danced with a boy with a snub nose and freckles. She called him Opie and he narrowed his eyes and stalked off. She danced with a beautiful black guy whose head was shaved. She watched the lights bounce off his gleaming skull. Her feet hurt so much she was surprised when she looked down not to find them bloody and raw. She saw George watching her, laughing at her. Her plan had gone awry, her beautiful, simple, essential plan. George would roam the streets of New York forever, untamed, undomesticated, an aging Lost Boy. She danced with Ben and noticed he had a scar above his lip. She asked him what it was from, but he didn't hear her, and she let it go. She danced with Geneva who was a head taller than she was, which made her drink more. And then she saw Chris.

He came in the door looking crisp and healthy, the replacement girlfriend on his arm. Her head is very small, Polly thought, enraged. And why is his collar turned up like Katharine Hepburn's? Polly was certain Chris had not seen her, and she slid over to George for cover, standing behind him, but that turned out to be where Chris was headed, too.

"Dude," Chris said.

Polly reminded herself how much she had hated that, his Dude greeting. But still his voice made her sad.

"Dude, you stood me up last night."

"What?" Polly said, stepping out from behind George. "You did what?"

"Oh God," George said.

"Oh, hey, Polly," Chris said. He turned pale, which gratified her.

"Hello," she said.

"Did you ever meet Diana?"

"Hello," Polly said to Diana.

Diana smiled lamely, and they all stood there.

"You 'stood him up'?" Polly said suddenly.

"No big deal," Chris said. "Just a game of pool."

George looked down at his beer.

"You 'stood him up,'" Polly repeated. "'Stood him up' as in 'did not show up for a prearranged meeting.'"

"He usually shows up," Chris said. George groaned. Chris, obviously realizing he had said the wrong thing, tried to smile. His face just twisted oddly, and he sighed and looked up at the ceiling.

Polly saw the guy with the shaved head approaching. She moved toward him. She danced with him and watched her brother, her ex-boyfriend, and the usurper girlfriend, who still stood together, though no one seemed to be saying anything.

"I hate him," she said.

The shining head turned and glanced at George and Chris. "Which one?"

Polly thought about this for a moment, but decided she wasn't ready to commit herself.

There was a bleary full moon that night as Doris and Harvey returned from a party at her sister's in Bedford. Doris found a space right in front of their building, and the evening, during which she had impressed a member of the local gentry with her impassioned call for uniforms in public schools, and so already a success, became, with the parking space, a triumph. She slid the car happily into the huge space.

"What a luxury," she said.

It was really delicious, a large parking space, like slipping into silk pajamas. She sat for a moment without stirring, enjoying the moonlight, the streetlights, the quiet, and the smell of leather. She knew she was considered a scourge by her colleagues and her friends and certainly by her husband. But I ask so little, really, she thought now. I enjoy simple pleasures. A distinguished meal. Intelligent conversation. The beauties of nature. A place to lay my head and park my car.

Harvey was asleep. She didn't trust Harvey's driving anymore, and he didn't seem to mind. He would sit in the passenger seat reading aloud—traffic signs, billboards, the sides of trucks, marquees. TORN AND SPLIT EARLOBE REPAIR . . . OUR CENTRAL LOCATION SAVES YOU TIME AND MONEY . . . SLIPPERY WHEN WET . . . Doris had been delighted when he fell asleep on the drive home, allowing her to be alone with her car and her thoughts.

"Out you go. On your way," she said, gently pushing Harvey. She felt a rush of tenderness toward him, which in turn gave her a sense of magnanimity and accomplishment.

At their door, Harvey fumbled with his keys while Doris waited patiently.

A full moon, an empty parking space, an evening of witty repartee and excellent wines. She recounted these blessings again.

She was wearing a short, sleeveless shift, a vintage Pucci that had been sitting in her own closet for forty years waiting to be resuscitated, and had been much admired that night. Her hair, a careful though rather too youthful strawberry blonde, not that distinct in tone from her complexion, was pulled back into a tight bun and the damp heat on her neck felt soft and caressing. She noticed a large Poland Spring bottle abandoned in the impatiens at the foot of her building's scrawny tree, beside a large mound of excrement. A thrill of outrage ran through her. She had to be more vigilant. The street was literally going to the dogs. And those impatiens—so 1980s. This is my neighborhood, my community, she thought. And she straightened herself up and glared up and down the block, as if it were a scruffy and recalcitrant block, squirming and avoiding eye contact as she confiscated its cell phone.

Jody saw Doris from her own doorway across the street. She waited until Doris and Harvey were inside their building, then led Beatrice to the SUV in its comfortable spot.

"Good girl," she whispered as Beatrice peed beside the front left tire.

Simon saw them. He was walking home from his poker night, at which he had won forty dollars. Beatrice shone, a ghostly white, in the moonlit heat. Beside the slick white SUV, the dog lowered her hindquarters, carefully, daintily, every inch a lady, he thought. He waited out of sight, for he sensed that what he witnessed was private. To intrude on this intimate act of defiance would be almost sacrilegious, a defilement of the purity of the white dog in the moonlight, the quiet, smiling woman, and the shining puddle beside the shining car.

George watched Geneva and Ben leave the club together. They were all over each other. He felt a stab of jealousy, then lapsed back into the heavy hopelessness he usually felt toward

the end of a night out. All those writhing bodies. All that
noise. All the fun. To what end?

Polly, her hair damp and disheveled, appeared beside him.

"You're a cad," she said.

"I'm sorry, Polly."

"It's, like, the definition of cad."

"I'm really, really sorry. I didn't think you'd mind so much."

"Well, I do."

They stood beside each other, both looking out at the
dance floor. George had known that she would mind very
much indeed. He almost thought she had a right to mind. He
didn't even like Chris that much. But he was used to him.
Chris had been at the usual bar at the usual time. What was he
supposed to do?

"It's not like we're married, Polly."

Polly actually stamped her foot, the way she used to when
they were children.

"Okay. It is like we're married."

"Did he say anything about me?"

George tried to remember—a word, a scrap that would
make his sister feel better. "He asked if you were okay." He
wasn't sure even that was true.

"Narcissistic shithead."

George hoped that would be the end of it and suggested
they leave, but Polly was not finished.

"Am I okay? Am I *okay*? He thought I'd crumple up and
die without him? Doesn't she look like a fool? I hate girls who
wear shrugs. I bet she got him those Gucci loafers, too. What
an oaf he is. With his turned-up collar."

"I told him about Howdy."

"Oh yeah?"

"He said he was bitten by a dog when he was little. So he's
terrified of dogs."

Polly smiled.

"Diana's severely allergic to dogs," George said, having no idea about Diana's sensitivities but feeling he was on a roll.

"Severely . . ." Polly murmured happily.

"*And* cats," he added for good measure.

George went home with Polly and listened while she verbally abused Chris. She sat in the subway, slumped but unbowed, quietly recounting the many faults of the man she had once lived with. She held out a finger for each transgression, trying to number them by heinousness, on a scale of one to ten, ten being the worst. She started small—Chris undertipped. She ran through his political crimes—he had voted for Nader, thereby causing war and famine—to his personal habits, which ranged from the obvious toilet-seat issues to his habit of leaving used tissues on the dining-room table. George noticed that some of the sins with the highest numerical value seemed far less important than some of the earlier lower-rated ones. Was the potential for a double chin based on Chris's father's double chin really an eight, when his unwillingness to give up his seat in the subway to an old bent-over woman carrying a new humidifier was a six? But George decided it would be best to keep his own counsel on her rating system, and by the time they got to their front door, Polly seemed more composed and more sober.

"And you," she said, spinning around and catching him by the collar. "You owe me sisterly allegiance. Brotherly allegiance, I mean."

"I know what you mean."

And the argument was over. George saw it on her face—a sudden calm—and he felt the same calm. He wondered if all brothers cared so much for their sisters. It had always been like that between them. No words. Just a sudden shared knowledge. What a drag it was, this bond, and what a relief. In all the world, wherever he was, whatever he was doing, there was one person who would care. Polly held out her hand. George shook it with ceremonial solemnity.

The next morning, Polly lay in bed and tried to swallow, but her mouth was too dry. Her head hurt and her eyes refused to stay open more than a slit. She forced herself to get up. Howdy was probably on George's bed. Polly felt a pang of jealousy. Even the dog preferred another. Then she stood in the shower and said out loud, "I will never be jealous again," holding her arms the way Scarlett O'Hara did when she vowed not to be hungry. Jealousy was of all emotions the least justifiable. It was ungenerous, it was painful, and it was useless. "I'm so happy George is so good with the dog," she said, trying out her new manner. "Chris was not right for me, and so, he and Diana . . ." She paused. "Should rot in hell," she said finally. I'm only human, she thought.

On the street, she met Heidi and Hobart. Polly told her that she had seen her ex-boyfriend the night before with his new girlfriend as they stood in the morning glare, their two dogs languidly sniffing each other's nether regions.

"Mmmm," said Heidi. "My first husband wanted a divorce. I told him to go in peace, as long as I could keep my son."

"Well," Polly said, "I don't have a son, so I guess that's okay."

twelve

"Someone who would be right for you"

Emily called Everett from Italy. She had acquired a taste for red wine as well as a pair of fabulous Dolce & Gabbana sunglasses. Everett was so happy listening to her voice that he thought he might swoon. Then she mentioned her mother's upcoming marriage plans.

"They're so old," she said. "What's the point?"

"Yes," he said, "quite ancient. Perhaps they will purchase color-coordinated walkers for the wedding ceremony."

"It's all your fault."

"Emily . . ."

"Don't even bother, Daddy."

He did bother, though, explaining yet again how people change, how they grow apart, how, of course, their feelings for their children could not change, but . . . Everett bothered, and he explained, and he listened to the words and thought how puny they were, how feeble. When he hung up, he thought of how it must strike Emily, this idea of change. People change, he had said to her. Why? he wondered. *Why* did they? It was so unfair. Emily would change. She would grow up and move somewhere far away and resent visits of more than three days. "You know what they say about fish and houseguests," she would say wearily to her husband, the way he used to say the same thing to his wife. And then Emily and her husband, too, would change, and they would get divorced. The idea of Emily divorced was too much for him. His poor baby. He became very angry at her husband, who obviously did not deserve her. How dare you treat my daughter this way? You're a scoundrel, he thought, the word rising up from some forgotten assigned reading. A scoundrel and a bounder!

He opened a bottle of Chianti in honor of Emily and considered calling Jody and asking her to come and share it with him. Or, even better, he could knock on the door of his young neighbor, Polly. It was not a very good bottle of Chianti and she would be less likely to notice. Still, her brother might be there and that would be awkward, somehow. By the time he had made up his mind to try Jody first and then, if she wasn't available, to ring Polly's bell, he found he had finished the bottle himself and rendered the question obsolete.

After the Geneva and Ben fiasco—the two were now seriously dating—Polly decided to temporarily concentrate on her own life of walking Howdy and hoping to bump into Everett. Instead of Everett, though, it turned out to be Jody whom Polly often bumped into, and they soon got into the habit of walking to the park together with their two dogs.

Polly liked Jody. Jody was always the same, perhaps that was why. She always had that smile, her laugh was contagious, and she smelled good, too, Polly noticed. Fresh, like soap. She was older, as well, and now that Polly had decided to leave her late adolescence behind, Jody seemed to be a good person with whom to practice.

Jody had become fond of Polly, too, on these walks, in spite of herself. Polly was so determined, so sincere in her proclamations. "This is the most beautiful tree in the park, and we must always take this route," she would say, and so they would always take that route. She made political proclamations and fashion proclamations. There were positions on Kleenex softened with aloe (the greatest invention since bagged lettuce) and on heirloom tomatoes (they were just as tasteless as regular tomatoes, but uglier). Polly declared, and anyone within ten feet listened. But Jody recognized, too, that Polly was just a kid, and that like a kid she, even she, was uncertain and afraid. She still talked constantly about the breakup with her boyfriend, which Jody personally found reassuring, but she saw also that the loss had startled Polly and made her suspicious. It was not, Jody thought, in Polly's nature to be suspicious: she seemed uneasy, jumpy in her own unhappiness. Jody sometimes timed her dog walks to coincide with Polly's. She instinctively and involuntarily felt herself wanting to put Polly's little world back together. In addition to which, Polly was Everett's neighbor, and Everett had become so elusive these days.

"Do you ever see Everett around?" she asked Polly on one of these walks.

"Do you want to hear a secret about that?"

Jody thought she probably did not want to hear a secret about that, but she simply nodded.

"Don't you think Everett's pretty hot? For someone his age?"

"Is that the secret?"

"No. I know this sounds so egotistical, but I want to tell someone. I can't even mention him to George. So . . . okay. Sometimes, I think there's a chance Everett actually likes me. He hasn't said so, but it's just a feeling. You know what I mean? That feeling?"

Jody did know what she meant since Jody, in the darkest moments of her dark sleepless nights, had that feeling, too: that Everett liked Polly. She said, "Beatrice!" just to be able to say something, and the dog looked up at her, bewildered.

"Look, I know he's too old for me," Polly said.

"And you're too young for him," Jody said. She regretted it immediately. Could Polly hear the misery in her voice, the bitterness in her words?

"Same thing."

No, Jody thought. It's not the same at all. You're taking advantage of him. People think older men prey on young women, but it's youth that is tyrannical. And irresistible. And finally, inevitably, fickle.

"Probably nothing will happen," Polly said. "But, you know, takes my mind off . . . things."

"Chris?"

"Him? I hate him."

They walked on in silence.

"Anyway, you need a boyfriend, too," Polly said at last.

"Do I?"

"I have to figure out who would be right for you."

Jody knew exactly who would be right for her. At least, she knew who she wanted. But what difference did it make if who she wanted, who was right for her, if that person wanted someone else, someone younger and more charming and outgoing?

Was this, then, the end of her affair? Was it to end before it properly began? She glanced at Polly. Yes, Polly was young. Yes, she was charming, in a boisterous sort of way. Yes, she was certainly outgoing. And wasn't that what every saturnine middle-aged man wanted? It wouldn't last, of course. Those things never did. For a brief moment, Jody thought of confiding in Polly. This is just a way of filling time for you, she would say. For me, it's serious. And we must think of what's best for Everett.

"Someone who would be right for you . . . ," Polly repeated.

Jody sighed, then forced herself to smile.

"That's very thoughtful of you, Polly," she managed to say.

Polly agreed. Everett wasn't even her boyfriend yet, and *still* she was offering to lift up her sister-in-arms. Jody was getting on in years and she wore flowered socks, but she deserved happiness as much as anyone. Polly smiled, pleased at the thought of her good works.

It was exactly one week later that Chris called. Polly heard his voice on the phone and was for a moment disoriented, as if she'd woken up from an odd but realistic dream.

"I have to see you," he said. "I need to talk to you."

"But . . ."

"It's kind of important."

Something was either important or it wasn't. Nothing was "kind of" important, she thought, and she almost corrected him, as she used to. Of course, she reminded herself, one did say "rather" important, or "extremely" important. A modifier could be used, certainly . . .

"Polly?"

"Oh!" She was talking to Chris. Chris needed to see her. He needed to see her and to talk to her. "Chris!" she said, as if to convince herself it was really him. "Yes, of course, if it's important." When she'd hung up, she went downstairs, stood on the sidewalk, and smoked. She brought Howdy with her and stood there, smoking and thinking. She hoped Everett would not come by just as sincerely as she usually hoped he would. Shaken and confused, she found she could not reconcile her crush on her neighbor with her excitement at Chris's phone call. She looked guiltily around her, but Everett was luckily nowhere to be seen. She felt sheepish and suspicious, as if she were having an illicit affair. But on which one was she cheating, she wondered, since she was involved with neither? It all means nothing, she told herself. Chris means nothing and Everett means less than nothing and I mean the least of all. She leaned against the rough brick wall and nodded hello to a man with two dachshunds named Sparky and Lucia. Howdy crouched down in a submissive position until the tiny dogs passed.

But try as she might, Polly could not help wondering about Chris. What could be "kind of" important? She replayed Chris's words, the tone of his voice. Perhaps he was ill. Or . . . But we all know what Polly thought next, what any one of us in that situation would have thought, the thought that is actually no more than the whisper of a hope. Perhaps he was ill, she thought. Or, or . . . he wanted to come back to her. She looked down at her feet and tried to ignore what she had just allowed herself to imagine. Then she admitted that she still missed him, almost six months later. Maybe he missed her, too. The hope whispered in her ear: maybe he missed her, too. Then she crushed her cigarette beneath her foot and, shyly, staring unseeing at the pavement, she smiled.

The building on the north side of the street, which housed the community center where the Alcoholics Anonymous meetings were held, was having a tag sale. To advertise the event, small porcelain objects were lined up in the window among the dusty plants, along with several unhappy-looking stuffed animals. Polly felt sorry for the stuffed animals, the plants, and even the souvenir saucer from Seattle and, on her way to work the next morning, she went inside to buy something. A wide woman in an official-looking pink smock told her the sale did not begin until noon.

"No exceptions."

With some relief, Polly left the community center, where oddly dressed old people were already gathering for bologna sandwiches and juice. Many of the old people lived in the same building, which, through a separate entrance just to the left of the storefront community center, provided some kind of subsidized housing for the elderly. There appeared to be a constant, inexorable turnover of these aged residents. Not surprising, perhaps, Polly thought, considering their years. She passed the Dumpster outside, which filled up each day with a new supply of battered bureaus, rusty lamps, faded plastic bed-pans, and crooked walkers. Polly hoped the woman in the pink smock would rescue something from the sad, dead-old-people's Dumpster for the tag sale. That record player, perhaps. But who would buy it? If no one wanted to take it off the pile out-side for free, why would anyone go inside to pay for it?

Glad that she did not have time to take the abandoned record player home herself, Polly walked through the oppres-sive heat past a large brown velvet sofa farther down the block that had been sitting on the sidewalk for several days. There's so much going on in New York! she thought happily. And she headed for the subway and a day of obsessive anticipation of her meeting with Chris.

As Polly descended the subway steps, Doris was fondly pat-ting her car in its convenient parking space. Doris continued on toward Broadway, past the disreputable sofa, but even that could not dim the pleasure she felt. She crossed to the south side and walked back toward Columbus and the embarrassing Dumpster with its cargo of private detritus. Doris was pa-trolling. As the first and only member of an all-volunteer force dispatched, by her, to protect the street, she wore latex gloves and carried a large clear garbage bag. She did not want to be mistaken for a homeless woman when she stooped down to pick up discarded bottles, so she wore Armani slacks and backless high-heeled shoes with pointy toes and a silk knit sleeveless sweater, all of which suggested, she felt, a dispenser of charity rather than a recipient of it. It was true that she took the bottles to the supermarket to collect the deposit money, just as the homeless women did. And frequently she was called upon to wait in a line behind ragged, unwashed men and women whom her husband referred to as her colleagues. But the change she collected was immediately deposited into a glass jar labeled "Beautification," which would someday be used to purchase plants and topsoil and, perhaps, recruiting flyers alerting her fellow residents to her project. Doris did not labor under the false hope that anyone would join her efforts, and had not, therefore, bothered actually to make up any flyers as of yet, but she had, with great perseverance, contacted her city councilman.

"It's a disgrace," she had told him.

He had sighed, and she had pressed him, and he had sighed several more times, and finally she had prevailed. She would escort him on a tour of the block that afternoon at 5:30, when the dogs and their owners would be out in full force.

As she completed her morning patrol, she remembered that she was trying to impress the councilman with how dirty the street was and wondered if she ought to replace the four or five bottles she had collected. But she could not bring herself to commit the crime she was protesting and decided to keep the bottles, instead, as evidence. She returned home and told Harvey her plan.

"Should I line them all up on the dining-room table? But then I'd have to wash them. Still, they'd make more of a statement that way than if they're just sitting at the bottom of a garbage bag . . ."

"What are you going to serve?" Harvey asked.

"I didn't think of that . . ."

"I was joking, Doris."

But Doris was not joking. She decided on Perrier.

"He won't want to drink alcohol on duty, of course," she said. "I think I'll offer coffee and a few cookies, too."

"What if he's on Atkins or something?"

"Oh, be quiet now, Harvey. He doesn't have to eat them. They just have to be there."

And she, like Polly, went off to work full of hope and anticipation.

thirteen

"No regrets!"

Polly and Chris had agreed to have dinner at Café Luxembourg that night, and Polly inserted commas into her magazine's copy even more generously than she usually did. The world was full of possibility. Her boss admired her bag—which Polly was too embarrassed to admit she'd gotten from a street vendor—then asked her to think about when she wanted her two-week vacation. Who knows? Polly thought. Anything can happen now. After work, she went to get her hair cut. The haircutter was on the second floor of a building on the corner of Sixty-first Street and Madison facing Barneys. Getting her hair cut was one of Polly's favorite outings and she walked happily up Madison Avenue in the heat, leaving her office behind, window-shopping as she went. Her plan was to arrive, ideally, with just enough time to take the elevator to the seventh floor of Barneys, where the less expensive stuff was, then head for the sale racks for an exhilarating half hour of shopping—with the safety net of not having enough

time to try anything on, much less buy it. Polly loved the muffled din of the other shoppers, the lush symmetry of the racks
of clothes, the rare, heady victory of a bargain. But there could
be no bargains at Barneys that day, and she took the escalator
down, strolling through each floor of smooth extravagance with
a sense of serenity and virtue, then finally crossing the street
to settle comfortably in a large chair, close her eyes and relax
as soft, warm water and competent hands worked their way
through her hair.

While Gian Carlo, her haircutter, snipped and chatted about
the house he'd just bought in Italy, Polly was soothed by the
buzz of hair dryers and the clicking of scissors. It was sticky
and glaring outside, but here the world was air-conditioned
and young women arrived with coffee or pushed wide, silent
brooms.

"I want to look more sophisticated," she said.

"By which you mean cuter."

"Well, not exactly."

He cut her hair just the way he always did.

"No regrets!" he said.

"No regrets," Polly replied.

The noise of the room was beautiful to her, the humid
summer evening hovering softly on the other side of the glass
walls, the fat round brush sliding through her hair, the scissors
rasping softly. There was a bowl of hard candy on the counter
in front of her. She remembered going with her father to a
barbershop when she was little. She had liked the combs soak-
ing in the jar of aqua-blue liquid. She tried not to think about
her dinner with Chris. She was too excited for her own self-
respect.

Gian Carlo began to dry her hair and the dryer roared and
swooped around her head, the rush of hot air breaking the
delicious chill of the air-conditioned room.

"*Bellissima*," Gian Carlo said.

Then, as if that were a command, all the dryers stopped. The noise, all the noise of all the dryers, disappeared. The music stopped. The lights went out.

Polly felt the heavy, slow-motion confusion of an emergency descend. A hushed murmuring began, which grew into a loud chatter as women with pieces of foil jutting up from their hair stood to look out the window, Polly among them. The traffic lights below were out. People were emerging from other buildings looking around in an odd, questioning way. The women on either side of Polly pulled out their cell phones. Not again, Polly thought desperately. Not again. She grabbed her cell phone, too, wondering where the terrorists had struck. She dialed George, but her cell phone got no service. No one's cell phone got service. The phones at the desk did not work. The elevator was not running.

Polly stood with all the ladies and all the hairdressers looking out the huge plate-glass windows. She tried to breathe normally. Her wet hair had soaked through the towel and her back was damp. She shivered.

"Maybe it's just this block," someone said. But they could see that it was not.

"Maybe it's just the East Side," someone else said.

"Maybe it's nothing."

People were mumbling incoherently. Maybe this, maybe that. Polly saw herself in the mirror, a pale blank face above the brown nylon smock.

Someone from the front desk had run downstairs. Polly stood rooted to her spot by the window. She saw the young receptionist whose name, she believed, was Jiffy, an unforgettable name in Polly's opinion, run over to a car and stand for a few minutes by its open door. Maybe Jiffy will get in the car, Polly thought dimly. And go home.

Jiffy came back upstairs and entered the salon with an air of almost frantic importance. "It's not terrorists! They said. The radio said! They said!"

There was more incoherent chatter among the women with wet hair. The hairdressers, waving their hairbrushes like batons, asked a hundred questions.

"I heard it on the radio. It's just a blackout, they said."

"Just!" someone said.

"It's the *whole* East Coast. And really far west . . ."

A blackout, Polly thought. She exhaled. Blackout. As if the whole East Coast had fainted.

"I'm so sorry," Gian Carlo was saying, looking at the useless hair dryer when Polly sat back in her chair. He smeared some gel on Polly's hair and pulled it back into a tight ponytail.

"Thank you," she said. She was so relieved. She felt giddy.

Gian Carlo shrugged. "Such humidity," he said sadly. "You will be frizzy." But he, too, looked relieved.

"No regrets," Polly said, and she paid, wondering why the credit card machine was still working, and walked down the stairs.

Simon was able to board a crowded bus. He stood, shaken, sweating, his briefcase between his feet. The air-conditioning was no match for the heat generated by the nervous, muttering crowd of bodies. By the time he reached home, over an hour later, his jacket was soaked, clinging to his body. He had wanted to remove it almost immediately, as soon as he got on the bus, but found himself too self-conscious to jostle his neighbors in order to do so. He held the rail above him and leaned his head on his arm and listened to the excited murmuring in the bus. He imagined Jody, who was giving private lessons over the summer, holding the hand of a frightened little child, leading it down dim brownstone stairwells to the chaotic street below. How worried its parents must be, their cell phones useless. He could not imagine the child as anything but a generic child, neither boy nor girl, just a small hand carrying a tiny violin case, the other small hand clutching Jody's larger, reassuring hand. This was a poignant image: Jody leading the faceless innocent down the dark stairs, the frantic parents yelling impotently into their cell phones. The fabric of the East Coast of the United States was rent because no one had an old-fashioned phone that did not need to be plugged into an electrical outlet. No one but Simon, whose office, run by the city, was supplied with only the oldest and most out-of-date equipment. He had, for this reason, been able to call his parents in Portland, Oregon, and tell them not to worry, calming himself at the same time. He had called Jody, too, knowing that her phone would not function, knowing he would not be able to leave a heartening message on her voice mail.

He noticed the rising, musty odor of the body of the man in front of him, then realized it might be the rising, musty odor of his own body, slippery with sweat. He closed his eyes and felt the bus sway. Perhaps today he would talk to Jody about horses, about hunting, about the freedom and the demonic speed of it. Perhaps he would kiss her tonight, in the dark, dark city. He would lead her to his apartment and throw her on the bed and . . . the phrase "fuck her brains out" came to mind. Simon frowned at his own absurdity.

When the electricity went out, George was splayed on his bed staring at the ceiling. He might or might not have fallen asleep. He was not prepared to say. It was hot. The old air conditioner had been struggling. Then it was silent and the room was even hotter. George tried all the light switches. He opened the fuse box. He opened the window and looked down at the street. Five or six people gathered around a car with its windows down. The radio was so loud he could hear it.

A blackout. He thought of Polly on the twenty-fourth

floor of her office building. She would have to walk down a dark, hot stairwell. Uneasy, he put the dog on a leash and went down to the restaurant to see what was going on there.

Doris had been too impatient to wait upstairs for the city councilman. She had posted herself in the lobby, and when the lights went out, she cursed her landlord and noted it was one more thing she could mention to Mel, as he was known to her in her thoughts, though she hadn't decided if it would be more efficacious to call him Mel or Mr. City Councilman when she actually met him. He had seemed an informal sort of person on the phone, but she did not want to be too forward. The lobby was heating up, and she went outside and noticed the traffic lights were out. Something was definitely wrong. Down the street, some people were clustered around a car listening to the radio, but Doris did not feel she could leave her post to join them. Whatever it was, she would take it up with Mel when he arrived.

Polly marched across the park. The sky was an unyielding pearl gray. There was no sun and so there was no shade. The heat was wet and heavy. Polly's shirt was soaked through. A blister was forming on her left heel. There was a heightened excitement in the park. It was crowded with flushed, anxious people. She tried three hot dog stands unsuccessfully and was beginning to panic before she found an ice-cream cart that still had water to sell. Then she worried about the ice cream, about all the ice cream in the city, melting and useless, soon to be abandoned. She felt sad for the ice cream but found herself growing elated by the blackout itself, as if it were a snow day and she would not have to attend school. She noticed a more and more festive air to the people she passed: It was not a terrorist attack! It was hot and all routine was left behind! It was a holiday!

At home, Polly changed into a camisole and shorts and flip-flops. When she saw that George wasn't home, she shuffled over to the restaurant. Tables and chairs had been brought out onto the sidewalk. Inside, at the bar, George was mixing up icy drinks.

"Hey!" he said, looking relieved.

Howdy leaped up and pushed his cold, wet nose in her face.

Jamie was pacing up and down the sidewalk in front of the tables. Noah had a long walk from Wall Street. Jamie knew he shouldn't worry. But he did worry. No, he wouldn't worry. Worry was useless. Noah would probably show up in a limo provided by one of his clients. And the babies were okay. And the big twins were splashing in a wading pool in the backyard with the nanny. Thank God Isabella had refused to go to day camp today. It had infuriated him that morning. So what if it was hot? So what if the bus made her sick to her stomach? So what if the playing field was a bald patch of dust, more and more of which made it home with her each day? That's what day camp was—a horrible nightmare that your parents think you like no matter how many times you tell them you don't. He had tried to explain this to her, but she had become hysterical, and Noah had come in and taken over, which meant Isabella had stayed home on the condition that she finish her lanyard. Jamie thought of the Billy Collins poem about a lanyard. This made him want to run home and take Isabella in his arms. Or was it that he wanted to be taken in Isabella's arms? Perhaps he should make her a lanyard, a useless uneven thing full of love. And one for his mother, of course. Then he saw

Noah staggering up the street in his wrinkled suit and he stopped pacing, stopped worrying, stopped thinking altogether. He put his arms around Noah and Noah put his arms around him.

"Were you worried?" Noah said, surprised.

"I'm only human," Jamie said, and he thought perhaps he would make Billy Collins a lanyard while he was at it, that he would make lanyards for all the world.

After seeing that George was okay and Howdy did not need her, Polly went to the corner store to rescue at least some of the Koreans' ice cream. There was a long line that extended out into the street. The heat had intensified. Her arms were glistening with sweat.

Behind her, Simon stood waiting to buy water and batteries. He did not recognize her from the back, perhaps because her hair was pulled back and gelled to her skull, perhaps because he was not paying attention: he was staring at her shoulders, unable to look away from the hundreds of haircut hairs stuck to her sweaty skin.

Mel the city councilman arrived at Doris's building, perspiring and disheveled and forty minutes late. Doris recognized him from an interview about magnet schools he'd given on New York 1. She waved excitedly.

"Can you believe this, Mrs. . . ."

"Doris," she said, taking his hand in both of hers, very much like a politician herself, she thought proudly. "I appreciate your taking time out of your busy schedule, Mel." Yes, Mel sounded just right. But why was Mel laughing and talking at the same time in such a high-pitched, agitated voice?

"Would you like some refreshment?" Doris asked.

Mel gratefully accepted, and Doris led him up the three flights of stairs after he informed her that the commotion she had noticed was caused by a blackout, that he had been caught on the subway when it happened and would not have shown up at all except that he had escaped the subway at Seventy-second Street and thought she might be kind enough to let him use her bathroom. Doris opened her front door for the city councilman, thinking that after her hospitality her chances of help from that quarter would be greatly increased. He would see her collection of discarded bottles and cans, and he would drink her Perrier.

Jody had gone to the Cooper-Hewitt to look at a wallpaper show and have tea in the pretty garden there. She walked home slowly, unnerved by the aimless bustle in the streets. The heat and the confusion struck her as almost one and the same. Beatrice would be miserable without the fan Jody had left on for her. She wondered if she had a flashlight. She would need one to read later that night when she couldn't sleep. The panic of insomnia rose within her. She reminded herself that it wasn't even dinnertime yet, much less bedtime. But insomnia without electricity would be even more boring than ordinary insomnia, and she took her place in the long line at the Korean market to buy a flashlight and some Tylenol PM.

It was only when Polly lit a cigarette and Simon coughed that Polly noticed him and said hello. He looked startled.

"Sorry," she said and put out the cigarette.

"No, no . . ."

"It's okay. I'm not a militant smoker. It's more of an affectation."

Simon thought how pretty she looked, even with hairy shoulders and larged gelled skull.

"Very becoming affectation," he said. He knew he was flirting, insofar as he was able to flirt. What about Jody? He should be faithful to Jody. He felt the guilt, and the thrill, of transgression.

Polly laughed. She would rescue several quarts of ice cream

and go home and eat them. Then she would meet Chris at Café Luxembourg. She knew he would be there, electricity or no electricity. He had been so urgent.

From her place in the line, Jody saw Polly leaving the market but did not call out to her. It was so hot. And Polly looked almost manic, a huge smile on her face as she dug into a carton of ice cream with a plastic spoon. She saw Simon follow her out. He didn't notice Jody, either, and she relaxed, making her way slowly into the dark, airless store. She was unsettled, almost panicked. She couldn't bear the thought of small talk, of turning on her cheerful smile. Even cheerful people have off days, and this was one of Jody's. Only after she unlocked the door to her shadowy, cramped apartment and received Beatrice's frantically joyful greeting did she start to calm down. She kissed the silky ear pressed against her lips. A dog in the dark, she thought, is still a dog.

Everett lay naked on his bed after a shower. He let the water evaporate and felt cool. He had walked home, sixty blocks. That was three miles. In his younger days, he had loved to hike in the mountains out west where he went to college, sometimes going ten miles or so, taking his time, noticing a translucent snakeskin or a bit of coyote scat or the indigestible remains of a hawk's meal, the little bones wadded into the feltlike fur. Now, a trek of only three miles on flat, even city sidewalks had worn him out. He was old. His daughter was in college now. It was her turn to hike. He savored this maudlin thought for a moment, enjoying the importance of his own pathos. Then he imagined hiking with Emily, envisioning a meadow of wildflowers, when into his fantasy meadow marched an uninvited vision of his ex-wife.

Go away, he thought.

You're allergic to wildflowers, she responded.

Everett sat up. The old cow, he thought. Then he looked down at himself. You're a bit of an old cow yourself, he thought.

He was in good shape for a man his age, but he was, neverthe-less, a man his age. He got dressed and opened the refrigerator and stood in front of it. The cool air had already begun to smell, although there was nothing in the refrigerator but two apples, a loaf of bread, a jar of olives, some mustard, and a few bottles of beer. He was better about marketing when Emily was around. She would be home for two weeks at the end of August before she went back to school. Everett opened a bot-tle of beer, went to the window and opened that, too. On the street below he saw the Italian woman in black inching her way along, leaning on her cane.

"*Buon giorno!*" he called.

She looked around her, confused.

Maybe when Emily was home she would speak in Italian to this woman. He was impatient for Emily to be home. Wait un-til she heard what her mother had done. Her mother had done what no mother can do with impunity, and she had done it for reasons no child could respect. She had given away the fifteen-year-old family cat because the successor, as Everett chose to call him, was allergic to her.

It was one thing to be allergic to wildflowers, something with which Alison had taunted Everett each spring, and con-tinued to taunt him within his own imagination. But the cat? Couldn't the successor take pills or get shots? It was selfish, and it was inhumane.

"Why don't you take her if you're so concerned?" Alison had said.

"Don't be ridiculous," he said.

"Yes, you have always hated her."

"I don't hate her. I just don't like it when she sits on me. And sheds. And tears up the furniture."

"You never wanted her in the first place."

"Exactly," Everett said.

It couldn't be good for an old lady like that cat to start life anew, he thought now, watching the Italian lady sit down to rest on an abandoned sofa. True, the cat had been given to a neighbor who was also an old lady and had recently lost her own cat. But you cannot simply exile a member of the family, and he happily shook his head again at the thought of how angry Emily would be at her mother.

The restaurant had become unbearably hot, and though it was not that much better outside, Jamie and George moved more tables and chairs to the sidewalk. At six o'clock, George was busy serving beer, still cold from the refrigerator, and mixing drinks with the ice that was melting fast. The gas stove was working, and the chef cooked by candlelight. Jamie decided to offer food free with drinks. The food would spoil anyway, he said. The atmosphere was loud and festive. George stood at his makeshift bar and made the drinks stronger than usual, imagining that everyone needed extra-strong drink tonight, or at least deserved it. He was worried about the old lady, Heidi, who usually walked by the restaurant at 5:30 sharp with her fat little dog, Hobart. She had not yet appeared. Simon was there, though, drinking bourbon. And there was Doris, that sinewy, excitable woman with the orange face, clicking toward them in pointy-toed heels, a short, round disheveled man in tow. They did not stop, though the man looked as if he wanted to. George made his drinks stronger and stronger, hoping the increased alcohol would compensate for the dwindling ice.

The darkness, when it came, was unfamiliar and profound. Tenants across the street set up a grill on the sidewalk, and its fire burned bright and fierce in the blind night, illuminating in flickering yellow the cluster of neighbors who sat on the abandoned brown velvet sofa, on the stoop, on folding chairs they had dragged down from their apartments. The candles on the restaurant's tables sparkled, their light miniature and lonely, and someone farther down the street, invisible in the dark, played the guitar and sang lilting folk songs that had been popular in the nineteen sixties.

Polly sat at a table at the restaurant surrounded by the plunging darkness of a powerful city without power. Above her, the stars had come out, startling and rich, stars not seen in the city's sky since the last blackout, before Polly was born. But Polly did not notice the stars, and if she had they would have given her no joy. Her knees were pulled up to her face, and she stared unseeing at the filmy skirt she had finally decided to wear for her meeting with Chris. Chris had been at the Luxembourg, as she knew he would be, blackout or no blackout, and at the sight of him, her heart had beat faster and she'd smiled, then stumbled. Chris held his hand out and caught her, and she apologized for her clumsiness, happy to be leaning on him. The Luxembourg was closed, so they made their way back to Go Go and sat at one of the little tables with flickering candles. George brought them martinis and Polly listened, more and more relaxed, as Chris chatted about an apartment he was thinking of buying. Then Chris took her hand and told her he had always loved her and always would, and her eyes had welled up with tears, and he had squeezed her hand, looked down, and said that he was getting married and wanted her to be the first to know.

For one brief moment, Polly thought he was getting married to her, Polly, and said to herself, with a combination of surprise, elation, and indignation, that, of course, she should be the first to know. Then she realized the truth: Chris was getting married to someone else. Without her.

At a table on the other side of the now outdoor restaurant, Jody was drinking whatever George brought her. The dog was panting at her feet, lying down, occasionally dipping her jowls into a large bowl of water that she seemed to be holding between her front paws. Jody slipped one foot out of its sandal and put it in the water bowl. The water was tepid but felt good. Beatrice licked her foot. Jody tried to pay attention to what Simon was telling her, but she realized she was a little drunk and could not follow his long narrative, which involved a large horse, a leaky flask, and a fox being chased by hounds.

"Hounded," she said, dreamily.

Simon nodded politely and said, "Well, yes. If you're a fox."

"Foxy lady," Jody said, in an absurd Jimi Hendrix voice.

Simon laughed. He put one finger beneath her chin and tilted it toward him. He leaned toward her.

But as Jody lifted her head, Simon saw her gaze slide past him. He saw her smile suddenly, raise her hand, and wave excitedly.

It was Everett, who had just appeared in the soft pool of candlelight around them. Simon let his hand drop back to his glass.

"Join us for a drink," he said sullenly, and to his dismay, Everett did.

Everett pulled a chair up between Jody and Simon. He saw Polly a few tables away with a good-looking young man. He felt a pang of hurt and annoyance, then reminded himself that it wasn't as if he had been pursuing her, it was she who kept making eyes at him. Girls were too fickle. He knew that. He should stick to his own age. He thought of his ex-wife. She had once been young. She had once made eyes at him. Seeing that Jody and Simon were already drinking cocktails, he thought it improbable they would switch to wine and ordered a good bottle of Pinot Noir.

George brought him the wine. As he poured, he watched through the dim candlelight as Chris got up and walked toward the street. He had not even paid the bill. I will never play pool with Chris again, George decided. For he could guess, from the look of horror on Polly's face, what had happened, or something very like what had happened. In the candlelight, she looked so soft and pretty. George went to her and touched her shoulder.

"He's getting married," she said. "I'm the first to know."

"I'm sorry."

"You're the second to know," she said. "Congratulations."

George noticed Everett looking their way. He thought of his pretty, vulnerable sister and the older man.

"Listen, Polly," he said quickly, "I have to check on Heidi. Why don't you come with me?"

"No."

"Yes, come. It will take your mind off things a little."

"No."

George knew that tone. It was the juggernaut tone, the no that ran roughshod over everything in its path, the no that crushed opposing armies, that had no mercy and spared not its enemies. He sat next to Polly and put his arm around her. He suffered a conflict of chivalry. Should he comfort his sister, who might throw herself at Everett the pedophile if he did not? Or should he rescue Heidi, who might be lying, helpless, in the dark oven of her apartment, her panicked dog whining and impotently licking her face?

"He asked if I had his iPod. As if I would have taken his stupid iPod. Can you believe it? Now he has to get married without an iPod. Ha!"

"If I go, will you promise not to leave here until I get back? I'm really worried about her."

Polly said where on earth did she have to go anyway?

George took this as an assent. "Okay, then watch the bar for me. I'll just be a minute." If he could not get her away from Everett's pernicious influence, he could at least keep her busy while he was gone.

Polly shrugged.

"Come on, Polly. I'll be right back."

Polly shrugged again. "I've just been jilted."

George kissed the top of her head. "Maybe Chris will come back and you can poison his drink."

"Okay," she said, brightening slightly.

"Can you make any drinks, by the way?"

"Sure. Long Island Iced Tea for everyone."

The cool aftermath of his shower seemed years away to Everett. He was glad it was dark, for he felt large patches of sweat on his shirt. The collar stuck to his neck. He felt alone and could not help thinking of the last blackout, when he had been young and lived by himself. Now he was old and lived by himself. His wife was soon to wed another. Surely that was a lyric to a song. Perhaps the wailing folksinger down the street would suddenly begin to wail out those sorry words. Everett tried to think of the next verse.

Jody watched his face in the soft, uneven light and noticed how ordinary he looked when he was sad, and she found this poignant, found his ordinariness as beguiling as his beauty. She liked the shirt he was wearing, neatly tucked in even in this heat. His hands were on the table, clasped. They were square, strong hands. Besides ordering the bottle of wine, Everett had said nothing. Jody wanted to reach out and take his clasped hands in hers. She wanted to hear his voice and feel his skin.

Simon tried to speak. The silence was unpleasant. "Everett is gloomy and Jody is moony," he said, but he was drunk, and the words came out a mumbled complaint that neither Everett nor Jody seemed to hear.

"My wife is soon to wed another," Everett sang softly, with rather more of a country-western twang than he had intended. "She's set a date and asked our friends . . ."

Simon closed his eyes. He didn't like Everett, he said to himself, and he would pretend Everett was not there.

"I guess my invitation's coming," Jody sang, surprised at herself but quite pleased. "Written with my wife's own poison pen."

Everett smiled at her, as wide and bright a smile as she had ever seen.

"Oh, they wondered who sent out all that anthrax . . ." she continued. This is the chorus, she noted to herself, to account for the change in meter. "Yes, they worried 'bout the uniletter bomb. But I said, boys, you can all sit back and re-lax, for the culprit is my darling daughter's mom."

Doris looked out the window. It was like some grotesque third-world slum down there. In the cavernous blackness, she could make out a bonfire burning in the kettle of a barbeque and old women sitting in the street on kitchen chairs like Calabrian widows. The natives were caterwauling. There was drinking and, yes, dancing in the street. Mel had been as good as his word and had allowed himself to be shown the unruly dogs and their scofflaw owners, but Doris could not help but feel that, in the midst of a major blackout with fires burning and guitars strumming and tequila flowing, her little show of discarded bottles and unscooped poop had been upstaged.

"Come to bed," Harvey said.

"It's too hot."

"It's too hot to do anything else. And too dark."

"I'm going to sit in the car with the air-conditioning on."

And Doris walked down the stairs with a flashlight to guide her, following the funnel of light along the sightless sidewalk, then settled herself in her perch in her car and sighed with pleasure as the icy air moved past her hands on the wheel to her flushed, smiling face. Harvey could laugh at her and her SUV all he liked, but she knew what she was about.

When George got to Heidi's apartment, Hobart began barking from behind the door.

"Hush," he heard Heidi say. "Hush, Hobart."

Relieved that she was alive, and a little guilty that he had imagined her dead, he rang the bell.

"I was worried about you," he said when she opened the door.

"Oh! You spoil me. You mustn't spoil me."

Heidi had been out earlier, it turned out, but she had not walked by the restaurant because of all the commotion. No, the stairs didn't bother her. Yes, nine flights, nine flights, she used the banister, you know, so there was no problem whatsoever, she did it slowly, that was the trick. It was so considerate of George to offer to walk Hobart, but he was quite all right until the morning. Would George like a drink, perhaps? He must be tired himself, climbing all those stairs. And so George entered the apartment with its tablecloths and doilies lit by candles in crystal candelabras, and he sat on a brocade settee and drank wine with Heidi.

Simon was sobering up, and he didn't like the scene that met the increasing clarity of his gaze. Jody and Everett continued to make up songs together, then laugh with uncontrolled hilarity at their own compositions.

"Howdy, neighbor! How's your chickens? Mine are doin' fine!" they sang.

Simon estimated that Everett was at least ten years older than himself. I could take him, Simon thought. Anytime, anywhere. But that sentiment, however sincere, felt uncomfortable to him, like someone else's shoes. One of his patients', perhaps. Brooding and ineffective shoes.

"The electric lights are all shut down . . ." sang Everett. "There is a blackout in your heart . . ."

"You once lit up at the sight of me," Jody answered. "Now your fuses are all blown."

"Oh my baby's had a power outage . . . Left me sweating in the dark."

"I called Con Edison and shouted, but this is all they would remark:"

"Unplug your love, unplug your dreams, shut off the switch of desire."

"Your batteries won't help you now. You're nothing but a dead, dead wire."

Everett and Jody found the song hilarious and congratulated each other, much to Simon's disgust.

"Barmaid!" he said to Polly. "Another round."

Polly brought them each another glass of the brew she had been concocting. She no longer knew what she was pouring in, or in what proportions, because she didn't care. They could all drop dead as far as she was concerned. Perhaps her mixology would help things along a little.

Simon made a face. "What is this?"

"I don't know. I don't care. I'm distraught."

Jody turned to look at her friend and saw that she really was distraught. Polly was crying, silently, the tears streaming down her cheeks. Jody reached out to take her hand when she noticed another hand reaching out. It was Everett's hand. It took Polly's hand in its grasp. Everett stood up. He put his arm around Polly. And, as if Jody did not exist, as if Jody had not been entertaining him and making him laugh and making him smile his beautiful smile for the past hour or so, as if he had not shone that smile again and again on Jody, as if Jody had not been falling in love with him all over again, Everett walked away with Polly, away from Jody, into the dark.

The instant Polly and Everett left the restaurant, they were surrounded by darkness so deep Polly felt as if she were drowning in darkness. Everett's arm was around her. Then both Everett's arms were around her. Then Everett was kissing her. He tasted of alcohol, every kind of alcohol ever distilled. His reading glasses were in his breast pocket, just like her father's reading glasses, and she felt them pressed against her.

"I'm sorry," he said, stepping back.

"Where are you?" He was suddenly lost to her, one step away.

He touched her arm. She started, then grabbed his hand, an anchor in the dark sea.

"Don't be sorry," she whispered.

"I'm taking advantage of you. Of your unhappiness."

"Yes," Polly said, pulling him toward her, pressing her lips against his neck. "And I'm very, very unhappy, so you have a lot of advantage-taking to do."

Everett thought this over as he walked with her toward his apartment. She was a pretty girl, and he had been flattered by her attention over the last few months. He was old enough to know better, perhaps, but he didn't like being old enough to know better. Couldn't he be young enough to be foolish? Just for a little while? Polly seemed to know what she wanted, and it seemed to him, even if she had been crying over her old boyfriend, that what she wanted was him. If he could comfort her, why shouldn't he?

Why, then, did he harbor in his heart this nagging feeling that he was moving through the hot, endless darkness toward trouble?

They passed a big SUV with its motor running.

They passed the folksinger.

They passed a woman, visible for a second in the lights of a passing car, carrying a schnauzer.

"Don't be scared, Rosie," the woman was saying. "Don't be scared."

"I forgot Howdy!" Polly said. "I forgot my dog!"

They hurried back to the restaurant, Polly muttering self-recriminatory curses, Everett roiling with silent dog antagonism.

I hope he's there, Polly thought, her evening plans forgotten. I will never forgive myself if he is not.

I hope he's there, Everett thought, his evening plans threatened. I will never forgive him if he is not.

Howdy was indeed there, lolling patiently by the bar. Polly relaxed, joyously hugging the dog. Everett looked guiltily around him and was glad to see that Jody was gone. So was Simon. Everett knew he had left the table a little abruptly. He hoped they would attribute his behavior to drink.

Polly's cell phone seemed to work now, for he heard her speaking into it. "I'm going home with the dog. Maybe not home, exactly. But I'll have the dog, so don't worry about him. Or me."

There was a pause, then Polly said, "That's none of your business, is it?"

Then there was another pause. "I know, I know," Polly said. "Yes. I hear you." And she hung up and put the phone in her purse.

"Everything okay?" Everett asked, though there was a blackout, her boyfriend was marrying someone else, her brother had obviously lectured her about going off with strange older men, and everything was most decidedly not okay.

"Some scholars believe that the word 'okay' was first used by the Anti-Bell-Ringing Society in Boston in 1939," she said. "Others attribute it to Choctaw Indians."

Everett looked, questioning, at her face, just visible in the candlelight around them.

"I'm a copy editor," she said.

He smiled awkwardly.

Polly looked at him with intense interest now and took his hand in hers. "There's also the Mandingo theory," she said. "But who cares?" And she led him away, with Howdy trailing behind them.

While Everett and Polly, hand in hand, walked the dog toward home in the dense, dark heat, George drank Heidi's wine, confided his worries about Polly to her, tried to take comfort in her observation that everyone was entitled to a foolish love affair, wondered why he wasn't in love with anyone, foolishly or otherwise, and, with the aid of a flashlight, looked at watercolors the old lady painted at night when she couldn't sleep. Doris contentedly watched the dials on the dashboard of her air-conditioned car until she was down to an eighth of a tank of gas. Simon, meanwhile, much to his surprise and delight, fucked Jody's brains out.

fourteen

Was She in Love?

There is a moment, even in New York City, when fruit on the trees begins to ripen. Crab apples appear one day, as small and green as grapes. The fruit grows bigger and pinker, overnight, and the day after that, it seems, the apples are crimson. Summer, tired and dusty and pale, gives way, and berries appear on bushes you don't know the names of. At least, I never know the names of them: red or purple or orange or, on one shrub at the bottom of the Seventy-sixth Street steps into Riverside Park, an unearthly, lingerie lavender.

For Simon, these blushing fruits were usually welcome, the first signs that the long, yearly hiatus was soon to give way to his real life. But this year, Simon saw them with dismay. Virginia, the green rolling pastures in which he had always thought his heart resided, like someone in a Stephen Foster song, was far from where his heart seemed to have recently made itself comfortable, which was here, on his street, with Jody.

He was a bit long in the tooth, you might think, to have fallen in love so completely, so deeply. The argument could be made that he was really both too old and too young—too old for an all-consuming romantic first love, too young for a desperate, midlife infatuation. But sometimes the numbers are wrong, and Simon was in love. He woke with Jody's improbable and unmelodious name on his lips. Her voice, which was melodious, echoed exquisitely in his head.

He sometimes thought Jody liked him, too. The rest of the time he hoped she did. But mostly, Simon dwelt on his own good fortune, and every time he saw her, every time he touched her, every time she spoke and he sensed the warmth and sweetness of her breath, he was overwhelmed with gratitude. She was not the first woman he had loved, but she was the first woman he had fallen in love with. He had courted her, in his accidental fashion. And in an accidental fashion, he had won her. The hot summer had been blissful for Simon. Now the autumn loomed before him, uncertainly.

Jody, in turn, did think about Simon, but her thoughts ran in another direction. Jody was, very simply, surprised by Simon's sexual brilliance. He was like someone who looks up at the clock and realizes it is 4:12 p.m., and he has forgotten both breakfast and lunch: his appetite was enormous, his pleasure boundless. He seemed ecstatic, like a Russian religious, like a child. She had headed out into the pitch of the night during the blackout not expecting much and not caring. She had already vanished that night, she felt, vanished from Everett's consciousness and so, to some degree, from her own. As Simon led her gently to his bed, Jody thought, I don't care what I do. Afterward, she thought, How can I be so fickle? Then she looked at Simon as he slept, smiled, and thought, I'm only human.

She was now, she realized, sexually enthralled. There was no other way to describe the tie she felt to Simon. To some it may seem inexplicable, even reprehensible, that she could transfer her interest so quickly from one man to another, and at first it was both inexplicable and reprehensible to Jody herself. You're so desperate, she thought, scrambling from one man to another, picking up men, any old men, from spinster to ho in one night.

But I find myself judging Jody less harshly than she judged herself. There she was on the night of the blackout, deserted suddenly by the man she thought she loved. And there before her was another man, a drunk, inarticulate, but kind and adoring man. He had taken her hand and led her through the blackness of night to his bed.

Simon worshipped at her shrine, she who never before realized she had a shrine. In the days that followed, this substitute lover overwhelmed her with the force of his feeling for her, with his passion and his attention. Is it any wonder the substitute should begin, in fact, to take the place of the original?

Then summer ended and school started.

"Are you all right?" the art teacher asked her on the first day back.

"Yes. Why?"

"You're sleeping?"

Jody paused. Was she sleeping? Was what she and Simon did sleeping? And yet she woke each morning, which implied sleep. And when she woke, the day met her graciously and gently, and she jumped out of bed grateful for the night and grateful for the hours that lay ahead until the next night could begin.

"Yes," she said. "Yes, I guess I must be."

The art teacher shook her head. "It's disorienting, that's all," she said.

"For me, too," said Jody, and when they went in to lunch she, the cafeteria Pollyanna, did not defend the wilted lettuce or the weak coffee. Quite the contrary.

"Leftovers from Snowball?" she asked, indicating the lettuce and alluding to the pre-K class bunny.

"This tastes like old bathwater," she said, lowering her coffee cup in disgust.

The art teacher stared at her, then put down the thermal flask of coffee she had been about to pour and reached for a tea bag instead.

On noticing this, Jody felt a rush of exhilaration, a sudden sense of power. She caught her breath. She thought, How pleasant to be unpleasant.

"You know what I think?" said the art teacher, pouring boiling water in her cup and swirling the swollen tea bag. Her voice was high and teasing. "I think you're in love."

Jody said nothing. She sipped the vile coffee thoughtfully. Was she in love? She couldn't say. What did that mean? And what did it matter? She was in an awfully good mood, and she was loved. Surely that was enough for anyone.

For George, the fall was not that different from the summer. He worked at Go Go, he went out on his nights off, he felt vaguely guilty and unfulfilled. The two biggest changes were that he had no girlfriend and he had begun to walk an extra dog. The incident with the pretty girl and the rottweiler mix had led to a short-lived romance with Laura, the pretty girl, and a long-term commitment to walk and tame Kaiya, the pretty dog.

The autumn blue sky was bright with shining white clouds and the wind was brisk and alert when George and Howdy and Kaiya reached the park. The dogs danced at the ends of their leads, barking at potbellied squirrels who bustled off like prosperous burghers, opulent in fur. George unclipped the leashes. The dogs stood absolutely still, then leaped crazily in every direction, it seemed, spinning in the air in pursuit of squirrels, of leaves, of life itself. A middle-aged man with a pug on a leash stopped and chatted with him about the weather. But then the young couple with their own pug came by, and George, with his large dogs of questionable breeding, was snubbed.

George wondered if he missed Laura and wondered why that had not worked out. She was a beautiful, buxom, hard-driving girl, almost as impatient as his sister. Were all girls like his sister? And if not, why not? Because, really, he thought, Polly is the best. He had been surprised at how much fun they had together. His friends at first thought he was crazy to move in with his sister, as he had himself. But they had come to see the wisdom of a comfortable berth and a comfortable friend, which is what Polly had turned out to be. He could talk to her or not, as the mood struck him. When he had a cold, she brought him orange juice and knew what over-the-counter drugs would make him sleep. She was always ready to go to the movies with him or order takeout late at night. They fought over the remote and the most comfortable chair in the living room. It was as if the two of them were back home, there had been no divorce, and their parents had gone out for a very, very long dinner.

On the other hand, if Polly were the best, why was she wasting her time with that dried-up old Everett? And even if Polly were the best, which, following this logic, she perhaps was not, would he really want to be seriously involved with someone like Polly? Probably not, he decided. For one thing, he already was seriously involved with someone like Polly: Polly.

And the whole point of Polly, he reminded himself, was that she required nothing more than what he had always provided: his brotherly presence. He would never be able to get away with that if he got involved with someone like Polly who was not actually Polly.

George wondered if everyone worried about the kinds of

things he worried about. He hoped not. He whistled for the dogs, who trotted amiably at his side.

Doris saw them go by, and though she knew the unofficial but well established courtesy of letting dogs run off leash in the park before nine in the morning, she stopped, made a clucking sound, and glared at George's back before resuming her power walk. She noted with approval some gardeners pulling out dead plants. She had a meeting later that morning with that ridiculous Margaret and her lovely husband, Edward. Their son, Nathan, was in trouble again. He'd brought his Swiss Army knife to school. Then there was a faculty meeting. And there were always those urban legend blow jobs in the bathrooms that had to be dealt with. Her day would be the uphill struggle it was every day, a thought that provided her with a swift, pleasant sense of her own necessity and a jolt of extra power for her power walk. Harvey was getting quite deaf, which was depressing. If anyone at school knew her real age, she would probably be forced to retire. But the day was bright, and the street on which she lived, so run-down, was filled with possibilities for improvement. Just yesterday, she had collected eight beer bottles, six water bottles, and caught a woman allowing her Jack Russell terrier to urinate at the base of a tree. "Curb your dog!" she had cried, pointing to a sign nailed to the tree, a sign she herself had placed there. Doris moved with heightened energy and pleasure down the bridle path, happily noting dangerous holes dug by some dog, no doubt. Doris was considered a negative person even by those who loved her, and that much more so by those who did not. But if negativity denotes despair, then Doris was in no way negative. In truth, the unfortunate world and all its stumbling, hapless ways was the source of all her considerable joy.

A woman pushing a baby carriage passed on the paved walk nearby. In the baby carriage was a wide-eyed, flat-faced dog with long white fur.

Doris stopped, caught between indignation and simple revulsion.

"Her name is Kissy," said the woman, patting the dog affectionately.

Doris moved on, even faster than before, invigorated and at peace.

Jamie sat at his table greeting customers with his customary smile. The evening was young and he was already halfway through a bottle of red wine. He would have to slow down.

"Lois!" he said, standing up to kiss a woman on the cheek. "Try the skate," he whispered to her. "It's new on the menu. Tell me what you think."

He sank back in his chair and waited for Noah to come. Noah's parents were in town and all of them—Noah, his mother and father, and all the children—were coming by to pick him up for some ghastly event, the circus or ice skating or puppets, he couldn't remember. Noah's parents hated Jamie, or so it seemed to him, but he found he couldn't really blame them. Everyone had dreams for their children. A gay restaurateur had clearly not been theirs.

More customers came in and Jamie stood to shake hands and exchange pleasantries. He enjoyed this part of his work. It was routine and unchallenging, but then so were most jobs. And Jamie had discovered over the years that people liked him, people were drawn to him. In his youth this had sometimes been a problem, causing heartbreak for his many admirers. But here, in his restaurant, he had found a way to be admired without causing pain.

He looked around him and could not help feeling a flash of pride. He could make people happy. One of his busboys, the teenage son of his Filipino bookkeeper, dropped a piece of bread on a customer's lap and looked, terrified, over at Jamie.

Jamie raised an eyebrow. The boy quickly recovered himself and the bread and continued with his work. Jamie wondered if he would have to be fired. He hoped not. He knew the boy needed money for college next year. Perhaps they could just move him to lunch.

Simon and Jody had just come in and he smiled at them and nodded hello. They were an odd couple, he thought. She, Miss Cheery Sunshine, and he, an anxious, lost, overgrown woodland animal sort of person, a disoriented stag. He tried to imagine them in bed and couldn't. They both struck him as utterly sexless. He amused himself by imagining other people in the restaurant together: the two young women, mothers on their girls' night out, he guessed, gossiping and drinking margaritas; the middle-aged couple on what seemed to be a first date; the parents of a well-behaved and nicely turned out little boy and his baby sister, probably European, he would have to drift by their table and see what language they were speaking. The restaurant was full, and full of amusing mating possibilities. His thoughts lingered on two gay men, one considerably older than the other, then turned back to Jody and Simon. They were both so earnest. Perhaps that was what drew them together, two lonely, earnest souls. He turned back to his glass of wine, feeling voyeuristic and ungenerous.

"There you are!" he cried, seeing his brood bundled through the doors. The littlest ones were in their unwieldy double stroller. The four-year-olds ran to the bar and climbed onto the high stools. Jamie's daughter threw herself into his lap and demanded zabaglione. The dogs began barking and running in circles. The babies cried. The boys spun on the bar stools. The girl sat glumly, her lower lip in a pout.

Simon watched Jamie's family with fascination. He had met Noah once before. Noah was even taller than he was, which had immediately drawn them together, he thought. Now he waved, but Noah, kneeling beside a wailing little boy, did not see him.

Jamie asked George to take the dogs home for him. He waited with his unsmiling in-laws—or, he supposed, un-laws was a better title. He offered them some wine and, to his surprise, they accepted. He seated them and Noah and the older children at the bar and served them from the other side. He caught Noah's eye and his heart expanded.

"Here we all are," he said, lifting his glass. "Here we all are."

George took the two little dogs down the street to Jamie's house. One of the nannies was there and let him in. She was a little old for him, but she was awfully good-looking. Did age really matter that much? he asked himself. Then he thought of Polly and Everett and remembered that, yes, it did. He handed over the dogs.

"Goodbye, Hector. Goodbye, Tillie," he said.

They sat and each waved a paw at him. He had taught them that.

"I taught them that," he could not resist saying to the pretty nanny who was clapping her hands in delight.

He returned to the restaurant and saw Jamie and his family lined up at the bar. Just like a real family, he said to himself.

"Wow," he said loudly to cover his unworthy thought, "what a great family."

Jody was watching Jamie's family, too, thinking how odd it was to have so many children in this day and age. Well, she reminded herself, in vitro, surrogates, all of that caused so many twins, didn't it? She wondered if she was too old to have children. Certainly not five children, but one or two. It still surprised her, almost daily, that she did not have children. Then the babies in their stroller both began to cry again, and she turned away, terrified suddenly that perhaps she no longer wanted children, even one.

"Sometimes I'm impatient with other people's children," she said to Simon, trying to make her thoughts sound more reasonable.

"Well, with all those kids at school . . ."

"Oh, no," she said quickly. "Not them. They're *mine*."

Jamie and Noah and the children and grandparents exited, leaving behind a sudden hush. Then the glasses and forks and plates began to clink and voices rose and fell as usual. Simon paid the bill, as he always insisted on doing. Jody made a show of resisting, but she enjoyed being treated, really. Jody had left Beatrice at home and now they stopped at Jody's apartment to get her. Simon had never been to her apartment. They always went to his.

"Just wait here," she said to him on the stoop. "We'll be right down."

She didn't want him there, in her one little room. She couldn't have said exactly why. But he waited docilely enough, and she ran up the stairs.

Simon, not really docile at all, watched her go with something close to panic. He couldn't stand to be apart from her. He tried to control himself. He never said anything to Jody about it, he didn't want to scare her, but even a short separation like this made him long for her. He tapped the concrete with his foot. He ran his hand through his hair. He sighed. He turned and looked up at her window. He turned and looked down the street. When she finally appeared, he was nearly vibrating with impatience.

"Beatrice!" he said, throwing himself at the dog to hide the state he was in.

Beatrice licked his face and wagged her tail, and Jody watched with a smile that Simon feared signified nothing more than benevolent amusement.

It was a warm, comfortable evening. Two big golden retrievers sashayed past. No collars. No leashes. The owner followed half a block behind, a haughty-looking woman dressed in fashionable *Field and Stream* clothes. Give me a break, Jody thought.

"Showoff," she murmured under her breath.

As they strolled along the street, she looked up at Everett's windows in spite of herself. They were dark, except for the flickering blue light of a television. She wondered if Simon noticed she had looked up at the windows. She would hate to hurt Simon's feelings. She had grown more and more fond of him. He was still shy around her, except when they were in bed, which she found charming.

"Isn't it beautiful?" she said, to call attention away from her glance at Everett's windows. "I love this time of the year."

Simon replied in his soft mumble.

"What?" She had still not gotten used to his inaudible speech and replied with obvious irritation, which she immediately regretted.

"I used to," he said, a little louder.

Now she was confused. "Used to what?" she said, trying to be pleasant this time.

"I used to love this time of the year."

"But now . . . ?"

"Now . . ."

"Now?"

"My whole life has changed."

Jody tried not to be angered by this declaration. It was unfair and unkind to be angry when someone was declaring his love to you, even in this stumbling way, especially in this stumbling way. But she found she was angry. Wasn't it possible to have a sexually moving relationship without muddying the waters? Don't ruin it, she wanted to say.

"I can't go," he said.

Virginia, again.

"Come on, Simon. You don't mean that."

"Come with me," he said.

She didn't answer. She knew he couldn't be serious.

He stopped and pulled her to him, accidentally yanking Beatrice's leash as he did so.

"Hey . . . ," she said.

"I love you," Simon said. "I want to marry you."

fifteen

"Just for a little while"

Just before Emily came home from Italy, Everett realized he had to have a talk with Polly.

"You understand, I'm sure," he said. "I mean, that we can't really see each other while . . ." He stopped. He found he could not say Emily's name in this context. It all seemed suddenly so sordid.

Polly looked at him skeptically, as if she understood all too well. "Don't want your daughter to know you're a cradle robber?"

"Exactly," Everett said. Why mince words? If Polly was old enough to carry on an affair, she was old enough to be discreet. He hoped.

There had already been one embarrassing incident. He'd been walking with Polly when he saw a woman he recognized from Emily's school, a mother of some friend of Emily's, he couldn't remember which one. All the little girls with their long silky hair and small hooded sweaters had looked the same to him. Nor could he remember the mother's name. But he did recognize her, and she obviously recognized him.

"Why, this isn't Emily, is it?" she said, in what Everett thought was a far too obvious prompt for information. "I saw you from across the street and for a moment I thought you were."

Polly had turned red, more with anger than embarrassment, Everett thought. Everett imagined he turned red as well. But there was nothing to be done about it. He had simply agreed with the woman that no, this was not Emily, Emily would not be home for another few weeks. Then, in an attempt to turn her attention from Polly, he asked what her daughter was doing these days and, successful, was forced to listen to the woman describe at some length her daughter's internship as a sports reporter.

"Come on, Pops," Polly said when the woman finally moved on. She laughed, a little maliciously, he thought, but she never mentioned the incident again.

"You understand, I'm sure," he said to Polly before Emily arrived, and she needed no further hints.

The two weeks with Emily were both blissful and excruciating. She was, as predicted, furious with her mother about the cat, which afforded Everett several moments of private satisfaction. But she was also furious with Everett about the cat, which caught him off guard. She had learned to love wine in Italy and drank a glass with him at dinner, when she was around for dinner, and claimed that she no longer enjoyed downing forty-ounce bottles of Budweiser through a funnel. Everett was not sure he believed this, but he thought it was progress that she felt she ought to say so. She had a lot to say about fashion, so inferior in the United States, and politics, so stupid in both Italy and the United States, and the histrionic girl in the group who almost ruined the whole trip. She had very little to say about art, he noticed, or the many museums she acknowledged having visited, but she drank espresso with conviction, and Everett thought that on the whole the trip had been a success.

She was so dismissive of her mother's impending marriage that Everett actually felt sorry for Alison and found himself defending her.

"They really aren't the first people in the world to get married, Emily. I know it's hard for you in theory, but it doesn't change your relationship with your mother."

"I'm not worried about *that*." She gave him a contemptuous look, as if he were insane, or merely stupid, for suggesting any man could come between her and her mother. "It's just so embarrassing."

She then snorted with disgust, and Everett prayed that she would not somehow find out about Polly.

He carefully avoided Polly during those two weeks, barely saying hello when they saw each other in the lobby, and Polly avoided him so dutifully that he found himself wishing she would slip up, just enough so he would notice—a quick loving glance, a rueful, secret smile, a late-night phone call. But she appeared to be in perfect control of whatever emotions she might be experiencing. Even so, Emily did seem to have a suspicion that something was up and an instinct that it had something to do with Polly.

"You're not very nice to that girl," she said one evening when they passed Polly and Howdy on the street.

"What girl?"

"Our neighbor with the dog that loves you."

"No dog loves me."

"Everybody loves you, Daddy," she had said, watching him closely.

He did not respond, but the next time they saw Polly he was careful to greet her in a casual, friendly way.

Now Emily was back at school and Polly was back in his

bed and he had been told to take the large, rambunctious puppy out, and buy some ice cream while he was at it. Everett put on his shoes and his jacket and followed Howdy around the coffee table, making several revolutions, before the dog allowed him to attach the leash. He had never been asked to walk the dog before, and at first he'd refused. Then, when he at last accepted somewhat ungraciously, Polly asked him to get her ice cream at the Koreans.

"What, with the dog?"

"They don't mind, Everett. I do it all the time."

Then why don't you do it tonight? he thought. And he left her watching one of the annoying TV shows she favored, a crudely drawn cartoon of hateful, foul-mouthed children.

But in the elevator, Everett's thoughts softened. Polly was tired. As well she might be. He shivered with pleasure at the memory of her exertions on his behalf. Polly. She deserved a little ice cream.

A round little moon hovered high above the buildings. In the Korean market, Everett self-consciously led the dog in, keeping the leash taut and the dog close to his leg, as if to hide him. He hesitated at the freezer, then decided on Häagen-Dazs strawberry. He was self-conscious because of the dog, who pulled on the leash trying to sniff everyone's shoes. This reminded Everett that he was still a little angry at Polly for making him take the dog, which made him feel guilty. He stepped outside and chose some yellow tulips. He remembered buying tulips the spring before and giving them to Jody, and he quickly changed the tulips for roses, pink ones, though they were more expensive.

Everett noticed the faint smell of stale cigarette smoke when he entered his apartment. Polly never smoked inside, to his knowledge, but her clothes sometimes carried the tobacco odor Everett associated with college dorm rooms. Perhaps because of the flowers, he thought of Jody again, her cigarette beneath the canopy in the rain, her fresh soapy smell. Polly was stretched out on his bed watching a movie. He noticed with annoyance that she had put on one of his clean, pressed white shirts, though she did look sexy in it, he had to admit.

"This movie is so incredible," she said, not looking away from the screen.

"*Annie Hall*? It holds up?"

"I guess so. It's hilarious."

"God," he said, laughing, as he watched Diane Keaton in her floppy hat and necktie. He sat on the edge of the bed. "The *Annie Hall* look. Remember that?"

"No," Polly said.

Then Everett realized that *Annie Hall* had been made before Polly was born.

He groaned.

"What's wrong?" she said, looking over at him.

Everett shook his head.

"Hey!" Polly said. "Strawberry! *And* flowers! You're the best." And she threw her arms around him and kissed him. Howdy, drawn by the excitement, joined Polly and Everett on the bed.

"Off," Everett said to the dog.

"Oh, come on," Polly said, pulling Howdy to her breast and kissing the top of his head.

Everett went into the kitchen to serve the ice cream and to put the flowers in water. He listened to her laughing at the movie, the sound floating lightly through the dark apartment.

Polly ate her ice cream and then got dressed, kissing Everett goodbye and leaving with Howdy but without the flowers.

"Don't let the door slam," she heard him call as the door slammed shut behind her.

She tossed a guilty glance back, then followed Howdy down the stairs. She liked Everett. He was a little cold, a little repressed, a little bleak, perhaps, but with some imagination one could think of him as a man of dry wit, and Polly had plenty of imagination. He had such a dry wit, in fact, that he made Polly feel gorgeously alive, a veritable life force, in comparison. He took her to good restaurants and gave her good wine. He was polite and unchallenging. She felt as though she were on a vacation relationship, lolling on a relationship beach in relationship St. Bart's.

At home, she took a leisurely shower, congratulating herself on finding such a restorative love affair after the heartbreak of Chris. When she got out, she rooted around in the closet looking for a bottle of moisturizer. She opened a gym bag. There was the bottle of moisturizer, as she suspected. Beside the slender, white Origins bottle, Polly noticed another slender white object. It was an iPod. I don't have an iPod, she thought, holding it in her hand. But she remembered something about an iPod. Chris had lost his iPod, hadn't he? Oh, yes, he had, and he had told her so when he announced his marriage. Chris was getting married and had lost his iPod. And Polly had found it.

During the next few weeks, Polly listened to the songs on Chris's iPod, trying to find some clue to what he had been thinking just before they broke up. She discovered nothing except an unfortunate taste on his part for Billy Joel. She knew she should call him to tell him she'd found his iPod, and several times she sat up in bed and reached for the phone before deciding it was too late at night or too early in the morning. He would just think she was stalking him, anyway. And why should she give Chris back his iPod in the first place? He'd probably gotten a new one by now. Even if he hadn't, surely she could borrow the thing for a few days before returning it to him. And so the days turned into weeks, and still Polly kept Chris's iPod.

"When did you get that?" George asked one day when she got home from the office still wearing the little white ear buds.

"I found it."

"Polly . . ."

"I did. In a bag in the closet. I guess it's Chris's."

"I guess it is," George said, laughing.

"I think I should keep it for, like, alimony."

"What does Chris think?"

"I don't know. I can't call him. He'll think I'm a stalker."

She turned the volume up, listening to a song by Billy Joel that she had liked in elementary school. "Roy Cohn, Juan Perón, Toscanini, Dacron . . ." Chris's taste in music was a revelation to her, and not an agreeable one. How was it that she had lived with him and never noticed his preference for puerile, pretentious pop? Was their whole relationship a lie? The iPod said it was, and she found herself listening to the iPod at every opportunity.

When she walked Howdy with Everett that evening, Everett asked her if she would please remove the headphones from her ears.

"It's a little rude, Polly," he said. "It's almost insulting."

Polly, who had become aware of a tendency on the part of her new boyfriend to offer up little lectures more appropriate to a father, put the iPod in her purse with the slow, sullen movements of a daughter. She had been in the middle of the "The Thong Song," fascinated that Chris had chosen it and rather enjoying it, as well.

They walked along in silence until they reached the park, where a woman pushing two minuscule children in an enormous high-tech double stroller stopped to pet Howdy.

"Oh, isn't she beautiful!" the woman said, then rolled her large vehicle past them.

"I can't believe she thought Howdy was a female," Polly said, offended.

Everett laughed. "That used to happen all the time with Emily."

He went on to suggest that Howdy wear blue, but Polly was not listening. She was wondering why he always had to talk about his daughter. It was unnatural.

Everett meanwhile was looking at Howdy and thinking of Emily, while the dog, who had taken the leash in his mouth, pranced gaily in front of Polly. Everett, still dreaming of Emily, experienced a confused surge of tenderness.

"Howdy!" he called out.

The dog stopped, dead still. He tilted his head. Then he barked and wagged his plumed tail, barking and barking until Everett reached out to pet him. On the walk home, Howdy placed himself beside Everett. Whenever Everett looked down at the dog at his side, the dog was looking up at him.

At first Polly had not taken the dog to Everett's very often, for Everett was fastidious and forever shooing Howdy off the furniture, which Polly thought cruel and old-fashioned. But she was feeling more and more defiant. The night before, for example, Everett had asked her not to sit naked on his Saarinen Womb chair, in spite of its name, and she resented it.

When they got home, Everett watched Polly disappear into the bedroom to watch TV. He made himself a martini and sat down in the living room with the paper. His was a lonely life, he realized, even with a nubile girlfriend. Polly greeted him and chatted with him and kissed him and made love to him with youthful energy and cheer, but it was as if she did those things from across a great divide.

The dog had followed him now and pushed his face between Everett and the newspaper, laying his muzzle comfortably on Everett's leg. Everett was too sad to scold the dog at that moment. He didn't stir. The dog didn't stir. A gentle quiet descended. Everett realized he liked the feeling of the dog's head on his leg, the warmth of a living being close to him, demanding nothing, just there. He patted Howdy with one hand and held the martini glass with the other. The dog had such silky ears, such a golden, silky face. He listened to the rhythmic tranquility of the dog's breathing.

"Howdy," he said softly.

Howdy looked up, his head cocked, his eyes dark and somehow reassuring.

Everett experienced an unfamiliar sensation. He looked into the dog's eyes, and he was suddenly, intensely aware of the room around him, of the soft order of his furnishings and his life, of the soft order outside where day was giving way to night, of the TV sounds and the cold wet of the martini glass, of the smudgy feel of newsprint on his fingers, but mostly he was aware of joy—the wild, clattering joy of being alive.

"Howdy," he whispered. "Howdy." Howdy thumped his tail against the floor, and the two of them gazed into each other's eyes, like lovers.

When Howdy jumped on Everett's bed that night, Polly said, "Off!"

But Howdy, instead of jumping down, turned and looked at Everett, as if for further instructions.

Everett did not know any dog commands. "Just for a little while," he said, which is what he used to tell Emily, but Howdy seemed to understand him perfectly and stretched out with a comfortable grunt.

"You've changed your tune," Polly said.

"I'm only human," he said.

sixteen

The Happy Couple

George was at work daydreaming about riding his bike beside the river after work. Then he wondered if he was a good bartender or, indeed, good at anything. It would be nice to be good at his job. But he suspected he was not. He knew how to make drinks, there were never any complaints, nothing sent back. But he didn't like to talk to the customers. He was sure you were supposed to talk to the customers. Every bartender joke, every bartender cartoon in *The New Yorker*, every bartender scene in a movie was predicated on the idea of the bartender talking to, or at least listening to, his customers. George was sure he was breaking some kind of bartender code, not living up to his bartending potential. He wished he was on his bike already, racing along the glassy river.

Jamie came and sat at the bar. George poured him a glass of wine.

"We have interviews this week," Jamie said. "For nursery school. There were no interviews when I went to nursery school. We went, they gave us a nap, then they gave us a graham cracker."

George nodded. He wished someone would give him a nap and a graham cracker. He used to lie on a blue mat the teacher put out and squirm, desperately waiting for the hellish rest period to pass. Now he would appreciate nap time. Youth is wasted on the young, it was true.

"Am I a good bartender?" George asked.

Jamie thought it over.

"You speak English," he said finally. "And you don't use too much vermouth."

George's cell phone rang.

"It's okay, take it," Jamie said when George acted surprised, as if he'd been sure he'd turned his phone off before starting work.

It was his mother.

"Mom, I'm working."

"You call that work? Is Polly okay? She's never home. Does she have a boyfriend? She never tells me anything. And what about you? You never tell me anything. No one ever tells me anything."

"I don't have a boyfriend," he said.

"Yet," Jamie whispered cheerfully.

"Very funny," George's mother was saying. "Now look, I want you and Polly to come home for my sixtieth birthday. It's on a weekend. And take a few days off on either end. I'll pay. You can get wonderful cheap fares now."

"Mom . . ."

"Tell Polly."

George agreed. He had no choice, but he didn't really mind. His mother's house was comfortable, she would dote on them, the weather in California was always nice, and it would be for only a few days.

"Where are you from?" he asked Jamie.

"Pittsburgh."

"Do you ever go back?"

"For holidays sometimes. My parents still live there."

"Do you say you're going 'home'?"

"I've lived here for twenty years, but, yeah, I guess I do say that."

George made some gimlets for a table of excited young women. One of them smiled at him. He smiled back. He would go home to California. Then he would come home from home, home to New York.

That night, Polly had gone to a movie with Laura, the owner of the rambunctious rottweiler mix. Usually when George and one of his girlfriends split, Polly would mourn her absence and wait for the next, much like George himself. But since Kaiya was now part of George's daily routine, Laura, even as an ex, came by every morning to drop the dog off, and Polly had gotten in the habit of offering her a cup of coffee. Then they began having dinner once in a while or going to the movies. She had been surprised to discover Laura was black. George hadn't mentioned it. She wondered if he hadn't really noticed, hadn't considered it worth mentioning, or thought he wasn't supposed to consider it worth mentioning.

She and Laura often talked about George. Polly loved to talk about George. She was proud of how sweet he was, how funny and good-looking he was. And she was exasperated at how hopelessly lacking in ambition he was. Laura seemed to share these feelings. She practically worshipped him for the work he'd done calming her frenetic dog. And she was impatient with his desultory life. She and Polly, therefore, had a great deal to discuss.

"It's true he's aimless," Polly said when they went to a quiet neighborhood bar after a movie. "But at least that leaves room for . . . something." She was thinking of Everett. He wasn't aimless. He was stuck.

"But that's why he's so frustrating, don't you think?"

Polly was about to defend George, out of habit, although she agreed absolutely with Laura, when Laura added, "But then he gets totally gallant, you know?"

Polly did know.

"I'll probably end up with some striving asshole, just like myself," Laura said.

"Or some striven one. Like Everett."

They laughed.

"Striven," Polly said again, enjoying the word.

"He is a little old," Laura said. Though she had never met Everett, she'd heard about him from George, who'd made him sound as though he were stooped and quivering with the weighty burden of his years.

"It's not that, you know," Polly said. "It's just his whole . . ." She paused, thinking. "Life," she said finally.

Laura nodded sagely, and the girls happily ordered a new round of drinks.

The next morning, George climbed out of bed to have a cup of coffee and announce their mother's invitation.

"A summons," he said. "Like traffic court. Might as well get it over with."

"Or we'll get hit with more fines?"

He nodded.

Polly shrugged. She had some vacation days due. It seemed a shame to waste them on family, but it would be fun to see her high school friends who had stayed in California. Then she had a startling thought.

"The dog!" she said.

George looked stunned.

"I forgot about him," he said, looking guiltily at the sleeping hulk in the corner.

The problem was resolved in a way neither of them would have predicted. Everett offered to take care of Howdy while they were away. Polly was pleased and felt her importance in having such a devoted boyfriend. On the other hand, she was a little disappointed that Everett didn't seem at all anxious about her impending absence.

"I'll only be gone for a few days," she said, prompting him. But he just nodded and said it wasn't much time for Howdy and him to get to know each other, but it was a start.

Everett, for his part, could hardly believe his luck. Howdy was coming to pad around his empty apartment. Howdy's big plumed tail would swish across his coffee table. Howdy would sprawl on his bed, his couch, his carpet. He immediately began straightening pictures on the wall and plumping cushions, as if Howdy were a fastidious houseguest.

George didn't like the idea of leaving the dog with Everett, but he saw no other possibilities. He had dropped hints to Jamie, but Jamie had responded with studied incomprehension. So on Friday afternoon, he gathered up Howdy's toys and food. Polly was going to the airport straight from work and he was to take the dog up to Everett.

Everett had left work early in order to be home when the transfer was made, and he opened the door when George rang, squatted down, and offered his face for Howdy's greeting. George watched with grudging approval.

"Here's his food," he said, handing Everett a shopping bag with dry food and several cans.

Everett looked in the shopping bag, which also contained Howdy's toys, a box of treats, and a detailed list of his schedule of walking and eating. Then Everett produced his own shopping bag and its contents: a new blue rubber ball, a squeaky plush hedgehog, and a ceramic dog dish with soft green stripes.

"Jonathan Adler," he said, handing the dish to George. George looked puzzled.

"He designed it," Everett said. "He's a designer."

George handed the bowl back to Everett.

"You can call to check up on Howdy," Everett said. "Do you want my cell phone number, too?"

This was the friendliest Everett had ever been to George.

"Howdy," Everett was saying softly. "Howdy, Howdy, Howdy." He patted his chest and Howdy immediately put his front paws there. The two of them stood gazing into each other's eyes.

George couldn't help but smile.

Everett saw the smile and smiled back. George felt suddenly happy, as if the sun had come out. Oh, he said to himself. I get it. This is what happened to Polly: the smile.

"It's so nice of you to take the dog," he said. He almost meant it. He watched Howdy wagging his tail, and he had a sudden realization. He looked at Howdy, now lying on his back, then at Everett, now scratching the dog's belly, and he thought, I am jealous of my sister's boyfriend. And not even because Everett was his sister's boyfriend, but because his sister's boyfriend was taking care of his sister's dog.

Oh, well, he thought, as he left the happy couple. I'm only human.

Everett clipped on Howdy's leash a few minutes later and took the dog for a celebratory promenade up the block. At the real-estate agency around the corner on Columbus he stopped as he often did to examine the placards displaying tempting photographs of loftlike gems and spacious sun-filled one-of-a-kind marvels. But he found he was less intrigued than usual and led Howdy over to a fluffy white dog, introduced by her owner as Lola, and he peacefully watched the two dogs in their amiable examination of each other's genitals.

seventeen

"It's urgent!"

As anyone who has experienced one knows, an October morning in New York is in itself a good enough reason to live in the city. To the east, a hint of daylight shows between the buildings, above a low bank of silver clouds softly gathers over the roofline, then a pale, milky, and delicate sliver of moon. To the west, the sky is deeper, more vibrant. The air is cold and clean. The windows on every side are still dark. The streetlights are yellow. The natural world, so often obscured in the city, seems preeminent, powerful, and benign. When Jody opened the door of her building and beheld the October morning, she did not indulge in such fanciful language, but she stopped and looked around her and took a deep breath of fresh autumn air, noticed the sky was the color of blue sea glass, and felt she was privileged to be alive. There was the taste of peroxide in her mouth, for she had decided to whiten her teeth, which looked rather dingy to her, and she had carefully peeled off two sticky treated strips of tape and pressed them against her teeth, upper and lower, before setting out with Beatrice for a run. At 6:00 a.m. she was not likely to meet anyone she would have to speak to, and she sucked contentedly on the whitening strips as she started toward the park. Perhaps it was vain of her to worry about the whiteness of her teeth, she thought. On the other hand, she smiled so much, often as a simple, meaningless reflex, that it seemed only fair to the world at large that she not burden it with a smile that was tired and gray as well as insincere. So she told herself as she crossed Columbus, Beatrice trotting at her side.

She had not yet given Simon an answer. If only he had not asked her to marry him. If only their friendship could have gone on, undisturbed and unexamined. Jody had never been asked to marry anyone before, and she was not above a feeling of triumph now, having attained what was supposed to be every girl's dream. She knew she could marry Simon. She liked him. She loved sleeping with him. He had endeared himself to her in many little ways. He had no money, but neither had she, so there would be no pecuniary adjustment necessary on either side. Neither of them was young, they had that in common, too. They could live in his apartment and she could keep hers as a studio or give it up and save money. Simon was kind to Beatrice. He was kind to Jody. She trembled with desire, literally trembled, when he touched her. When she laid these arguments out, her way seemed clear.

But there were arguments against the idea of marriage, too, chief among them her own feelings, for she found that, in spite of all the arguments in favor of the match, she did not want to marry Simon. Perhaps she did not want to marry at all. Perhaps she did not trust Simon's infatuation with her. Perhaps, simply, she did not love Simon.

Her parents would be so happy if she married Simon. They

referred to her not as "Good Old Jody," the way her colleagues did, but as "Poor Jody." Simon called her "Darling." Surely her path was plain.

She and Beatrice passed the spot where the tree had fallen. They passed the bench on which Simon used to wait for them. They jogged along Philosopher's Walk beneath a canopy of whispering orange leaves. Beatrice had begun slowing down on their morning runs. Now Jody noticed her limping a little and stopped to examine her paw. She put her arms around Beatrice, pressing her face against the dog's neck.

It's you I love, she said silently to Beatrice.

Beatrice held up her left back leg and gave a short cry. Worried, Jody led her slowly homeward. She would call the vet and take Beatrice in that afternoon after school. She would play the Vivaldi piece that Beatrice loved, the one that made her thump her tail against the floor and stare lovingly at Jody. She would go to Citarella and buy her a Newport steak.

By the time Jody reached Columbus, she had made herself so nervous she was sure Beatrice should go straight to the vet. Jody would call in sick at school.

Then, as the traffic light changed and she began to cross, Jody saw Everett just as she had seen him on the day of the snowstorm except that this time he, too, had a dog on a leash— Polly's dog, Howdy.

He stood in the middle of the street, smiling, golden as a god in the sunlight, his golden youthful dog beside him.

"I'm dog sitting," he said proudly.

Jody wondered if he remembered their first meeting. She had heard all about his relationship from Polly, who seemed to find some comfort in Everett but still talked about her old boyfriend with regularity. Polly was a sweet and engaging girl, Jody had to admit. She wondered if the sweet and engaging girl was making the older man happy. He looked happy, standing there in his dark suit petting the two dogs, one of them wriggling with puppy energy, the other tense with pain.

Jody felt suddenly old and sad.

"I have to take Beatrice to the vet. She's limping."

As Jody spoke, she felt the whitening strips, wrinkled and sagging, on her front teeth. She hurried away, then, cheerless beneath the beautiful blue sky.

Everett took Howdy home and fed him, listening to the quick wolfish gulps with the same kind of tender satisfaction he remembered from listening to Emily's infant lip smacking. He didn't pay too much attention to Beatrice's ailment. She was an old dog. Probably a little arthritis. He did remember the first time he met Jody and Beatrice on the snowy street, though. He remembered the attractive woman and the ghostly dog. How much had changed since that stormy afternoon. He had arrived home that day to discover that a neighbor he'd never known had hanged himself downstairs. Now he was sleeping with the new neighbor who'd moved into the dead man's apartment. He was walking that dead neighbor's dog. Everett had been a middle-aged man bored with his work and bored with his girlfriend. Now, he was a middle-aged man still bored with his work. What about his new girlfriend? Was he bored with her?

Everett marched disconsolately toward the subway. He wished he could turn around and spend the day with the dog, watching Howdy sleep by the heat riser in the kitchen. He dreaded the day Polly returned to take the dog back, to rip the dog from his bosom, as he described that event to himself. He was ashamed of these thoughts. He pushed them out of his head, went down the steps, and stood on the platform, felt the odd, dead rush of air as the train came in, elbowed his way onto the crowded train, and arrived at work where, with great relief, he threw himself into the urgent business of intimidating his younger colleagues.

At the vet, whose office was just around the corner, Beatrice sniffed the resident cat, then lay down to wait while Jody paced the small waiting room until the receptionist led them into an examining room. Jody lifted Beatrice onto the stainless steel table with some difficulty, which difficulty she found consoling, as if the strain meant she was doing something to help. The vet was a nice-looking young man who thanked her for the referral of Polly and her dog.

"Oh," Jody said. "Them. Yeah." She didn't care about his referrals. She thought it vulgar of him to bring it up at this moment of crisis. "Is she okay? Is she going to be okay?"

The vet gave her an anti-inflammatory for Beatrice and said if she was still limping in a few days, she should come in for X-rays. Jody carried Beatrice up the stairs to her apartment. She gave her peanut butter as a treat. She played Vivaldi for her. She let her maneuver down the stairs herself when it came time for her next walk, and she noticed that the dog seemed to limp a little less. The two of them shared a steak that night and got into bed to watch *Antiques Roadshow.*

Simon had hoped to have dinner with Jody to further press his courtship, for he was becoming impatient. He had never asked anyone to marry him before, so he had no personal experience of the matter, but the novels he had read and the movies he had seen taught him to expect a swift and sure answer, whether it was yes or no. This uncertainty was unsettling. And it made him wonder, too, what married life would be like. Would all decisions be mutual now, and prolonged? Did that mean he would have to wait and wait, to hang on anxiously while his bride decided whether they should get term or whole-life insurance? Whether they should build bookcases? Whether, rather than when, he should go to Virginia? What about which side of the bed they should each be allotted? At her apartment, once she allowed him up there, Jody preferred the left side. At his, she chose the right. Would she switch back and forth when they were married? He could sleep on either side of the bed, but he did cherish consistency, and consistency, it seemed, was exactly what would be under siege. And while on the subject of annoyances, he thought, he had to admit that Jody's toiletries were especially disheartening to him. So many bottles, so many tubes, so many brushes and small pots and zippered bags. He liked the smells that came out of Jody's shower—the fresh scent that he associated with her. But the lineup of plastic containers on the side of the tub and wedged in each of its corners was surely excessive.

Even so, he missed her when he was not with her. He wished he could have her without all her bottles, without her gusto for red meat, which he did not eat, without her occasional cigarette, without her need to practice her violin several hours each day, which took her precious attention away from himself. But even with those drawbacks, he wanted her, and he was reasonably sure he would get her.

He sat in his leather chair in the dark that night, angry that Jody had refused to have dinner with him. Some weeks ago he had put his saddle back on its high shelf, returned his boots to their felt bags and placed them in the back of his bedroom closet. He'd put off his friend Garden in Virginia, too, delaying with vague excuses. But perhaps he should just retrieve his saddle and his boots from their ignominious hiding places and get on a plane for Virginia that night. There was nothing to stop him. And perhaps there was no one to stop him, either. He pictured the guest house that Garden, his college roommate, invited him to stay in each November. Garden had inherited a horse farm soon after they graduated. Every year, Simon would take his four weeks of vacation in the cottage that stood small and pristine among rolling green hills, neat wooden fences, blazing sunsets, and a lattice of fragrant late roses by the back door. Now he indulged himself in the memory of the sounds

of the horses, snorting with excitement, their hooves pound-
ing the turf. The creaking leather of scores of saddles and boots
and bridles, the hounds baying frantically, the snap of branches,
the sting of the fast, cutting air. Simon was a romantic. He
trudged to work he did not relish each day and trudged home
each evening. He murmured shyly in response to the loud,
busy world. But in his heart, there was a bright, surging expectation. Expectation of what, you might ask? And I would
ask you in return, Does it really matter? It didn't matter to
Simon. This secret excitement was undefined, something like
yearning, something like hope, something like peaceful satisfaction. In the dark, in his armchair, dreaming about the soft
jolt of his horse's hooves as it landed on the other side of a
stone wall, of a fence, of an icy brook, Simon sighed with
pleasure.

He sat like that for a long time, dreaming of the joys he was
denying himself in his pursuit of new joys, until he realized he
was hungry and went for a late dinner at the restaurant down
the street.

He was surprised to find Everett there alone at a table with
the large dog who belonged to the bartender and a bottle of
red wine. He was more surprised when Everett waved him
over.

"Sit," Everett said, motioning toward a chair. The dog, who
had been lying down, immediately sat up. "Not you," Everett
said gently to the dog. "You." And he smiled at Simon.

Simon sat down without a word. Everett seemed suddenly
quite a decent fellow. Simon had thought him a great bore in
the past, but now Everett smiled so warmly, and he had already
gotten another glass and begun pouring Simon some wine.
Everett was, perhaps, a little tipsy, but he was also involved
with that young Polly and so no threat to Simon, and Simon
decided that as he had no one else to eat with that night and as

he was disappointed, or at least delayed, in love, he was happy to join his new friend Everett.

"What are you doing here all alone?" Simon said.

"What?" Everett said, as people often did when Simon spoke. Simon noticed that if he waited, people usually would process his words, as if it took longer for the sound of his soft voice to travel the distance to their ears than it did other people's voices. "Oh," Everett said, "I'm not alone. Howdy is with me." The dog looked up at the sound of his name. "And you're with me. Have a steak. We're having steak, Howdy and I."

Simon did not mention that he never ate red meat. He hated the explanations that declaration always lead to. Is it for health reasons, or a moral statement? people would ask. Do you eat chicken? What about fish? Don't you miss bacon? Simon ordered pasta. He drank a glass of wine. He began to feel better.

"I usually go away in November," he said.

Everett had leaned in at the first word, listening intently. "Polly's away now. With her brother. With George. I'm dog sitting," he said, reaching down to touch the dog's head.

Simon tried to look sympathetic. But really, he thought, these people and their dogs. Get a life. Then he noticed a good-looking girl come in, her hair blown by the wind, her cheeks pink. How pretty she was, bringing the outside in with her.

"How is poor old Beatrice?" Everett asked.

"Beatrice?" Simon had no idea how Beatrice was. He could only assume Beatrice was as Beatrice generally was: dignified with a tendency to jump up and look one in the eye.

"Well, Jody was so upset. I saw her this morning. *We* saw her, didn't we, Howdy?"

He talks to the dog, Simon thought. In that horrible baby voice they all use. Simon watched the pretty girl unfurl her scarf. Then he took in what Everett had said. This morning, he repeated to himself. Everett saw Jody this morning. That didn't seem quite fair.

"She was coming back from the park, I guess," Everett was saying. "The dog was limping. Jody was taking her to the vet."

"She's okay," Simon said. Jody hadn't mentioned Beatrice to him. She hadn't said anything about being upset or about the dog limping or about going to the vet. He had no idea how Beatrice was. She could be dead, for all he knew, euthanized that afternoon, an event, like so many events, he could only assume, about which he was not considered sufficiently intimate to be informed. Not liking to be less knowledgeable about his girlfriend's dog than Everett was, Simon said, "Beatrice is fine."

The pretty girl was asking for George.

"Are you George?" she asked Jamie, who was substituting at the bar while George was away.

"No, thank God," Jamie said.

The girl glanced around the room.

Jamie felt suddenly self-conscious, as if she were assessing his business. It's a slow Monday night, and it's late, he wanted to say. What do you expect?

"George is away," he said, instead.

The girl looked so let down. Simon saw it from across the room. He recognized helpless disappointment when he saw it. He felt a self-pitying kinship and called out, "This is George's *dog*."

Everett looked at him, alarmed. "That's not quite accurate, you know."

The girl came over to their table. "So you know George? I need to find him. It's urgent."

From the girl's manner, Simon would have assumed she was

pregnant and wanted to confront George, the father of her un-born child, but she had not even known what George looked like. She had mistaken Jamie, a forty-year-old gay man, for George. Surely even one of George's many girlfriends would recognize him, or at least would see the difference between young dark-haired George and the shorter man with the gray-ing buzz cut behind the bar. Simon was intrigued. A pretty girl in distress.

The girl was kneeling down petting Howdy.

"I'm dog sitting," Everett said defensively. He pulled the dog a little closer to him.

"I have a dog," the girl said. Then she burst into tears.

Jamie headed toward the disturbance, hoping he would not have to call the police. A man had come in a few months ago and taken all his clothes off in the men's room. Almost all his clothes. He had kept on his sneakers and his kelly green socks. He'd come waltzing out and sprawled on his back on the newly reupholstered bench along the restaurant's wall. Jamie had called 911 and an ambulance had come and strapped him onto a stretcher and taken him, smiling, away. This girl, though, had thankfully not begun to undress. Yet.

Everett looked with horror at the girl who had brought her tears under control and sat on the floor sniffling weakly. He thought longingly of his tranquil apartment, dark and cool and unruffled by female passions. There were some benefits to be-ing alone, he thought. But when he was honest with himself, he had to admit that his apartment was just as tranquil and un-ruffled by female passions even when Polly was in it. It wasn't that his life was too full of female passions. It was that his life was empty.

Everett looked down at the weeping girl. He looked down at Howdy. Howdy was licking the girl's cheek. Everett put his hand out and patted the dog. "There, there," he said to no one in particular.

Simon, wearily slipping into social-worker mode, helped the girl up and into a chair. She wiped her eyes on a napkin offered by Jamie. She smiled pitifully.

"George will be back tomorrow," Jamie told the girl.

Tomorrow, Everett thought. Tomorrow he would see Polly, a prospect that should have made his heart leap with joy and anticipation. But tomorrow Howdy would leave him all alone, just as his wife had, just as his daughter had. He felt suddenly, sentimentally, overwhelmingly sorry for himself. He would cease to have an excuse to walk in the park at dusk and hear geese calling out to one another as they flew overhead. The old lady in black inching her way painfully along the street would no longer stop and call out to the dog in Italian, ending inevitably with, "*Chichi, chichi*," as she reached unsteadily to pet Howdy's silky head. Everett would no longer watch Zappa the Chihuahua climbing Howdy's leg while its owner, a dapper old man in a straw hat, admonished it in tender Spanish. The Frenchwoman would not greet him, the old woman from Germany who'd survived the Holocaust would have no excuse to stop him, and he would have no excuse to persuade her to tell him her courageous tale. The Irish woman with the sensible shoes and overweight Boston terrier, the dashing young Belgian with the Brussels griffon, the tattooed man with toy poodles, the eleven-year-old boy with Truly, the shepherd mix—these neighbors would no longer even notice him. The garbagemen would not wave to him each morning as they hung off their lumbering green trucks. The prancing, muscular boxer, the dainty miniature pinscher, the bouncing Labradoodle puppy—none of them would wind their way among Howdy's legs and between Everett's, their leashes busily twisted and intertwined. All of this would stop when Polly came home.

It seemed almost incomprehensible to Everett. He had lived with this dog for five days. In five days, his life had come alive for him. His street was full of people, and his city was full of streets. His park, once nothing more than a grand exercise track, was now a landscape, a lawn, a garden, a thicket, a boulder, a swamp.

Everett watched the mysterious girl stand up to leave. "There, there," he said again gently, half to himself.

eighteen

"Just my luck"

Simon walked home in a thoughtful mood. He did not welcome drama in his life. He saw enough of it at work. He had long associated intense feeling with the socially maladjusted and the mentally ill. He felt sorry for the girl in the restaurant, but he felt sorry for himself, too. He had gone there in a foul mood and he had left in an equally foul mood. It was just his luck to be accosted by a hysterical female. She had dried her tears, apologized in a genuinely touching manner, and hurried out the restaurant door. Simon wished her well, but the encounter, his whole evening, in fact, left him unhappy and ill at ease. Why hadn't Jody told him about Beatrice?

He called her when he got home, ostensibly to find out how Beatrice was but really to make her feel guilty about not confiding in him and, if possible, to wake her up.

"Why didn't I tell you? I guess I didn't think you'd be interested," she said.

Now this was unfair, and Simon knew it was unfair, and he told her so in a voice that sounded peevish even to him, but he could not stop himself. He was interested in every aspect of Jody's life, he said. He always asked her about her students, about faculty meetings, about a difficult passage she was practicing.

"You're right," Jody said. "I'm sorry."

Simon was inclined to continue the argument but had to settle for winning it. He said goodbye and sat in his chair for another twenty minutes sulking before he went to bed. Even I can't wait forever, Jody, he thought. I'm only human.

While Everett tucked a pillow under Howdy's head and went to sleep, one arm thrown over the dog's shoulders, and Simon sat in his chair brooding, and Jody, awakened, as Simon had hoped, by his call and unable to fall back to sleep, sat up reading a magazine article about the strange death of a Sherlock Holmes scholar, Doris lay in bed beside her husband and rejoiced. Tomorrow night was the City Council meeting at which she would present her petition to post extra officers from the Parks Police to ticket scofflaws and their defecating, leashless canines. In addition, and she was especially excited about this one, she had decided to introduce a motion, if one did such a thing at a City Council meeting, to liberate the park from canines altogether, except between the hours of midnight and 6:00 a.m., during which hours, plentiful enough, surely, the canines could, and probably would, run in frothing packs as far as she was concerned. This, Doris felt, was inspired. This would be her legacy as far as the canine blight was concerned. She always called dogs canines now. They were canines under the law and under the law is where Doris wanted them all to be.

"It's a rather unpopular position," Mel had warned her. "I can't support you on this."

"Oh, I understand you can't support me *publicly*. It would be political suicide," Doris had said, enjoying the back-room nature of the conversation. "It will be enough to know that you support me in your heart."

Mel had not exactly replied, but she understood that he had to protect himself. You never knew who was listening. And so she had accepted his unspoken endorsement.

"One owner doesn't even leave his building," she said. "He just stands in the lobby, lets the canine out, then gives a holler about ten minutes later, and the canine comes home, bold as can be, leaving behind . . . well, what they leave behind . . ."

"Obedient dog, huh?"

"That is hardly the point," Doris said.

"No, of course not," Mel said quickly.

Doris visited his office frequently these days. Mel himself had become one of her community projects, and he seemed to be progressing nicely. He often mentioned her civic energy with what she took to be almost awe, though I am not sure he was quite as gratified by her participation in local government as she imagined, for his most vociferous praise invariably occurred as he ushered her out his office door. But Doris was content, and she turned over in bed, pressed herself against Harvey's warm, familiar bulk, and fell asleep with visions of infrastructure improvements and statutory reforms dancing in her head.

The trip home to California had been as George expected—a loving combination of guilt and indulgence. Polly had dragged him back and forth between their long-divorced and still bickering parents just as she always had. They had serviced both mother, in Santa Monica with insufferable boyfriend, and father, in Encino with innocuous wife. George and Polly had been fed and made much of, and had then, with a slight pang of sorrow and a vibrant sense of relief, escaped.

On the plane back to New York, Polly asked George why

he didn't like Everett. In an attempt to avoid the real conversation—Everett was too old for Polly, she was using him to avoid having a real life, he was superior and rude—and remembering how sweet Everett had been with Howdy, George murmured something about being jealous over the dog. Polly gave a loud laugh and the man beside her woke up with a jerk.

"So. You're home," Everett said when Polly appeared at his door. "Darling," he added, giving her a kiss on the cheek.

Polly registered some coolness on Everett's part but was enveloped by the noisy whirl of Howdy's greeting and put it out of her mind.

"Did you guys have a good time?" she asked. She was addressing Howdy, but Everett answered with sudden animation. He told Polly about Howdy's happy encounters with squirrels and ducks and schoolchildren. He described acrobatics in pursuit of Frisbees and baseballs. He elaborated on the amount of dog hair harvested each day with the several different types of brushes he had tried. And finally he said, very simply, "I'll miss him so much," handed Polly the shopping bag of unused food and new toys, turned abruptly, and closed the door.

Howdy gave a confused whimper, looked at the closed door, then followed Polly down the stairs to their own apartment. Polly wondered if Everett was drunk. His behavior really had been bizarre, sullen and then almost manic. She watched the dog sniff at the furniture. She filled Howdy's water bowl and watched him drink, the mechanics of which, with its noisy splashing, she always found fascinating. Then she brought Howdy outside. They took a long walk together, leaving muddy tracks by the edge of the lake, then standing, side by side, watching the setting sun glint off the windows of the tall East Side buildings. A hawk floated high overhead. A flock of goldfinches flew by, flashing and improbable. There was a rustling in the bright fallen leaves. Howdy growled. Polly looked down, expecting a bird scratching in the underbrush, or a busy squirrel. Instead, she saw a long skinny rat tail flash beneath the leaves, then disappear. She smiled. She was home.

When George returned to work that evening, Jamie took him aside and related to him the preceding night's drama.

"But who was she?" George asked.

"I don't know, but she was frantic."

"What did she look like?"

"Tall, blonde, kind of fabulous looking."

George brightened. That didn't sound so bad. But what did she want with him?

"She thought you were me?"

Jamie nodded, rolling his eyes. "Then she went over and saw Howdy and started crying hysterically."

George thought this over. The girl didn't know him, that was clear. But she knew his name and where he worked. And something he had done had caused her to be hysterical and distressed.

"The dog made her cry?"

Jamie nodded again.

George had a frightening thought. What if she were related to the man who killed himself? What if she had come to claim Howdy?

"I really don't think I want to see this person," he said.

"Maybe you're her sperm donor."

"You're the one with all the children," George said. "Not me."

He went behind the bar and began cutting limes. The mysterious blonde woman wanted Howdy. That sounded so ominous. What if Howdy had secretly been cloned in Korea and the woman was an agent for the government? Which government? The CIA . . . Or perhaps Howdy was not cloned. He was not even a mutt. He was a very, very rare breed, worth a fortune, and the blonde woman was coming to claim him, her only inheritance from her . . . father? Uncle? A distant cousin . . .

He pulled out his cell phone and called Polly.

"The man in your apartment? The dead guy? He had no relatives, right? Was he, like, a scientist? Was he Korean?"

"Why are you bringing him up? Why are people always bringing him up?"

At that moment, a tall blonde woman came in the door, and George knew at once that she was the blonde woman of the night before who was looking for him.

"Never mind," he said and hung up.

While George was watching the blonde girl walk across the restaurant, Everett was sitting at his kitchen table, having been interrupted in the preparation of a martini by a phone call from Emily.

"I'm coming home next month," Emily said.

"Yes, I know."

"For Mommy's wedding."

"Right."

"I wish you were coming."

"Don't you think that would be a little awkward?" Everett said.

"I think the whole thing is awkward. I think they should live in sin."

Everett hung up, put away the bottle of gin, and went across the street for his drink and his dinner, hoping he might see Howdy there. Polly had called to say she was tired and jet-lagged and going to sleep. She had sounded irritable and truculent and Everett had not challenged her, though really it was a short trip, not as if she had come from Hong Kong. And he missed Howdy already. Perhaps George had brought the dog to work with him.

Simon and Jody were also headed to the restaurant. Beatrice had been left at home, however, for her leg was still bothering her. Simon had found himself less sympathetic than he might normally have been, simply because he had not been immediately informed of the dog's ailment.

"She'll be okay," he said, when Jody fussed over the dog as they left. She shot him a look that made him wish he had been silent. He bent down and kissed Beatrice goodbye to try to make up for his coldness. Jody smiled then, and Simon kissed her, too.

"I've been thinking a lot about . . ." Jody paused, obviously embarrassed. "About your . . . proposal."

How odd it sounded, put like that, a proposal, a modest proposal, as if he had suggested Jody eat her children.

"I kind of like things the way they are," she said. "For now."

Sometimes Simon thought he liked things just the way they were, too. Sometimes he had wondered what he would do if Jody actually accepted him. Ever since he'd asked her to marry him, he had noticed things that would almost certainly bother him once they were married, things that had never even registered before. The way she left her coat on the chair, the toast crumbs in the butter, her love of early music. Yet when he looked down at her now as they walked along the street, at her quick footsteps and windblown hair, when she looked up at him and smiled uncertainly, then took his hand in hers, he wanted to be with her every moment, he wanted to actively deposit toast crumbs in the butter, whole slices of toast, entire loaves, if that was what it would take.

"Let's go home," he said, suddenly overcome with desire.

Jody smiled a very particular smile that he knew and cherished. Without a word, they turned and retraced their steps.

Jody lay in the darkness beside Simon, who had fallen into a soft sleep. She was happy and she was hungry. How nice to feel such unequivocal feelings: happiness, hunger. Beatrice lay beside the bed on the rug, also asleep. Why shouldn't it always be like this? Marriage would spoil it, put too much weight on the soft airy fabric of her time with Simon, tear it to skimpy, ragged pieces. Jody was sure of it. But why? She had always thought she wanted to get married. She had certainly wanted to have children. But now, somehow, when it came to it, all she really wanted was to lie in the darkness just like this, with Simon beside her. Was that so wrong?

Perhaps it was not wrong, Jody thought after a while, but now I seem to be wide awake with worrying. She worried that she had hurt Simon's feelings. She worried that she was, simply, making a mistake. She worried that she was hungry and she worried that she was gaining weight. She worried and turned over and then back again and then worried that she would wake Simon. Carefully, she slipped out of bed and took the phone into the bathroom. She called the cheap taco place and ordered a pound of chicken fajitas. Simon liked them. And there would be leftovers for tomorrow. When she hung up, since she couldn't turn the lights on in the studio apartment without disturbing the sleepers, she thought she might as well take a bath.

She put in bath salts and waited for the tub to fill up, enjoying the steam. She slid into the water and closed her eyes and thought, yes, she wanted everything to stay the way it was.

Simon had woken up the instant she left the bed, but he lay where he was, not moving, savoring the quiet of someone else's house. It was different from the quiet of his own apartment. He heard the bathwater go on. He imagined Jody submerged, only her head and the tips of her knees visible above the milky water. The smell of the bath salts wafted into the room. How mysterious women were. Scented, stubborn, and unfathomable. She was so beautiful, so soft, so hard of heart. He was angry and hurt, and he was sated and full of love all at once.

She had refused him. He tried to twist her words to give himself hope. Leave things as they are. For now. That left some room, perhaps, but it was hardly the ringing endorsement of his matrimonial plan he had hoped for. Why wouldn't she marry him? What possible difference could it make to her? She would still have her job and her dog. She would still sleep beside him every night, still make love, still play her violin. He couldn't see what was keeping her from him, and he grew more and more angry.

He thought about calling his college roommate in Virginia. He could still go down there. It was only for a month, after all. Jody would be right where she always was when he got back, in her little apartment with her big dog and her scented soaps. Perhaps she would have changed her mind by then. Perhaps "for now" would be over.

Jody closed her eyes and lay her head back against the cool enamel. She wished Simon would wake up and come and join her. It would be romantic. She imagined him opening the door, the steam curling around his naked body. He would step into the tub, lower himself into the water . . . and there would be no room for me, Jody thought, envisioning the water sloshing onto the floor, the great tangle of knees and elbows and uncomfortable slippery limbs. And she wondered if that was what marriage would be like—two naked people in a bathtub, the water turning cold and gray.

Simon knocked on the door.

"I have to leave," he said softly.

Jody pushed the door open with her foot. He was dressed. He bent down to kiss her.

"Don't worry," she said, not sure why.

"Worry? No. No, I won't worry."

The buzzer rang and Simon waited by the door until the delivery boy climbed the stairs. The sight of Jody in the bathtub had softened his heart.

"There's money in my bag," Jody called from the bath-room, drying herself quickly.

"Allow me," Simon said in mock grand tones.

She put on her robe and came out of the bathroom to find the take-out containers neatly arranged on the table. A place had been set for her with plastic fork and knife on their proper sides of the paper plate, the fork resting on the thin little paper napkin.

"You won't stay?" she said, sitting down and serving herself without waiting for an answer.

Simon did stay. The smell of the fresh, hot tortillas was too tempting. He gratefully ate several fajitas, then just as gratefully made his way home to his own bed with his own familiar quiet.

Unlike Jody and Simon, Everett did make it to the restaurant, and he saw immediately that Howdy was nowhere in sight. But there, almost as interesting as Howdy, was the girl who had cried so pitifully the night before. She was at the door near the kitchen, her coat still on, staring at George. George, blushing a deep red that was visible from the front of the restaurant, stared back.

What did George do to that poor girl? Everett wondered. Polly was always complaining about him, about what a wom-anizer he was. But how can you womanize a woman and then have her not even know what you look like? Perhaps he was harassing her on the Internet. Everett came closer and sat at the bar, hoping to overhear something.

"*George?*" the girl said in a shocked voice.

"Alexandra," George said, for there she was, Alexandra, his old boss, as imposing as ever.

They faced each other with almost identical expressions of horror.

"Just my luck," Alexandra said then, and she burst into tears.

nineteen

"He bites"

When Alexandra began to cry, George handed her a napkin. He didn't know what else to do. It seemed almost impossible to him that his high and mighty boss lady was capable of tears.

"I'm sorry," she said from behind the enormous white napkin.

"Oh," he said. "You are?"

"Laura said . . ."

"You know Laura?"

"We were roommates in college. She said there was this guy she used to go out with . . ."

Oh, God, George thought, what did I do wrong?

"And she said he was really great . . ."

Laura said he was really great? He grinned.

". . . about her dog," Alexandra went on. "She has this dog, Kaiya . . ."

George's grin faded somewhat.

Alexandra began to cry again, and George poured her a glass of water, then a glass of wine. He gave them both to her, and she stood with a glass in each hand, sniffling. George steered her over to the bar. She sat down next to Everett. George wished she had chosen another seat, but at least she was sitting now, sipping the water, gulping the wine. And Everett seemed as oblivious as ever, not even nodding his head in greeting.

"Do you want anything to eat?" George said gently.

Alexandra shook her head.

"I'm really sorry," she said. "It's just that I was expecting to find this dog trainer guy and instead it was you."

George didn't really like the way she said "you." Pitiable as she was with her tear-stained face, he could not help but think she had betrayed an unacceptable level of contempt in the pronunciation of the word "you."

Alexandra heaved a big sigh. "What a stupid mix-up. I'm sorry to bother you. I'm looking for this guy Laura told me about and he's incredible with animals and I have this dog . . ." She trailed off, staring into her empty wineglass in obvious misery.

Now George saw that he must forgive the scornful delivery of the word "you." Now he understood that she was there not to accuse him of anything. She was there to ask his help, and his gallantry kicked in immediately. He sat down beside her and softly questioned her about the dog.

It was a mutt, a rescue dog, part Chihuahua, part pug, part beagle, part terrier. It was the cutest dog in the world. People stopped her on the street to ask what kind of dog it was, that's how cute it was.

"That's wonderful," George said.

"No. No, it's terrible. They stop to ask what kind of dog he is, and they reach out to pet him and . . . and he attacks them." She looked down in shame. "He bites," she whispered. "He bites . . . me, too." She looked up at him suddenly. "But then he's so sorry," she added, speaking quickly. "He whimpers and licks my face . . ."

"What's his name?"

"Jolly. But what's the use? I just thought, as a last resort, that this guy . . ."

"But that's me. I'm the guy. I'm the one who helped Laura with her dog."

Alexandra tilted her head, the way Howdy did when he was confused. "You?" she said.

He still did not like the way she said "you," but his chivalry overcame his resentment and he said, "Yeah. Me."

Everett overheard all of this and told himself that some of the mystery was cleared up. It wasn't a paternity suit, at any rate, though there was some reason Alexandra didn't think much of George. He considered joining in the conversation, backing up George's claim. But he didn't like to reveal that he had been eavesdropping, so he continued to eat in silence.

"I walk Kaiya every morning," George was saying.

"You do?"

"God, I thought you were related to the guy who killed himself in my apartment."

"What?"

"I thought you wanted to take my dog."

"You have a dog?"

"No, actually."

Alexandra stood up. "What's the use?" she said.

"He's my sister's dog," George said.

"Did you train her?"

For a moment, George thought she meant his sister. Then he said, "The dog is a male."

Alexandra said, "I certainly don't want to take him. Don't you want him? Does he bite, too?"

"No, of course not."

Alexandra gave him a fierce, defiant look.

"He's just a puppy," George said, trying to cover his insensitivity. "And I trained him, I guess."

"And you trained Laura's dog?"

George turned this question over in his mind. Train? It seemed to him that Kaiya had simply calmed down, spontaneously. She grew more obedient, the way Howdy grew bigger, imperceptibly, a little each day. It had just sort of happened. Or had it? George admitted that he'd recently acquired the habit of reading everything he could get his hands on about animal behavior and dog training, spending hours at the Barnes & Noble at Sixty-sixth Street and hours more in the library and online. He read books by an autistic woman who designed humane chutes for cattle on the way to slaughter; he watched CDs of dog-trainer monks running across icy fields, their respectful German shepherds with magnificent sloping shoulders following swiftly on wide, sure feet. He read books about pack behavior and behavior modification for horses and children and parrots. He had gone through an ethology textbook and Virginia Woolf's memoir of Elizabeth Barrett Browning's dog, Flush. He had read Elizabeth von Arnim and J. R. Ackerley and Cesar Millan. He had spoken softly to Kaiya and he had listened to Kaiya and he had watched Kaiya and responded to and rewarded and ignored Kaiya, and Kaiya had calmed down.

"Yes," he said, finally. "I did train Laura's dog."

Alexandra sat down and looked at him piteously.

She's heartbroken, George thought, and just the word, heartbroken, made him sad and made him want to help her. And, too, George had to admit he liked having his old boss imploring him for help. He did, therefore, wait just a fraction of a second longer than he had to, enjoying this unaccustomed feeling of superiority and strength, but at last George felt he had to tell Alexandra that although he had happened to help Laura's dog, he simply was not a real dog trainer.

"I have no experience, and no credentials."

"I don't care. I've already tried three dog trainers. With experience and credentials."

"I could help you find someone, maybe."

Alexandra stood up and wrapped her scarf around her neck. She had never even taken off her coat.

"What's the use?" she said. "The vet said to put him to sleep. I just thought I'd try this one last thing."

George, with his fondness for the chivalrous gesture, gestures that were frequently evident to him alone, heard now unmistakably the trumpet calling him to the lists, and he longed to respond. Poor, lovely Alexandra. He took her hand.

As he did so, he looked into her eyes and knew that poor, lovely Alexandra's distress was too real for his chivalrous fantasy. This was not a medieval contest with prancing horses. This was not a matter of gestures and manners. This was heartache and pain, and George understood that he was less drawn to a lady's heartache and pain than he was to opening a lady's door or fetching her a glass of wine.

There was also the matter of Alexandra herself, a cold, hard lady if ever there was one, someone who had made his life difficult and had seemed to relish that, someone who had humiliated him at every opportunity. Yet now she was practically begging him for his help.

She was so sad and so vulnerable, wiping her eyes now with a cocktail napkin. George felt a surge of protectiveness that was usually reserved for Polly.

The thought of Polly made him remember Everett. George turned to look at him, but Everett was preoccupied, fascinated, apparently, by his tortellini.

"Stay," George said then to Alexandra, taking her other hand in his. "Stay and eat something. Then maybe I can meet

Jolly. What if I help you out while we look for a real dog trainer?"

The look Alexandra gave George, a naked, unguarded look of newborn hope, was not lost on Everett, though he still dutifully faced his plate of pasta. Imagine someone looking at you like that, he thought, with some envy.

Everett listened as Alexandra ordered the bread pudding. Good choice, he wanted to tell her. The bread pudding was both delicious and comforting.

"I already had dinner downtown," she was saying to George.

"You still work there?"

She nodded, then burst out, "I'm sorry I was such a bitch, but you were a really bad waiter and what was I supposed to do?"

At this, Everett could not help but glance up at George. George looked as unruffled as if Alexandra had asked for another glass of wine, which in fact he was pouring for her.

"I guess you're better with animals," Alexandra added uncertainly.

twenty

"But what I really meant was love"

Perhaps you're wondering what happened to Doris and her plans for canine reform. Well, the City Council meeting was not as successful a meeting as Doris had hoped. There were, in fact, those who, after gasping in disbelief, began to attack her in what she considered an unhealthy, nearly psychotic verbal barrage. They were certainly very loud, these fellow citizens, but Doris stood with her head tall until the meeting was called to order and the brouhaha calmed down. "A cry for help," she murmured then, shaking her head sadly at the rowdy behavior. Then, louder, firmly, "Somebody *must* set limits." Mel, she noticed, was as silent as the tomb, and seeing the reaction of the others in the room, she could not really blame him. Politics is politics, she thought, but civic duty was also civic duty, and with her shoulders back (she had decided on a vintage Chanel jacket and skirt and was at that moment buoyed by the simple, smart cut of the little navy suit), she smiled patiently, shot Mel a quick wink, and ended her presentation with the declaration that a petition could not be ignored, the people would be heard, and she would return in the future with enough signatures of those people to shake the powers that be from their complacent pedestals of ignorance and prejudice.

"This is not Paris!" Doris proclaimed as she sat down, her fist raised in defiance of that city's dog-defiled sidewalks, and there was no one who would argue that point.

There was, further, a small but real faction of her supporters on the block. There are, certainly, few citizens who would actively take a stand against clean sidewalks, or in favor of excrement on the streets. Even those with dogs, blaming the occasional mess on the professional dog walkers, were sympathetic to Doris's ideas about enforcing the pooper-scooper laws. Her efforts at cleaning up had been noticed and had been appreciated. If her followers were not aware of her more extreme proposals, Doris thought, they had at least begun to greet her with thanks when they spotted her on her rounds, and so, even after the unsuccessful and unpleasant meeting, Doris felt assured that her day was coming.

Jody, always careful to clean up after her own dog, was not, needless to say, one of Doris's supporters. To Jody, the orange face and the ominously shaking fist and the big white SUV were hostile and alien—recurring, menacing apparitions on her nice, friendly block. And how very, very friendly her block had turned out to be, Jody thought one afternoon as she moved her baton up and down, up and down, and listened to the singing schoolchildren arrayed before her. This was not a gifted group, these kindergartners, but they were earnest, and their little faces were almost comically expressive. The first kindergarten group she had ever taught were now college seniors. She had been doing this for seventeen years. That was a disquieting thought. But why was it disquieting? She was, after all, a thirty-nine-year-old woman. Her fortieth birthday was a week away. Then, truly, would she be a spinster. When, she wondered, would she stop thinking of herself as someone who was seventeen years old and start accepting not only that she was an adult, but that she had been an adult long enough to have seventeen years of history of adult work, to have a whole lifetime behind her?

"I've got a mule, her name is Sal . . . ," she sang along with the children, exaggerating the movement of her lips and mouth to help them remember the words.

Not the most distinguished lifetime, either. She was not a successful musician, at least she did not earn her living by performing. But this was not something she had ever minded before. As long as she'd been able to play, she had been happy. And teaching had its own pleasures. There was something to be said for being adored. The children had always adored her. Now, Simon adored her.

"Good job!" she said brightly.

The children left the music room, some of them skipping, one of them, a little boy with dark red curls, stopping to kiss her hand before running off to catch up with his friends.

Of course she liked having admirers. Who among us does not? But did that mean she ought to marry Simon? She straightened the chairs and gathered her sheet music into her bag. Although she had already given Simon her answer, she continued asking herself this question. She knew that if she wanted to marry anyone, it was unlikely she would find a better husband. He was kind and honest. And sexy. He was tidy, too, perhaps a little too tidy, as well as a little too used to living on his own. So was she, for that matter. But they could work that out, surely. Two only children at the center of their own worlds. She tried to imagine living in Simon's apartment with him. He would sit in his leather armchair. She and Beatrice would . . . lie on the floor at his feet?

"You can bring a chair from home," she said to herself, forgetting that Simon's apartment would then be her home.

That night, beside Simon in his bed, she watched him sleep. Her insomnia had returned recently, and she had not yet figured out how to cope with it when she was at Simon's. The window was closed, as Simon preferred it to be, and the room was too warm. The sheets felt coarse and creased. She could not turn on a light and read because it would wake him. But Simon looked so peaceful, and she was moved, though she reminded herself that people always do look peaceful when they are asleep, even terrible people. Stalin probably looked like an angel when he slept, if angels ever had large, heavy black mustaches, which she supposed they probably did not.

She put her hand out and stroked Simon's head. She had still not gotten used to the pleasure, the certainty of having this man beside her.

"I really should marry you," she whispered.

Simon stirred.

"What time is it?" he said.

"Three."

"Why aren't you sleeping?"

"I was thinking," she said, surprised as she was so often by her own cheery tone.

"Oh . . ." And he was asleep again.

The next morning, Jody looked at him closely, remembering that predawn moment when she knew she should agree to marry him.

"Have you been thinking about getting married?" she asked. "Still?"

Simon, opening the newspaper, stopped. He held it, spread out in the air, like a man holding a map, like a man who is lost, Jody thought.

He had indeed been thinking of marriage. He had been thinking of it at that moment, but what he had been thinking was that perhaps, after all, Jody was right. They had spent a glorious night together. They would have a chummy breakfast.

Then she and her enormous dog, who was sniffing at his bare feet with unwelcome interest, would go home and leave him to his solitary male sit-ups, his shower, his shave. Simon enjoyed these private activities, and part of his enjoyment, he realized, was that they were private. If we were married, he had been thinking, she would be there, smiling and encouraging, while he did his sit-ups. She would be waiting, with patient good humor, for the shower and the sink. She would be in every way loving and gentle and agreeable, but she would be there, an intruder.

"A little," he said, straightening the paper to hide his confusion.

"Me too."

Jody pulled her chair closer to his. Simon noticed her fresh, soapy smell. How pretty she looked, even in the morning. Then she scratched her head rather violently, which reminded Simon of Beatrice, who now lay across his feet. Jody slid over and sat on his lap. He could now smell coffee on her breath and the stale, sour odors of sleep. He felt uncomfortably warm. The radiator began to bang. How could they have turned the heat on? It was not even . . . November.

"November," he said out loud.

"November," Jody repeated, not paying much attention. She was gazing down at the paper at an article about global warming.

"It's so hot," he said, holding his arms out in front of him on either side of her and rolling up his sleeves with considerable difficulty. He liked his apartment warm, but this was impossible. He would have to speak to the landlord. "It's just too hot."

Jody just nodded and said, "Soon all the fish will die."

Simon noticed he was having trouble breathing. He tried to inhale deeply. He began to cough.

"Want some water?" Jody said. She did not seem to expect an answer.

He gently pushed her off his lap. She slid the paper along with her.

"Sorry," he said.

"Mmmhmm," Jody murmured, still absorbed in her article. Simon stood up.

As she read, Jody absentmindedly ran a finger across her plate, collecting toast crumbs. Beatrice lifted her head and seemed to stare directly at Simon, her eyes full of sadness. Simon turned guiltily from her gaze.

"Why is it so hot?" he said.

He struggled with the kitchen window, bulky with ancient layers of paint, tugging violently until it opened, letting in a gust of cool autumn air.

"That's better," he said, staring out at the brown, barren garden.

Not too many days later, Jody and Polly were walking with their dogs toward Central Park. Beatrice still limped occasionally. Jody watched her now with some anxiety.

"She's great," Polly said. "Look at her. You have to admit she's better now."

Although Polly's remark sounded, as usual, like a command, although, too, it was a command Jody would have been overjoyed to obey, she noticed, nevertheless, that Beatrice was favoring her back foot. She said nothing, but her heart sank, and the crisp air and playful breeze seemed to disappear. She could not bear the idea of Beatrice in pain. Howdy gamboled beside the old white dog, then ran a few feet ahead, then wheeled around to bark and invite her to play. Beatrice walked gloomily past the big puppy. Jody knew something was wrong.

Far ahead of them, Jody noticed an older woman, incongruous in a short black taffeta evening coat, dragging a matching black garbage bag and staring down at the sidewalk. Jody thought something about her was vaguely familiar. Her un-earthly peach-tangerine hair, perhaps.

"Polly," she whispered, "I think that's the stalker lady."

They watched the woman reach down to pick up a beer bottle, pour out the remains of its contents, then drop it offi-ciously in a bag.

"Gross," Polly said. "What is she doing?"

Jody crossed the street, motioning Polly to follow, and slinked away from the orange woman toward the camouflage of the park.

"Chris is getting married in two weeks," Polly said as they walked through the entrance. "And so is Everett's ex. On the same day!"

"Really? You can console each other."

"Everett's a little bummed, I think. He doesn't exactly say so, but you know, you can sort of tell."

"How about you? About Chris?"

"Oh, I hate his fucking guts, that's all."

"That's all."

"He invited me to the wedding. Can you believe that?"

"No, actually."

"Yeah. He did."

They walked on without speaking. The leaves made a swish-ing sound around their feet.

"Yeah. He did invite me," Polly said at last.

"Going?"

"Yeah."

Jody laughed. "Polly, I was joking . . ."

"I don't care," Polly said. "I'm going."

The dogs sniffed and peed in turn at a corner of the statue of a Civil War soldier. It was insane for Polly to go to Chris's wedding. Struggling for a reply from her reserves of blithely optimistic generalizations, the only response Jody could come up with was, "But . . ."

"I'm taking George."

"Not Everett?"

Polly made a face. "I don't know," she said. "Everett is so . . ."

Dry and funny? Jody thought, remembering his comment about the floating debris at the first thaw. Mordant and witty? She remembered the songs they sang together during the blackout. Handsome? That smile. Tender? She recalled him walking hand in hand with his daughter, and proudly taking Howdy to the park.

"Old," Polly said at last.

They turned back toward home. Everett was old compared to Polly, there was no denying that, yet Jody found herself on the verge of arguing the point.

"Perhaps he would feel uncomfortable, too," she said—diplomatically, she thought.

"Oh, people always think he's my father. So I guess he's used to it."

"Are you used to it?"

Polly mulled this over. "I guess I'm a little sick of it."

"Not quite the same as being used to it. Maybe he's sick of it, too," Jody said.

"Maybe," Polly said. "I hadn't thought of it that way."

Beatrice was limping, now, unmistakably, and Jody lost interest in Polly and in Chris's wedding, even in Everett. Beatrice stopped and whimpered. She held up her back left leg. Jody knelt beside her dog and gently held the quivering paw.

"Beatrice," she said softly. "Oh God, Beatrice."

The dog nuzzled her cheek and whimpered again.

Polly said something about getting a cab, but Jody, not even bothering to explain that no driver would stop to pick up an eighty-five-pound pit bull, picked up the dog herself and carried her the two blocks to the vet.

"Can I help?" Polly said, following, occasionally reaching out as if there was something she could do.

Jody barely heard her. She felt that she could not stop or she would never again find the strength to carry Beatrice so far.

"I know!" Polly said. "I'll get Everett." And she turned back, dragging Howdy behind her.

She rushed toward the apartment. The image of Jody, small and feminine, with the colossal dog dangling from her arms, disturbed Polly. Her own helplessness depressed her. She had to do something. The taxi idea had been a good one. Typically, no one had cooperated. It is difficult to rescue people when they won't obey. Polly was frustrated, but she was unbowed. She marched forward. Howdy cavorted beside her, turning annoyingly to look back at Jody and Beatrice, planting his feet, whimpering.

"Come on," she said, yanking on the leash, her voice harsh and loud, and a passerby, a cute guy about her age, gave her a disapproving look.

Mind your own business, she thought savagely.

"Let's go, Howdy," she said in a kinder voice, but surreptitiously, when the guy could no longer see, she did give the leash another, though milder, yank.   ,

She thought Everett would be home by now, and he would know what to do. He was a wealth of platitudes, she had discovered. Surely he would have one for a sick dog.

But all he said was, "Poor Jody," and dashed off, leaving her to brush Howdy for the first time in several weeks, careless of the tufts of hair that tumbled across Everett's rug, blown by the breeze from the open window. She gently massaged each leg as she finished grooming it, as if in this way she could protect her own dog from the misery that afflicted Beatrice.

While she brushed, Polly's thoughts turned from Beatrice and Jody to what she would wear to Chris's wedding. She decided on a dress she'd seen in the window of a shop in SoHo. George, her escort, had no suit, of course. Nor had she mentioned to him that he would be accompanying her, or even, truth to tell, that she had decided to go. Maybe she should take Everett, after all. He would also lecture her on her folly, but he looked so comfortable in a suit, of which he had many, more comfortable than he did in his one pair of ill-fitting and unstylish jeans. She had gotten him a fabulous polo shirt, but all he wore were golf shirts, which he tucked in tightly. Maybe, after all, she should go with George.

She got up and paced around the room, wondering what was happening with Jody's poor old dog. Everett had been so nice about going to help. He had set off without question, like a hero, she told herself. And yet she could not see him as a hero. She conjured him up in her imagination again. He wore a dark well-cut suit and stood beside her as she introduced him to her ex-boyfriend. And she knew in that imagined instant and without any doubt that she could never, ever, take Everett with her to Chris's wedding.

Everett, meanwhile, had rushed out of his building, not at all sure what he could do to help Jody, not at all sure his help would be welcome. As he got closer to Broadway, he noticed a small crowd gathered around the Go Go Grill. Were they chanting? Perhaps they were singers from the church down the street. He had no time to stop and find out and was hurrying on with his doubtful mission when one of them, an older church lady in a flimsy, dressy black coat, crossed the street to hand him a flyer.

Religious flyers. Everett shuddered. He deposited the folded paper in the trash as soon as he was out of the woman's sight. But, as you may have guessed, the flyer had nothing at all to do with religion and was, in fact, a petition, the very petition with which Doris had threatened the City Council at the ill-fated meeting she had earlier attended. "SOS," it read. "Save Our Street." The call for more enforcement of the pooper-scooper law was there, in big bold letters. In smaller print, there was a plea, cleverly worded, Doris thought, that dogs be allowed to roam the park freely, as nature meant them to do, but only, in even smaller letters, between the hours of midnight and 6:00 a.m.

"This is not Paris," the protesters chanted outside of Jamie's restaurant.

Jamie offered the little group, which numbered about ten including Doris herself, bottles of water.

"We are not here to dine," Doris said, waving him away, though several of her supporters accepted his donation. It was typical of Jamie, she thought with outrage, to thoughtlessly provide sustenance for his enemies. He really had no boundaries. She had chosen the restaurant as the backdrop to her gathering for just that reason—his lack of boundaries, allowing dogs where dogs ought not to be—as well as the fact that so many people came in and out of its doors, not to mention a glimpse of Jamie laughing at her, she was sure of it, just the other morning, as she passed by with her sack of discarded bottles and politely handed him a flyer. He had been standing on the sidewalk with his two dogs, who began barking as she passed, and Doris had distinctly heard him say, "Shush. Leave the harmless old cat alone." Looking back and seeing no feline on the street, seeing no one but Jamie chuckling to himself, Doris could only surmise that the harmless old cat in question had been herself, and this, she found, had hurt her feelings, and hurt feelings, she had long ago discovered with regard to herself, could not be forgiven, only avenged. She did not like being called a cat, even less being called old, and least of all being called harmless.

This man, this smiling, complacent man, was really a kind of criminal, wasn't he? There was no getting around it. He broke the law, every day, every hour, polluting his restaurant with illegal canines. And though Doris knew she would miss the delicious pea soup, this Sunday's at least, a boycott and today's picket had duly been arranged.

She turned now from Everett's receding figure to the man who had made the fatal mistake of thinking her harmless, then narrowed her eyes threateningly at a bewildered couple going into the Go Go for an early supper.

When Everett arrived at the vet, Jody and Beatrice were still in with the doctor. He sat and waited, trying to discourage a gray cat from rubbing against his legs. He wondered if he would have to carry Beatrice home. Perhaps he and Jody could each take one end, the way he and Emily had once carried home a Christmas tree.

Jody came out pale and stricken and without Beatrice.

"Oh, hi," she said, showing neither surprise nor warmth.

Everett felt foolish. What was he doing there? Polly was crazy. Jody didn't want a witness to her unhappiness. Misery longed for solitude, not company. He knew that, he practiced that in his life, yet here he was, like a rubbernecking motorist at a crash.

"Do you need help getting Beatrice home?" he said.

"They're taking X-rays." She stood by a chair but did not sit down. "She's in so much pain."

Everett stood beside her feeling awkward, like a boy at a dance. "Polly thought perhaps . . ."

Looking directly into his eyes, as if she had just that moment noticed him, Jody said, "Thank you. You're both so thoughtful."

Everett thought how odd that sounded, as if he and Polly were one entity. He wanted to correct Jody, to say, No, *we* are not thoughtful at all. Polly responded with her version of thoughtfulness because she is impulsive and young and grandiose and I because I am pessimistic and old. He felt the distance between himself and Polly at that moment more even than he normally did.

Jody was teary now. "Excuse the melodrama," she said. "I know she's just a dog. But . . ."

"I know," Everett said. He wanted to put his arm around her to comfort her, but he hesitated. Privacy, he reminded himself. Privacy for grief. "I do know," he added, thinking of Howdy.

"I feel, in some way, that she's the only one who understands me," Jody said. "Do you know what I mean?"

Everett nodded. He thought of the moments when Howdy would gaze into his eyes or push his nose against his hand or just sit, patiently, by his feet.

"Silly, isn't it?" Jody said.

Everett was about to say that it wasn't silly at all, it was almost mystical, when the vet came in. He was younger than Everett had expected and quite good-looking. He did not wear a white coat, which Everett thought unprofessional.

"It's the ligament, as we suspected. This does happen in these big dogs," he said. "I've given her a shot again, and we'll think about the surgery, Jody."

Everett had not gotten used to doctors calling him by his first name. He had never before considered the propriety of a veterinarian addressing someone so informally. He stood closer to Jody, protectively.

"She should be able to walk home. She'll be a little slow . . . ," the vet was saying.

"Can she make it up the stairs?"

The vet sighed. "Maybe you should leave her here tonight."

"Use my place," Everett said. "There's an elevator. I can stay with Polly . . ."

He tried to imagine himself in that dormlike apartment with George and his girlfriends, the sink full of dishes, the counter stacked with pizza boxes, tables lined with empty Corona bottles, wedges of sodden lime rotting in the tall necks. He had seen the apartment in that condition only once, after a party, but the memory was a powerful one. Still, under no circumstances could Beatrice be left in a wire crate at the vet's.

"You really are kind," Jody was saying, her tone of mild

surprise suggesting there had somewhere at some time been an actual debate on this particular issue. "Truly, deeply kind. I'm overwhelmed."

Everett smiled, pleased with himself even as he dreaded staying on a futon in a room with a bare overhead bulb.

"But Beatrice and I can stay at Simon's," Jody continued. "He's on the ground floor. We're used to it there."

Everett said, "Of course." How stupid of him. They were used to it there. Simon lived on the ground floor. He pushed the gray cat away with his foot, then waited self-consciously until Beatrice appeared and the enormous bill was paid.

On the walk home, he stopped and waited with Jody while Beatrice sniffed a lamppost.

"When Emily was little, she used to tell her troubles to a little stuffed dog."

"I suppose this isn't too much different, is it?" Jody said, pulling gently on the leash until Beatrice stepped gingerly forward.

"Just a whole lot of projection?"

"Well, yes. But what I really meant was love."

Everett noticed with relief that the church group was gone, and he left Jody and Beatrice at Simon's door, then walked thoughtfully across the street. Love. Projection. Who was to say they were not the same thing?

Howdy met him at the door carrying a squeaking rubber ball, bouncing it insistently at Everett's feet. Everett felt his heart leap. Not in a metaphorical sense, but a physical, joyful leap.

"Howdy!" he said, kicking the ball after a series of energetic soccer fakes.

"Everett," Polly said, stepping aside to avoid the running dog. "We have to talk."

twenty-one

"We have to talk"

Soon after his encounter with Alexandra, George went to her place in Brooklyn Heights to meet her dog, Jolly. The subway was overheated but restful, and the sun was shining when he emerged at Clark Street. A small dog, an attractive woman, a beautiful day, he thought as he arrived at her quiet little street. He had no formal training, he had no credentials, but he entered the brownstone where Alexandra and Jolly lived with a conviction that he would be able to help Alexandra with her troubled little dog.

He climbed the three flights of stairs and rang the bell. Jolly didn't bark. That was a good sign. Wasn't it?

Alexandra opened the door. She smiled slightly and took his hand.

"Thank you," she said.

George thought how dignified she was, tall and intense. Her hair was still a little damp from a shower, the blonde darker. The apartment glowed with sunlight. To his astonishment, he saw the Statue of Liberty through the window.

"Are you kidding?" he said, walking to the window. "That's amazing."

The apartment was a studio, smaller than his room at Polly's, as he still called his home. The walls were a soft rosy color.

"This place is beautiful," he said. In his excitement at the view he had almost forgotten the dog. But then he saw him. Jolly was a questionable choice for a name, perhaps, as the dog's wrinkled brow gave him a sad and troubled expression. But Jolly was, as Alexandra had said, very cute. He looked up at George with round dark eyes of infinite curiosity and possibility. He wagged a disproportionately long tail, which curled improbably like a loosely coiled pig's tail. He wriggled his tough, muscular body and let out a sweet musical yodel, full of longing.

"Alexandra," George said. "He's so unbelievably . . . cute."

"Yes," Alexandra said sadly.

"I have to ignore him at first. Just to let him get used to me. We can sit down and pretend to talk or something."

"Or we can sit down and actually talk."

"Right," George said. Her tone had been friendly, but George was still suspicious of her after so many nights of being at the mercy of her sarcasm and disapproval when she was his boss. He had to remind himself that he was the expert, or at least the fake expert, and need not quail before the magnificence of Alexandra. "Right. Let's talk."

They did talk, for several hours, and George watched the sun set behind the Statue of Liberty. They talked about behaviorism and conditioning and dog packs and dominance and wolves and dog food and antidepressants. Alexandra made him coffee and gave him a slice of lemon cake. The dog watched him warily at first, then lay down beside Alexandra with a grunt and went to sleep.

George felt as though he were on a vacation. The glowing light from the autumn sunset, the silence broken only by birdsong now and then, the pretty apartment with its simple stylish furniture—it seemed a long way from Manhattan.

He looked over at the sleeping dog. He thought that after he made friends with Jolly, he would start by approaching the dog the way someone on the street might. Then he would show Alexandra some exercises that would help Jolly get used to people approaching him, that would teach him that a hand approaching did not mean a hand approaching to hit him. George had brought an old leather glove and a wooden spoon with him for this purpose. Jolly's side rose and fell rhythmically with his breath. One ear fell softly over his eye. How sweet he was, George thought.

Then, as if in answer to that thought, Jolly leaped toward his own tail, spinning and whirling, a spiral of unearthly growls and yelps, a demon, a thousand demons battling a thousand other demons, all in motion on the rug. George sat, paralyzed with shock. Blood spattered onto his pants.

Then, just as suddenly, Jolly stopped. He whimpered. He trembled, panting. Alexandra picked him up and spoke to him softly, stroking his head as she headed for the bathroom. George followed her. She handed him a washcloth and he wet it and reached toward Jolly's foot. Jolly looked at him and curled his lip. George pulled his hand back, just escaping Jolly's bared teeth.

"Holy shit," George said.

"Do you think he has bad dreams?"

I think he is a bad dream, George thought.

But Alexandra held the dog so lovingly. For the first time he noticed her hands were scarred and scraped.

"Alexandra . . ."

"I know." She sat down with Jolly and dabbed at his foot with a wad of cotton dipped in witch hazel. "I know."

"We have to talk," Polly said, and Everett headed for the refrigerator. Howdy followed him with the ball, dropping it at his feet.

"No more," Everett said to the dog, his voice impatient and loud, and Howdy slunk away, making Everett feel like an ogre. He took out a beer and opened it. The cap flew onto the floor. Everett bent over to pick it up. His back hurt. He straightened up with difficulty.

Polly had followed him into the kitchen.

"I think we should stop seeing each other," she said.

Everett waited for the sick, sinking feeling of rejection, and it quickly arrived. Then panic followed. Howdy, he thought. What about Howdy? He sat down at the kitchen table.

"Why?" he said. Of course he knew why. They were so utterly unsuited to each other. They were tired of each other. He was too old to hold her interest, and she was too young to hold his. They embarrassed each other. They very nearly disliked each other. "Why?" he said again.

"I'm sorry." Polly sat across from him and put her hand on his.

Everett drank his beer in silence.

"You know it's the right thing," Polly said.

Everett pulled his hand away. He was speechless in his misery. Polly was a diversion, and though she was getting on his nerves more and more these days, she was a sweet girl and he would probably miss her. But Howdy . . . Howdy was his newly discovered love. Howdy was what he thought about all day. A stroll with Howdy was what rewarded him for his long dull day at work.

"We can still be friends," Polly said. She didn't really see how they could still be friends, since they never had been friends in the first place, but Everett looked so distraught. She was surprised and rather gratified. She'd had no idea he felt so strongly about her.

Everett looked up now, his eyes full of hope.

Poor guy, Polly thought. It's true he won't find someone else so easily at his age. He's a lonely old coot even when he has a girlfriend. He'll be desperate without me. This didn't really fit with the self-sufficient and independent man she had known Everett to be, but at this moment it made sense to her, and she patted his hand indulgently.

"We can walk the dog together," she said.

"We can?" Everett said eagerly.

"Sure. Whenever you want."

And Polly left with the comfortable feeling that she had let Everett down as easily as any girl had ever let any man down. She even let Everett take Howdy to the dog run that day, hoping that activity would at least momentarily take his mind off his sorrowful loss, which, I think we can assume, it did.

That same night, Jody moved in with Simon, not as a prelude to marriage but as a necessity for Beatrice. The question of marriage hung in the air, to be sure, but it hung like a cloud or a cooking odor, perhaps, rather than as a possibility. As the weeks passed, Jody thought only of the dog, whose condition was worsening. Simon thought only of Virginia. They smiled and politely passed the salt and passionately made love, but their proximity seemed to push them farther apart than they had ever been.

On her fortieth birthday, Simon brought Jody red roses. She arranged them in a vase and remembered the bright unexpected yellow tulips Everett had handed her on the street. What an odd man Everett was. She hadn't seen him much lately, perhaps because she walked Beatrice for such short distances.

"I got an e-mail from my friend Garden," Simon said that

night at dinner. He had insisted on taking her to an expensive restaurant in the Village, though she had begged him to let her celebrate her birthday closer to Beatrice. But he said she needed a break, and she had not wanted to disappoint him.

"Garden," Jody said, and she laughed as she always did when she heard the name of this Virginia fox-hunting friend.

"What?" Simon said.

"Just his name. It's a funny first name."

Simon frowned.

"What did Garden want?" she asked good-naturedly. She was not by nature sarcastic. She just took pleasure in the small absurdities of life, and Garden as a first name seemed to fall into that category. Her own name was nothing to brag about, but it wasn't someone's backyard either, or so she thought to herself as Simon ordered a bottle of champagne.

"Thank you," she said, smiling.

"It's not every day you turn forty," he said.

They were quiet then, Simon staring at the menu and Jody silently reeling from the word forty, until the waiter returned and poured the champagne. It was good champagne, as Jody had expected. Simon had no money, but he had learned his lessons in Virginia among those who did. Jody, sipping from her glass, thought of Beatrice home at Simon's sleeping on the rug. The vet had scheduled surgery for her hip. It was to be next week.

"He wants me to come down now. For a month or so."

Jody turned back toward Simon at the sound of his voice. She had almost forgotten he was there. A month. Beatrice would be convalescing in a month.

Simon watched her carefully. He thought she was pretty, gazing vaguely at him, the candlelight softening her chirpy good looks. Then she dutifully flashed her cheery smile at him, the one she used to fend off the world at large, and Simon grew angry. Did she understand what he was saying? She seemed not to be listening, much less understanding. There was a time, not so long ago, when he found her inattention refreshing. She put so little pressure on him, allowing him to make his way toward her in his own time, his own slow rhythm. How gracious she had seemed, patient and indulgent. Now he realized that she had not been patient and indulgent at all. She had been . . . inattentive.

"So what do you think?" he said.

"About what?"

"Jody, for God's sake . . ."

"Oh. Virginia?"

"Do you want to come with me?"

Jody leaned her head back and closed her eyes. Interesting that he said, Do you want to come with me? He didn't ask, Should we go? Nor did he exclaim, Let's go! He said, Do you want to go with me? He was going, and she could come along or not, as she pleased—that was the meaning of his question.

"I have to work," she said.

"That's true, you do."

Jody opened her eyes and looked at him. She had time off for Thanksgiving. He knew that. It then occurred to her that Simon didn't want her to go with him to Virginia.

"Wow," she said.

Simon was sick of her. There were so many signs. He went into the bedroom when she was in the living room. He went into the living room when she was in the bedroom. When she came back from Beatrice's short, painful walks, he would look up from whatever he was doing with an expression somewhere between apathy and dismay.

He was scratching his chin now, looking off into the distance.

"Wow," she said again, shaking her head. She could hardly

believe it. When had this change come about? When she wasn't looking.

"What do you mean?" he said coldly. "There's no wow. Garden asked me to come down in December. Period."

"Simon," she said, suddenly tender and full of love, "it must be so hard having two houseguests like us."

"How did the dog come into this conversation, Jody? I'm not talking about that at all. And you know it."

He waved his hand at the waiter. He was feeling so hot, the way he had the other morning. He had to get outside and get some air.

"It's so hot," he said, fanning himself ineffectively with the check.

"You must be going through the change," she said, giving a short, forced laugh.

But Simon did not laugh with her.

"Oh, baby," she said, putting her hands out across the table, taking his and holding them up to her lips.

Simon tried to smile. He didn't want to ruin her birthday dinner. But, he realized with awful clarity, he didn't want to be at her birthday dinner, either.

"Simon," she said, "please don't give up on me."

"Don't be ridiculous."

When they got home that night, Jody immediately kneeled beside Beatrice, kissing her, petting her, whispering soothing words. At the same time, she watched Simon pacing the small, crowded room. He was so kind. He was so attentive. He loved her so much. These were things she had often said to herself in an attempt to convince herself to marry him. But now, as she repeated her litany, she thought, He is still kind, he is still relatively attentive, as attentive as anyone can be when you live on top of each other like this, but he no longer loves me.

Simon no longer loved her. As she thought this, she felt her own love for him swell up until she could hardly breathe. What had she done? How had she let this happen? The kindest, sweetest, sexiest man had been devoted to her, had asked her to marry him. She had hesitated, and now all was lost.

She put her face close to the dog's but addressed Simon, who was pacing above her. "We'll make it up to you, Simon," she said. "Won't we, Beatrice?"

Beatrice thumped her tail without even lifting her head.

"You and that dog," Simon said bitterly, sounding not at all like the kindest or sweetest of men.

Jody stared silently at the worn carpet.

Simon poured himself a glass of bourbon, not offering one to Jody. Not that I would have wanted one, she thought irrelevantly. But it is my birthday. She felt sick, almost dizzy.

"I'm sorry you can't come to Virginia with me," he said, "but I'm not going to lose this opportunity. I'm leaving. Of course you can stay here with the dog while I'm gone if she's still having difficulty."

"We can?" She tried unsuccessfully to smile. "Thank you," she said weakly.

Simon, obviously confused by the tone of misery in her response, said, "Or even if she's not having difficulty," then finished his drink and poured himself another.

twenty-two

The Spinster

While her neighbors played out their personal dramas behind the brick and limestone walls of their buildings, Doris was more and more engaged in her own adventure, which was more and more of a public nature. She had now started an official Block Association Task Force. Having used up her recycled-bottle change to print the earlier petitions, Doris dipped into her own funds to pay for new fly-ers, piles of which she and her supporters distributed beneath the front doors and in the lobbies of the buildings on the block. The flyers, formal-looking pamphlets on cream-colored paper, described the resolutions made by this new advisory body and the progress of the SOS campaign to create canine-free people hours in the park. Professional dog walkers were warned to clean up after their charges, with the threat of tick-ets and bad publicity if they failed to do so. Local dog owners were reintroduced to the city's leash laws and reminded of their civic duty in the matter of curbing their animals. Pit bulls were singled out for their inevitably violent behavior, and the law banning them in Toronto was quoted in full. Restaurateurs were reminded of city health ordinances that banned animals from their premises. Readers were instructed to recall that they were not in Paris, and that a brigade of concerned citizenry would be making citizens' arrests when appropriate. Any questions or complaints should be addressed to the City Council. The motto, printed to look like the revolutionary New Hampshire motto, complete with snake, was DON'T URINATE ON ME.

There was considerable discussion about all of Doris's leaflets when they first began to appear. Some people warned that a mysterious old man with dyed red hair who lived on the block was sprinkling rat poison on the sidewalks to kill off all the local dogs. Others said the poisoner was a middle-aged woman from Greenwich who had stepped in dog excrement on the way to a wedding at the Catholic church and, never having forgiven the dog in question, whoever it might have been, was bent on wholesale revenge against all dogs in the neighborhood. Still others, skeptical of the poison report, were convinced the mayor was behind what they called a violation of civil rights. A few people were insulted that they had not been personally asked to join the Block Association Task Force, while others were outraged that flyers had been left on their stoops when there were signs requesting that no take-out menus or paper of any kind be deposited there. Altogether there was a great flurry of attention paid to the mysterious appearance of the announcements—far more, I'm afraid, than to their actual contents. Doris's followers tried to clear up the confusion, after which several neighborly quarrels took place, and at least one couple stopped speaking to each other for a period of three days.

Jody knew immediately that the Block Association Task Force was actually the woman who watched her from the white SUV. If she had not guessed beforehand, a sign posted on the SUV's window, printed on cream-colored paper identical to that of the flyer, might have tipped her off: PLEASE PREVENT YOUR CANINE FROM URINATING ON MY CAR. AFTER ALL, MY CAR DOES NOT URINATE ON YOUR CANINE.

Nor was the mention of pit bulls lost on Jody, and she continued to bring her big white dog to urinate on the big white car, if anything increasing those visits. They went late at night or in the wee hours of the morning. The car soon became Beatrice's favorite place to pee out of sheer habit. Wherever it was parked on the block, Beatrice would head toward it, then squat. Jody taught her to pee always by the driver's side, leaving a glistening, pungent puddle, a ritual that was one of the very few things that made Jody happy these days. Beatrice could hardly walk. The vet had begun the surgery only to find the dog was riddled with cancer. Surgery would be useless. Beatrice's days were numbered, and the number was a small one.

Jody and Beatrice continued to live at Simon's apartment on the ground floor, and Jody was grateful for that. But Simon himself was not present. He had gone to Virginia just as he planned, and Beatrice was left to live out her last days with the only person who really mattered to her. On the first night after Simon left, there were moments when Jody felt that Beatrice was all that mattered to her, as well, but there were other moments when she would remember some evening with Simon, or some night, or the way he looked at her on a morning when sun spilled in the window onto the bed, and she would know that Simon meant something to her, too. And now he was gone.

She could not bear to be away from the dog and rushed home from school each day. One afternoon, when Simon had been gone just a week, Jody took Beatrice for what passed for a walk these days. They made it out the door, they shuffled down the sidewalk until they spotted the white SUV, then Beatrice did what she had to do, and they painfully made their way back home where Beatrice dropped heavily to the floor and fell asleep. Jody decided this would be a good time to take a minute to go to her own building to get her mail and pick up some clean clothes and decent sheets. It was a beautiful fall day, the air clear and bright, but she was glad to get into the shadowy lobby. The sun had begun to depress her. She had always been told she had a sunny disposition. Since Beatrice had fallen ill and Simon had taken himself off to Virginia, she almost hated the bright, mocking sun.

When she turned the little key and opened the metal mailbox door, she saw that there was a letter from Simon inside. The appearance of personal mail always cheered her. And she missed Simon, even more than she had expected she would. She wondered why he hadn't sent it to her at his address. She held the letter tenderly. It was the first letter from Simon she had ever received. She walked up the stairs and entered her own tiny space. It's good to be home, she thought, sitting on the bed. It was so stuffy, though. She stood up and opened a window. She leaned against the window, remembering how she'd sat there knitting, watching for Everett. Then she opened Simon's letter.

There was a great deal about hunting. There were some passages about the magnificent weather. There were two anecdotes about rich, inexperienced riders of horses that were too much for them. There was a paragraph asking about Beatrice's health and offering the experience of a member of the hunt whose dog had undergone chemotherapy and had gone into remission.

Then, finally, at the end of the letter, as if he were working himself up to it, Simon said he missed her. He said how much he loved her, how his life had changed since meeting her, how much richer his existence was with her by his side.

Jody reached this part and smiled, imagining Simon in his tall black boots and his slender riding coat. Which one? The black one with the special buttons? Or the bright red one he'd recently bought secondhand? He was so proud of them both.

His life was richer, the letter went on, but did that mean he was happier? He had come to the conclusion that he was not. Perhaps he was not meant to have such an emotionally rich life. He had always kept to himself. He was not young, and it was difficult to change old habits, to teach an old dog new tricks.

Jody involuntarily thought of Beatrice as she read this. Beatrice had learned many things as an old dog. Or had she? Maybe she knew them all before, and Jody had just reminded her how to come when she was called, how to sit and stay and shake hands.

Jody was so full of life, Simon's letter went on. But he, Simon, had realized something when they were living together the last few weeks.

"I am an old maid," Simon wrote. "I am a fussy, intolerant old maid. I am a spinster, and I like it that way."

Spinster, Jody thought. She suddenly hated the word. It was not a quiet, easy word, as she had thought. It was a selfish, pinched, and ugly word. Simon had taken her word and changed it. He had taken everything and changed it. And she had let him.

He went on to say how sorry he was if he'd hurt her, but that he felt their relationship had proceeded too quickly, had become too intense too fast.

"Whose fault was that?" Jody said out loud, hoarsely, for she was crying.

And so, Simon wrote, he felt they should slow down. By slow down, Jody realized as she read on, he meant stop seeing each other altogether.

In fact, Simon wrote, he was planning to stay in Virginia. Garden had offered him a job as the head of personnel at his law firm. It paid much better than his current job, it was cheaper to live down there, and he would be able to hunt the whole season—especially as Garden had offered him a two-year lease on the guest cottage. He meandered on about the back injury of Garden's wife—thank God it was not serious, he wrote; thank God, Jody thought absently—and her generous request that Simon hunt her mare for her that season. Then he seemed to remember what the purpose of the letter was, saying that of course Jody understood he could not give up this opportunity. He would always remember her. She had changed his life, and she had given him the courage to change his life still more.

He signed the letter, "Yours truly, Simon."

Jody walked back to Simon's apartment in a wrathful daze. She realized she had left the window open, but she didn't go back. What difference did it make? Rain or wind or snow or thief—let them come. She had pushed away the only man she had almost wanted to marry.

Polly did go to Chris's wedding, taking neither George nor Everett, deciding it was a challenge she must face alone, like a Native American boy with thorns through his nipples, attached to a pole by a string, dancing and singing through the night. She put on her sexiest dress that would still be appropriate for a wedding, had her nails done, took a train, and found the wedding to be as dull as any other wedding she had ever attended. The wedding one enjoyed was the wedding that was one's own, or so she had said to Chris each time she was forced to appear as a bridesmaid in yet another ghastly dress, and she had thought herself clever. She still thought herself clever, but it did not help her survive the tedium of someone else's happiness, especially Chris's. Chris looked handsome, which brought home to her the pain of losing him. The bridesmaids wore purple and her heart went out to them. She was a stranger, which was always uncomfortable. There were only one or two of their friends from when they were a couple, and these, Polly realized, were Chris's friends after all, not hers. They looked surprised to see her and asked her to dance, then disappeared. She was a stranger, indeed. But at least I am a stranger in a strange land, she thought, for one contingent of the wedding seemed to be gorgeous six-foot tall women in skimpy dresses, and another pasty men with patchy beards and black hats. When Polly mentioned this to one of the guests, a good-old frat boy whom she had always rather liked, he said, "Oh yeah. The sister? She's a model. And there's some Jews from some-where," then spotted another young man waving two cigars and went off to smoke with him outside under the trees. Whose sister? Polly wondered. Whose Jews?

She had wanted to go out of curiosity, and her curiosity had been appeased. But she'd also felt that she had to go to this wedding, if only to assure herself that it really took place. And, too, there was a narcissistic pleasure in the pain. All these rea-sons she had been aware of. The reason she had perhaps been less conscious of was that she wanted to see Chris, just to see him. There was nothing to be proud of in any of her reasons, and yet she was proud, as if she had climbed a mountain or gone swimming with sharks. She had dressed with care, and she held her head high even among the Amazonian models, who looked as bored as she was. There were speeches at the actual ceremony, which Polly found odd, especially as they seemed to be recitations of the bride's and groom's résumés. The event took place at a country club in Connecticut, in the town where Chris's parents lived. Seeing Chris's parents was exquisitely distasteful, for they had never liked Polly and so were friendly to her now, when she was no danger, for the first time. But confronting Chris, when she finally did, was, all in all, she thought, a success. He came up to her and put out his hand, as if she were a distant cousin, and she looked at him, his hair neatly cut, his tuxedo fashionable and well fitting, and she thought, I've lost you, and that makes me sad. Then she took his hand, shook it, and wished him well.

"I'm glad you came," he said.

"Really? Why?"

It was an honest question. She knew why she had come, but she could not imagine why she had been invited.

Chris shrugged. "I don't know," he said, looking embarrassed.

Polly laughed, then reached into her purse and pulled out Chris's iPod and aimed it at him.

"Bang," she said.

Chris took the iPod from her. "You found it."

Polly began to sing one of the Billy Joel songs.

"Hey, I don't know how that got on there, dude."

Polly continued her song, enjoying his discomfort. It somehow made everything about the wedding worthwhile, the awkwardness, the wallflower moments, the ghastly parents, even the loss of Chris.

"Okay, okay," he kept saying. He pushed the iPod back at her. It turned out he did not want it, after all, for Diana had gotten him a new one with twice the number of gigabytes.

"So I guess you can keep it," he said.

"Yes," she said happily. "To remember you by."

Jody never went anywhere now unless she could take Beatrice with her, and they had already, in the days Simon had been gone, become familiar figures at Go Go. On the evening of Chris's wedding, while Polly drank to the happy couple's health, Jody went, as usual, to the restaurant. Jamie noticed the woman with the short, tousled blonde hair and the white pit bull and thought how lonely they looked. Of course they had been to the restaurant many times before, but always with Simon. Jamie realized he didn't even remember the woman's name. The dog, yes, certainly, that was Beatrice. But who was this woman who had always seemed so sprightly and now looked so drawn and forlorn?

"Can I sit with you for a bit?" he asked.

Jody looked up, surprised. She gave him a feeble smile.

Jamie sat and a bottle of wine instantly appeared with two glasses.

"Oh. Thanks," Jody said when he poured her one.

"I'm so glad you let dogs in here," she added after a moment. "I can't really leave her." And then she heard herself tell him the whole story in a confused rush. She listened with horror as she told this man whom she did not know about Beatrice limping, about the surgery, the cancer, and then about Simon, his proposal, his hunting, her refusal, her uncertainty, his letter, her sorrow, her unmitigated sorrow. She hated herself for revealing her intimate thoughts and feelings. She couldn't stand the sound of her voice.

She stopped finally, in horror, and stared at Jamie.

"Can I give Beatrice a steak bone?" was all he said. He summoned the handsome waiter and said something to him in a foreign tongue that sounded Scan-dinavian and soon a large raw bone appeared. Beatrice held it between her big paws and gnawed on it with obvious satisfaction. Jody watched her affectionately. When she looked up, Jamie was gone, but he'd left the bottle of wine and by the time she got up to go, Jody had finished it. She went home that night feeling better than she had in a long time. She got into bed and, though Simon was not there, she felt the world was warm and welcoming, and she slept.

The joys of walking Howdy did not come as easily or as frequently to Everett as he had hoped. Polly turned out to be far more possessive of the dog than she had disclosed that day she had let Everett down easy. And George—when George was not off with the hysterical blonde girl's dog, he stuck close by Howdy. Even today, when Polly was out of town at a wedding, Howdy was not put into Everett's care. It was as if there were a conspiracy to keep Everett and Howdy apart. Like Romeo and Juliet, he thought. Sometimes he walked without Howdy, but it was not the same. He found himself stopping people in order to fondle their dogs, which did provide a momentary diversion from his loneliness but made him feel eccentric. And when the dog and its owner moved on, leaving him standing alone in the middle of the sidewalk, he felt worse than he had before. At work he had become intolerable, even to himself. He had gone from being curmudgeonly and fierce to being merely obnoxious. He sneered openly at his colleagues' mistakes, he sought opportunities to humiliate those working under him, he kept everyone late and insulted them to their faces.

At home, he drank his martinis in silence, not even turning on the television. He went to the Go Go Grill now and then, but the friendly noise and bustle, not to mention the sight of George and, often, Polly, were not welcome. Mostly, these days, he ordered Chinese food and ate in bed, something he had always disapproved of, watching Animal Planet.

Alison is getting married today, he thought, watching a llama give birth, as he ate fried rice with a spoon, and he felt even more like an ex-husband than usual.

twenty-three

He Had Come for the Dogs

The dreary days that were not quite winter, the days that drew in firmly and never really seemed to draw out again, passed slowly for Jody. She spent less time at school than she ever had before, resentful when she was asked to chaperone the fifth-grade dance and to organize the penny drive. She had already begun teaching the lower grades the songs for the winter holiday pageant, making certain there were references to Hanukkah, Christmas, and Kwanzaa but none to Jesus or to God, but her heart was not in it. Her heart was broken, the pieces home with her ailing friend, her dying dog, her Beatrice.

She bumped into Everett one night, but even he did not make her feel better. Who was he, after all? A neighbor, a stranger, a man for whom she had once harbored a schoolgirl crush, the absurd, rejected lover of a ridiculously young girl.

"Simon's in Virginia," she said in answer to his question. "He's moving there."

Everett looked surprised. Not as surprised as me, she thought.

"I'm sorry Beatrice is so ill," he said. "If there's any way I can help . . ."

But she had just shaken her head and walked slowly on with the old white dog.

After that night, Everett found himself walking by Jody's building more often than he had ever found it necessary to do before. He lingered at her door sometimes, wondering if he should ring her buzzer on the off chance she would be home and want to take a walk. He never did it, but he did see her at Go Go, she and poor Beatrice. He asked for her cell phone number, not wanting somehow to call her on Simon's phone. And he called her on her cell phone, offering to make dinner at his apartment.

She came, on a drizzly night, leading the slow, bony white dog, and Everett was struck by the memory of the two of them coming through the veil of snow that day they'd met almost a year before, Jody's cheeks pink and the dog muscular and sleek. Everett put out water for Beatrice in the Jonathan Adler dog bowl. The bowl and the sound of Beatrice sloppily drinking made him miss Howdy.

He had cooked for the first time in years and was rather nervous about the meal, though it was just a simple roast chicken with roast potatoes and a salad. But he wanted the evening to be a success. He asked himself what he meant by success. Was it getting Jody to go to bed with him? Or did he just want to feed her and make her comfortable, as he would a wounded animal, as he would Beatrice?

"I saw a squirrel eating a croissant in the park today," he said. "A big fat croissant. He could hardly hold it with his little paws."

That made Jody smile, and Everett thought how pretty she was.

"What were you doing in the park?" she asked. "In this weather?"

"Pretending I had a dog."

Jody smiled again, and the evening had been on the whole a pleasant one. The chicken was fine, a little greasy, he thought, but flavorful, and she had stayed and talked for several hours drinking the excellent wine he'd gotten. He did not try to get her into bed. There was something too vulnerable about her, and at the same time too intimidating.

He feels sorry for me, Jody thought when he invited her to his house a second time for roast chicken. As well he should.

"You're very kind," she said, but what she meant, she realized, was, What difference does it make? It's too late. It's too late for everything. How maudlin she had become. She tried to concentrate, but she found she had difficulty concentrating on Everett, Everett whom she had once tagged after so loyally in her imagination. Now her imagination seemed to have moved to Virginia with Simon.

"Shall we go out tonight?" Everett said.

"Out?" It was a dark, chilly evening. They were sitting comfortably in his living room. Was he too embarrassed to serve roast chicken again? "But I love roast chicken," she reassured him.

"Well, but, the chicken didn't defrost, actually . . ."

Why would he have frozen it in the first place? she wondered. Beatrice had limped painfully across the street and into the elevator. The dog lay sleeping now beside Everett. Surely it is just as easy to stop at the market on the day of dinner as on any other day, Jody thought. She hoped the earlier frozen chicken had been antibiotic-free. But perhaps chemists were less concerned with such things.

"Yes, all right, that will be fun," she said, though obviously nothing would ever be fun again to someone as self-pitying as herself, and they finished their martinis and left Everett's clean and effortless apartment for the damp night and the restaurant across the street.

Everett watched her settle the dog by her feet. How gentle and calm she was with the big sick dog. He poured wine into Jody's glass, then held the glass up to her, as if she were an invalid, and said, "Drink."

Jamie watched them curiously, then turned to a large party of women, a book club he supposed, and seated them at the round table by the window. He suggested a wine. He smiled. They smiled back. Admirable, a book club. Or was it a Weight Watchers meeting? No, they would hardly gather in a restaurant for Weight Watchers. And they were all quite slim.

"Look at those adorable dogs," one said, pointing to Jamie's own dogs who had emerged from behind the bar.

He was contemplating what to present to the nice book ladies—complimentary grappa? Calvados?—at the end of their meal, when the door to the restaurant swung open with a loud and dramatic swoosh of cold, damp air. There, silhouetted in the doorway, arms akimbo, face set savagely, swaddled in a long fur coat, was Doris.

She stepped consciously, dramatically, aside. Behind her, like an enlarged late afternoon shadow, loomed a heavily muscled man with a square jaw and an incongruously purple plastic clipboard.

"There!" said Doris. She pointed at Jamie.

The portentous shadow moved forward. He jutted his chin at Jamie—in some sort of greeting, Jamie supposed. Jamie held out his hand and was about to introduce himself, when the shadow, who was now quite well lit, pulled a badge from his pocket and held it out, as if to fend Jamie off.

"'New York City Department of Health,'" Jamie read out loud, "'and Mental Hygiene.'"

"This," Doris said, her voice high with excitement, "is a raid!"

"Inspection," the man corrected her, his voice flat and ominous.

Doom, Jamie thought, but did not say, in the man's article-free cadence.

"Book him!" Doris said.

Mental hygiene, Jamie was thinking. Odd. From the corner of his eye he could see his staff jump into action. They would tape signs in the bathroom, throw things in the refrigerator, whatever they thought they should do to keep one step ahead of the inspector. But Jamie knew it was all useless. The inspector had not come for properly posted signs reminding the waiters to wash their hands. He had come for the dogs.

Jamie waved to George. "Please show the inspector . . ."

"*Sanitarian*," the man corrected him.

Jamie stared at him. The Sanitarian stared back.

"Please show the Sanitarian whatever he wants to see," Jamie said at last.

George came out from behind the bar. Maybe Sanitarians were like Quakers—simple, peaceful folk who invented electricity.

Doris looked proudly at the scene before her. She had worked so long and so hard to make this moment happen. She had called the Health Department more times than she could count, explaining that the inspector must come at night in order to be sure to catch Jamie in flagrante, so to speak, until finally, at long last, she had found a sympathetic official. But nothing worthwhile ever comes without hard work, she reminded herself. She had picked up trash and educated her fellow citizens and exercised her democratic rights. And now, after all, she would make a real difference. Triumphant, she stood before her conquered enemy. He did not meet her eye. He turned

his back on her. He walked away. Doris felt the sting of this. She felt the injustice. But no good deed went unpunished, as they say, and someday Jamie would thank her for getting him back on the straight and narrow. How many people avoided eating at Go Go because of the dogs lying everywhere they stepped? She didn't know how many, but certainly it was a considerable number.

"Aha!" Doris cried, pointing to Tillie and Hector, who came trotting toward her.

The Sanitarian rumbled something incomprehensible, though clearly of one syllable.

"They were just leaving," George said, hurrying after the dogs.

But the two of them had already rolled onto their backs by the Sanitarian's heavy boots and were kicking their little feet in the air.

The Sanitarian nudged one with his boot.

"*Why* are you petting the violations?" Doris said.

Jamie was a mild man. He was a moderate man. He had spent his whole life in the pursuit of other people's happiness with as little trouble to himself as possible. But now he felt something rise within him, something he thought he recognized as his gorge, whatever a gorge was. Did Sanitarians carry guns? he wondered. Perhaps Sanitarians were prone to outbreaks of violent madness, like postal workers. Perhaps this Sanitarian would draw his gun and shoot his obnoxious patroness and Jamie would watch her fall, bleeding and gasping unsuccessfully for breath.

"Look!" the patroness was saying. "*Another* violation." Doris had spotted Beatrice. She approached the old, sleeping pit bull. "In Toronto," she said, "you would be euthanized."

"This is not Toronto," Jamie said firmly.

"New York," the Sanitarian said, clarifying the issue.

He had begun writing on his purple clipboard in pencil.

Pencil, Jamie thought. Pencil, pencil . . . Pencil can be erased. Somehow, perhaps, his summons or whatever was being written out in pencil would get erased. That was what Noah, with resigned contempt, called "Jamie's Magical Thinking." Well, so what? Nothing else was going to work any better. This would be his third citation for dogs. He'd be lucky to pay a fine and not be closed down. It would never again be possible to let a dog walk in. He would not be able to afford the risk. If the restaurant was even allowed to stay open. Magical thinking? Yes. Why not? The atheist's prayer.

The customers were all aware that something was going on and had gotten very quiet. Everett had taken Jody's hand at the mention of euthanasia. Of course it was outrageous that Jamie let dogs into the restaurant. It was a miracle he had not been stopped before now. But, really, what harm was Beatrice doing, an old dog lady sleeping heavily, snoring just the tiniest bit? What harm did the amusing terriers do?

Jody was flushed. She pulled her hand back and ran it through her hair, which stuck up oddly afterward. "That woman," she was saying. "That appalling, monstrous woman . . ."

"Come along, now," Doris was saying to the inspector. "Write your tickets. Or whatever it is you do."

The Sanitarian eyed her with such cold antipathy that for one moment, one blissful moment, Jamie thought the Sanitarian might just forget the whole thing, might defy the enraged citizen who had brought him there, might smile and shake hands with Howdy, who had just appeared from the kitchen and offered him a paw, might nod pleasantly at Jamie, walk out the door, file a whitewashed report, and go home to what must assuredly be a happy, loving family and a large, delicious dinner, though judging from the Sanitarian himself there probably wasn't all that much conversation at the table; still, people communicate in so many different ways . . .

Jamie's daydream came to an abrupt end.

"Vi-o-la-tion," Doris was saying, addressing Howdy, who had ambled over to sniff her fur coat.

The Sanitarian turned to face Jamie. "Four," he said in his toneless voice. Then added, with sudden emotion, "Where the *hell* do you think you are, buddy? *Paris?*"

twenty-four

Thanksgiving

Everett looked forward to Thanksgiving, when Emily would be home. But when the time came, even Emily did not cheer him up. She tried, and he was aware of that and was touched. But Emily had her own life. He told himself this as he watched her prepare to go out on Wednesday night. He understood his feeling of emptiness on this occasion, and he reprimanded himself. What he didn't understand was why this same feeling of emptiness, of hollow ennui, had been there as he watched Emily and her friends sprawl on his furniture earlier that evening. He was flattered that they felt comfortable enough with him to occupy his apartment like an invading army. And yet he had sighed to himself and felt alone.

This year it was Alison's turn to have Emily for Thanksgiving dinner, and when Thursday night came, Everett, somewhat abashed, took himself out to Go Go. He had always felt sorry for people who ate at restaurants on Thanksgiving, all alone over their dry turkey dinners. But he could not bear to stay in his apartment and eat takeout. That would not only be humiliating, it would be cowardly.

Jody, too, had gone to eat her Thanksgiving dinner at Go Go, but not alone. Jamie had invited her to join him, his children, his partner, his staff, and, most important, his dogs.

"And Beatrice, too, of course," he said.

"What if that horrible woman comes? And that man?"

"On Thanksgiving?"

"I guess not," Jody said.

"You know what?" he said, suddenly serious, suddenly angry. "She almost closed me down."

He took a deep breath. Then he laughed, looking more like himself.

"Just once more," he added. "For fun."

"For fun," Jody answered, but she saw how much the raid ("Inspection," she could hear the Sanitarian saying) had troubled Jamie. Unshakable, complacent Jamie. She had become quite friendly with Jamie since that day he gave her dog a bone and threw her a metaphorical bone in the form of a bottle of wine. She had gone home happy, and though the happiness had not lasted, the sense that happiness was possible had, and Jody felt she had made a friend. She could not fly down to Florida to see her parents for Thanksgiving because of the dog, and she was too depressed to join any of her colleagues, but she found herself almost excited at the prospect of the illegal Thanksgiving gathering with Jamie.

She arrived exactly at seven, as if she had a reservation. When she was introduced to Jamie's boyfriend, Noah, whom she had seen on the street and in the restaurant countless times, she realized for the first time that he was an American, which surprised her. He was also about six foot seven. Jody wondered how many people asked him if he played basketball, for she had been on the verge of asking him herself. How enraging that must be, she thought, and she felt such sympathy toward him the entire evening that she had the sense that she and Noah had become great friends, though they barely exchanged two words from the beginning of the meal to the end.

Jamie was a little tipsy, Jody noticed. He knelt down and addressed Beatrice face-to-face. "We shall overcome," he said happily. "Shan't we?"

He put on some ancient disco music and began dancing with his children until Noah nodded to one of the exes who changed the CD to Stephin Merritt.

"What?" Jamie said, turning to Noah. "What's wrong with Donna Summer?"

"Calm yourself, darling."

"This is a celebration. Of innocence."

"Those innocent seventies," Noah said, smiling. He took Jamie's hand and pulled him close. "It's okay," he said gently. "Everything is okay."

Jody quickly turned away and saw, with a sinking heart, that Everett was coming through the door. Perhaps she should go home, away from these men, these children galloping round the table, this family, this intimacy. Away from Everett, one of her failed intimacies.

When Everett walked in, he saw Jody with the rowdy international group, and he was all the more conscious of his own isolation. He almost turned on his heel and walked out, but Jamie had seen him and loudly called him over, standing at his place at the head of the table, gesticulating with so much enthusiasm that Everett imagined the wine had already been flowing for quite a while. He walked awkwardly to the table, acutely aware of his own failure to be festive, or even drunk.

Jamie introduced Noah, who stood up and startled Everett with a greeting from high above. Then the children were presented. There were so many of them, and so many of them looked alike. Jamie did not bother introducing the staff seated at the table. He just asked one of them to move so Everett would have a seat.

"No, no, please, I don't want to disturb anyone," Everett said, but it was in vain. The young man had already gotten up, changed the place setting, and moved himself down to the other end of the table.

Everett saw that Jody was sitting across from him, and he smiled at her, though he wondered what she was doing there and almost resented her presence, it was so unexpected. He had prepared himself for a miserable evening and felt disconcerted and sheepish.

"Beatrice!" he said, leaning down to pet the dog, who was stretched beneath the table. Her tail thumped on his shoe. "You're here!"

Jody nodded.

"Up the Revolution!" he said, seeing the cairn terriers and smiling again. He was happy to see the dogs, but how reckless Jamie was. Well, it was not Everett's problem, though it would be if the Go Go was closed down. He would have no place to go next Thanksgiving! Ha! How amusing you are, he told himself sarcastically. He turned his attention back to Jody. "How is Beatrice?" he asked.

Jody shook her head slowly, sadly.

Everett wondered what was wrong with Jody. Had she taken a vow of silence until the dog recovered? He shrugged, somewhat put out, and tried to engage Noah in a conversation on the importance of afternoon daylight to a child's circadian rhythms, something he had just read an article about.

Jody had not, of course, taken a vow of silence, but when Everett smiled at her, she experienced all over again that rush of joy she had felt when she met Everett on the stormy street so many months ago, and she found herself momentarily speechless. I remember now, she thought, confused, almost ashamed. I remember. Before my heart was broken, my heart longed for you.

"You have a wonderful family," Everett was saying to Jamie.

"I think of it more as a cult," Jamie replied, but he was flushed and smiling and very much the proud paterfamilias, Everett thought. Hector and Tillie were sitting as still as statues, their longing stares fixed on him as he carved the turkey. His children, whose names Everett could not keep straight though he was moderately confident of a Dylan and an Isabella, were lolling or crawling or running, according to their ages. His staff was drunk. His boyfriend was rich and benign, if unusually tall. Jamie was a man to be envied, and Everett envied him.

"Where is your daughter?" Jody said, finally finding her voice.

Everett turned to her, no longer smiling. "With her mother," he said drily.

Jody looked down at her plate. As usual, she had said exactly the wrong thing.

"Simon in Virginia?" Everett asked, rather cruelly he realized, and Jody now looked even sadder than before.

"Still in Virginia," she said.

"Right. Sorry. He's moving there."

"And I'm taking over his lease!" Jamie said with great relish.

"So, here we are," Everett said to Jody.

"Yes," Jody said. "Here we are."

They didn't say much to each other for a while after that. Jody felt Beatrice's heavy head on her foot and drank too much wine and thought about Everett who was sitting across from her and Simon who was still in Virginia. She wondered what Thanksgiving would have been like had Simon not taken off. Perhaps they would have had a quiet dinner at his apartment. Perhaps they would have come here. Did Simon even have family nearby? She realized she didn't know. He was an only child, and his parents lived on the West Coast, but there might have been some cousin or aunt to invite. She felt Beatrice's breath on her ankle.

Everett was watching Jody. She looked so despondent. She always looked sad now. He remembered the way she looked on the street when he stupidly handed her the yellow tulips. He didn't like it when she looked sad. She was a cheery, chipper sort of being and was meant to look happy. When she looked so troubled, it was like seeing a despondent bird. Birds could not be sad. It was unnatural. Then he remembered there were sad Romantic poems in which birds featured prominently. And what about *The Raven*? That was hardly cheerful.

When dinner was over, Jamie, drunk but triumphant, toasted canine violations everywhere. Everett walked Jody and Beatrice home. She was still staying in Simon's apartment.

"Not for long," she said. She looked despairingly at the dog. "It's just because of Beatrice, and soon . . ."

Everett put his arm around her. He took her inside and made a pot of herbal tea. They sat in Simon's living room, he on the ottoman, she on the leather chair, drinking their tea, the old dog, breathing heavily, on the floor between them.

Polly and George were having Thanksgiving dinner at their own apartment. They had dealt with the divorced-parent aspect by inviting both parents, confident that neither of them would come. Alexandra and Laura were also invited and did come, as did their dogs. Kaiya ran through the apartment, followed by an overexcited Howdy, while Jolly was sequestered in George's room and could be heard snarling intermittently. The turkey, which Polly had insisted she would make, was ordered, fully cooked, at the last minute from Fresh Direct. When dinner was over, and they moved from the table to the couch and chairs right next to it, Polly surveyed her domain with pride. She lived in a place to which guests could come for Thanksgiving. This was her apartment, with the exception of George's room, and that hardly counted since it was she who had installed him there. Her eye swept across the unremarkable room and her heart swelled with domestic triumph. She glanced at the window, where the IKEA votive candle shrine was lit for the unfortunate previous tenant, and she was sorry he had been so unhappy in this place that she had come to love.

Alexandra was keeping a chart, at George's suggestion, of Jolly's behavior, and she carried the notebook over to him now as he sat on the couch eating a piece of apple pie she had supplied.

"Where'd you buy this?" he said. "It's really good."

"I made it."

She opened the notebook.

"It's really good," he said again. Alexandra always had delicious baked things at her apartment. It was like going to Grandma's house—muffins and cakes and pies. It had never occurred to him that Alexandra made them. His grandmother certainly never had.

He looked at the page of the notebook:

Wednesday

6 a.m. woke up growling

8:00 walk—lunged at runner; sat when told at passing bicyclist; growled at child, did not lunge

8:30 ate, attacked tail 2 minutes

slept on rug in sun

10:15 woke up, attacked laundry bag I was carrying, small bite on wrist

10:30–12 slept on dog bed; 4 spins on dog bed (counterclockwise; 4 min., 2 min., 1 min., 3 min.)

12–1 walk (snapped at skateboarder, but not at man in wheelchair!), then played with toys

1–2 worked on "off" command and "stay"; snapped at my hand (right hand, coming from above—no blood!!!)

2–3 slept underneath desk—2 spins (clockwise; 2 min.,
     3 min.)
3:00 very affectionate
3:30 tried to brush him, snapped at me
4:00 jumped on bed; got off when told
growled with intermittent spinning, bloody back left paw,
     until 4:40
4:50 walk, no incidents, went to work
2:30 a.m. on the bed, growling and whimpering about
     1 1/2 hours.

"So, what do you think?" Alexandra said, her voice a little uncertain but still hopeful.

George thought that "spin" was an interesting choice of words for what Jolly did, that's what he thought. The word made it sound as though the dog went out for a little drive in his little automobile. In fact, what Alexandra called a "spin" was a kind of furious, violent fit, the snarling eruption George had witnessed on his first visit to Alexandra's apartment in Brooklyn. He looked at Alexandra's record of Jolly's behavior, and he wanted to cry.

"Well . . ."

"Look," she said eagerly, putting her finger on the page. "He had a walk with no problems. And fewer spins than the day before."

They went over the behavior carefully, charting what happened in the morning, the afternoon, and at night. Did food trigger it? Sleep? Exercise? There were no clear patterns, and George was getting discouraged. But he did not want to let her down. Alexandra's notebook was as meticulous as Darwin's tracking the growth of climbing plants. How could he give up on Alexandra's dog?

In the past few weeks he had devoted almost every free

minute to Jolly. He had taught the dog to be petted by the glove on the end of the wooden spoon, and then by his own approaching hand, to sit when a wheelchair approached instead of attacking the occupant, and to stay alone in a room without tearing his own skin off. But as soon as he taught Jolly one thing, as soon as he desensitized him to one obscure trigger for his violence to himself and others, Jolly would immediately come up with a new idea. Now he attacked strollers and runners. Now, when people went to pet him on the street, he no longer lunged at their hands, he lunged at their faces. The sizzle of pork chops in a pan triggered a vicious attack on his own legs, as did Reggae music and the sound of the shower. After Jolly bit the man on the ground floor of Alexandra's building, who owned two Chihuahuas and so was extremely understanding, George tried getting Jolly used to a soft muzzle. But the dog could not bear it for more than a few seconds before he would lunge at himself maniacally, foaming at the mouth in a flurry of terrifying snarls.

George had devoted himself to this dog, this cur, as Polly called him, and in the process, without really meaning to, he had devoted himself to Alexandra. He saw her every day, even when he didn't see Jolly. He had never asked Alexandra out or put a hand on her or even flirted with her. But trying to help Jolly had become almost a courtship.

"I'll e-mail this guy at Cornell I told you about," George said. "He thinks the vet is right—it doesn't sound like epilepsy. But he sent me some studies of autism that are kind of suggestive." He sighed. He had no ideas left. "We could always try the pet psychic," he said somewhat bitterly.

"Poor George," Alexandra said, putting her hand on his.

Polly was in the kitchen wrestling with the turkey carcass. But she was close enough to hear her brother and Alexandra talking.

Poor George? she thought. Alexandra was living with a rag-
ing psychotic dog, and she said poor *George*? Then Polly smiled
and wondered if perhaps her worries over finding a suitable
girl for her brother could for the time being be put to rest.

Doris and Harvey were in Bedford at her sister Natalie's for
Thanksgiving dinner, and it was a grand affair, crowded with
neighbors bringing their elaborate contributions, delicious smells
and a competitive culinary buzz giving the house a festive air.
Doris had made a stuffing rich with nuts and oysters and bourbon and artisan breads. Her sister, in a clean, starched toile
apron, greeted them at the door. Doris handed her casserole
dish to Natalie and placed on top of it one of the flyers from
the Block Association Task Force. She could hardly wait to tell
Natalie of her great victory over the dogs of the Go Go Grill,
with the assistance of that very efficient Sanitarian, of course.

"The recipe?" Natalie said, noticing the flyer.

"No, just . . ."

But Natalie had already put down the casserole dish and begun to read the flyer. Though her face was not the same unearthly orange as her sister's, she did tend toward a deep ruddy
hue when she was exercised in any way, and Doris, who had
known that color and what it meant since girlhood, watched
with alarm as she saw the purple rise from her sister's neck to
her forehead.

"This is outrageous!" Natalie said in the rounded tones she
adopted for the very worst offenses. "Good God . . ."

"Yes, *I* thought so, and . . ."

But Doris had barely begun speaking when her sister
reached down into the pocket of her apron and pulled out a
small furry ball.

"*Isn't* it outrageous, Fredericka?" she said to the ball. "And
vulgar. 'Don't urinate on me,' indeed."

The ball, which turned two tiny black eyes toward Doris, merely shivered in reply.

"This is my sister," Natalie said, again addressing the ball. "And this," she said, holding the bit of fluff toward Doris, "is my Fredericka."

Doris slunk back. What was it? A lemur?

Fredericka barked, a high-pitched, surprisingly loud squeak of a bark.

Doris looked from what she now recognized as a dog to her sister to the dog back to her sister and, divining what was expected of her, she tentatively held out her hand and touched the dog's fluffy body. It squealed at her and she pulled her hand back, but in that brief touch she had felt the soft fur and the birdlike body, fluttering and shivering, beneath.

"Is it cold?" she asked. "It's shivering."

"Good God," Natalie said again, looking back at the flyer. "How can anyone be so cruel? 'Canines'? And threatening the poor little things. Of course you've shown this to that councilman friend of yours."

"Oh, yes," Doris said meekly.

Harvey had been standing beside her silently. But now he said, "Doris has devoted herself to this," grinned at his wife, gave her arm a reassuring squeeze, and went off to check the score.

Doris watched him go as Natalie handed Fredericka to her and explained that the dog was a teacup Pomeranian and could actually fit into a teacup, though not a traditional-size one but definitely one of the café latte–size things people used nowadays.

Doris barely heard her. She was still shaken by the terrible misunderstanding that had almost been understood. Harvey had protected her. Like a knight, he'd stood up for her honor and kept her secret.

Natalie sneezed and put Fredericka back in her apron pocket, exchanging the dog for a Kleenex.

"Doesn't Harvey look handsome tonight?" Doris said as her balding husband walked off with his familiar stooping shuffle.

"Harvey?" her sister said, a little surprised, blowing her nose.

"Yes," Doris said softly, almost reverently. "Harvey."

twenty-five

"I don't just mean the dog"

The sun seemed to have given up almost entirely, barely bothering with the short winter days. On this particular short winter Saturday, Polly and Laura were walking beneath the sad, leaden, gray sky, returning from a shopping trip to the Lower East Side. The air was cold without being invigorating. Anonymous bundled figures passed one another in shadowy haste.

"This is what hell would be like if hell wasn't hot," Polly said. "Or freezing. If hell was just . . . not nice."

Laura did not bother to respond, but Polly didn't mind. She was pleased with her formulation and smiling to herself, which may have been why she walked past Jody without noticing her.

Jody saw her young friend from half a block away and had been about to greet her, going so far as to widen her eyes and open her mouth the way one does before calling out a hello, but seeing that Polly didn't notice her she relaxed, closed her mouth, and continued on her way. She had been forced to attend a performance of a cellist who was an old friend, and now she was hurrying guiltily home to Beatrice.

Even before she opened the door, she knew the dog was dead. There was something missing as she turned the key, a shuffle of old paws, a jingling of tags—a welcome. She found Beatrice lying on her new dog bed, her big head on her curled front paws. Her eyes were closed. Jody lay down on the floor beside her and sobbed.

She did not leave the apartment for days after that. Someone came from the vet and took Beatrice's corpse away, but Jody stayed. Everett called several times to ask how Beatrice was, but she did not pick up the phone, letting him talk to the answering machine. Her parents called and she forced herself to speak to them in a calm, affable voice so that they would not feel the need to call again anytime soon. She sat in Simon's chair day after day trying to ignore the grueling notes of the piano lessons upstairs as she looked out at the grim winter garden. She slept in Simon's bed, or tried to, tossing and tangling herself in the sheets, staring at the dark ceiling, clutching pillows to her face to muffle the sounds of her crying, which was so frequent and so violent as to alarm even herself. She ordered her meals from the coffee shop and then could not eat. The school was told she had the flu, because how, she thought, can I tell them I must mourn my dog?

After a week she went outside and walked where she had once walked Beatrice, roaming through the bare muddy park, sitting on cold benches. The lake was dull, dun colored and claustrophobic, the trees sodden and gloomy. Even the birds, just a few crows, struck Jody as Gothic, funereal almost, with their black silhouettes and harsh cries. She crept back to the apartment and lay on the floor, trying to imagine what Beatrice's last thoughts might have been. But she didn't know what dogs thought on the best of days. She didn't know what anyone thought, really. Jody put her face on the dog bed, purchased to make Beatrice's last days more comfortable, which she had not been able to bring herself to move. After a few minutes, she got up and looked around at the room in which she had spent so much time. She was moving back to her own apartment the next day and thought she had better begin packing up what had migrated from there to Simon's in the last few months. She wondered if she should take the dog bed home with her. It was made of memory foam and covered in a pink and brown stripe. Of course she would take it with her. It was Beatrice's bed. She couldn't leave it here. And she certainly could not throw it away. Would that strike others as odd, a large pink and brown dog bed in a small apartment with no dog?

There are no others to be struck, she thought, and began carefully packing Beatrice's chew toys in a small duffel.

George was at that moment rushing from the subway to the restaurant. He had spent the day in Westchester working with an unruly wheaten terrier who belonged to a friend of Alexandra's mother. Bored and underexercised in her own fenced-in backyard, the dog was both rambunctious and frightened on those rare occasions when she was taken out on the street. Suburbia was difficult and unnatural even for pets, George thought.

He walked quickly down Broadway, breathing the thin, bitter air. The sky had gone from its daytime color of dirt to sad winter darkness. People huddled and huffed in their drab, bulky coats. And George was filled with joy. That morning he had joined the Association of Pet Dog Trainers. He had registered for a seminar called New Dog Trainer Development. I am a New Pet Dog Trainer, he thought, shaking his head in disbelief, then pulling his wool hat lower over his ears. And at the ASPCA, where he'd begun volunteering, the trainer he assisted had offered him a real part-time job. He, George, the lousy waiter and mediocre bartender, the drifter, the secret prodigy without portfolio.

"Because, George," she said, "I think you're, well, I think you're . . . gifted."

At last, George thought, almost shyly, looking at his feet as he scuffed across the street that sparkled unexpectedly, a sprinkle of mica in the asphalt. At last, at last.

He arrived at work twenty minutes late, and Jamie gave him a forlorn look but said nothing. George hoped that he would soon be able to quit this job, but he was not ready to get fired. He vowed he would be more careful in scheduling his freelance dog training and made himself look particularly busy, arranging glasses and wiping down the bar with great energy. Just as he began to slice a lemon, Jody came in. He hadn't seen her in weeks. She looked terrible, thin and pale, with dark circles around her eyes. He wanted to ask her if she had been ill, but he wondered if that was like asking someone if she were pregnant, when in fact she might just be fat.

Jody sat at the bar and ordered Jack Daniel's, in memory of Simon, and some lamb chops, in defiance of him.

"Beatrice died," she said to George. "My Beatrice."

George looked down at the floor where Howdy used to lie, and he thought that at least the awful visit of the Sanitarian had brought about this one good thing: no robust puppy lying there, an affront to Jody in her grief. Even Jamie's dogs, no longer allowed to snore lazily on the floor beside George's feet, though less threatening because, in George's eyes, less beautiful, might have added to Jody's misery.

"I'm so sorry," he said.

Jody thanked him for his concern, but she didn't seem to want to talk, so George returned to his bartending duties, which had progressed to cutting up little pieces of lime. The smell of the lime made him cheerful in spite of Jody. He couldn't help but be cheerful. Yesterday he had gone to Brooklyn to teach Jolly how to jump through a yellow hula hoop that he had carried out with him on the train to the admiration of a small boy sitting opposite him. Today, as antic as a clown, he felt as though he would like to jump through hoops himself.

"I don't know what I would do without you," Alexandra had said to him when the training session was over and Jolly had stretched out on the rug.

"I haven't done anything," George said, wondering how long the poor dog would be able to rest so peacefully. An hour? Three hours? Fifteen minutes? Perhaps the hula hoop had tired him out, and he would sleep all night. Perhaps not.

"I don't mean the dog," she said. "I don't just mean the dog."

And he had grabbed her and kissed her, as he had wanted to do for months, and she had kissed him back.

After work tonight he would pick her up downtown at her job, and they would ride on the subway to Brooklyn. They had all day tomorrow to spend together, lying in bed beneath the window framing the Statue of Liberty.

Doris stood in the doorway of the restaurant with an expression of faint disapproval on her face. That bartender was daydreaming, as usual. Jamie really ought to run a tighter ship. She had done what she could to encourage him, to put his house in order, but the rest was up to him, surely.

She noticed the woman at the bar, who looked vaguely familiar, and though Doris couldn't place her, she had a nagging feeling that she did not trust her. Still, she might try to recruit her for the campaign. City councilwoman. It had a nice ring to it. Of course Mel was not pleased, and perhaps it was a bit disloyal after all he had done for her, but there was no stopping progress, and when the school had suggested she might consider retirement, the idea of running for political office had come to her, and she had not been able to shake it.

"How do you do?" she said to the woman, a sad, lonely-looking soul. Doris thought she must have startled her, for the woman shrank back, almost in fear. "You live in the neighborhood, don't you?" Doris continued, and as she waited for her soup to take home to Harvey, she told the silent woman of the upcoming primary and gave her a leaflet laying out her platform.

Jody stared at her in disbelief. This was the woman in the white SUV, the euthanizer of pit bulls, the restaurant scourge, the tattletale whistle-blower snitch, her nightmarish nemesis, her sworn enemy, yet Doris was chatting and smiling and soliciting her interest in some local political race. She thought of all the times Beatrice had peed on the tires of the big car. What a good dog Beatrice had been, heading for the car as if by instinct. Jody watched, rather than listened, with horrified fascination as Doris spoke. The face, orange as a tangerine; small, suspicious eyes; a wagging finger; and then . . . from the front of her coat, in the gap between two buttons, at a level where a woman's breast might reasonably be expected to reside, a small furry head suddenly appeared.

"Fredericka!" said Doris. She petted the little head. "Are you getting too stuffy in there?"

Fredericka gave a high-pitched yelp.

Jody could not help but laugh. It was the first time she had laughed in a long time.

"My sister gave her to me. Isn't she adorable? Natalie was allergic to her. Who could be allergic to little Fredericka? I never appreciated doggies until my Fredericka came to live with me, did I, Fredericka? No, I didn't. Poor, poor Auntie Doris did not . . ."

"Dogs are not allowed here," Jody said, her voice dripping, she hoped, with sarcasm. "Anymore," she added pointedly.

"I took her to school with me, too, and the headmaster didn't want you there, either, did he, Fredericka? But we paid no attention to him, no attention at all."

Jody stared at the woman babbling in baby talk to the

teacup Pomeranian lodged in her coat. Perhaps she was testing Jamie's compliance with the health codes. Or was she merely insane?

"No dogs," George said wearily from the other end of the bar.

"Dog?" Doris replied innocently, pushing the little fur face back into the fur coat. "Dog?"

Jody watched with relief as her enemy and her enemy's fur coat and the illicit rat-size dog it sheltered left the restaurant, then she finished her dinner in silence, missing Beatrice and fondly remembering the desecration of the white SUV.

Everett saw her sitting there with a faraway expression and he hesitated before joining her. Jody had not answered his calls, which had made him think of her all the more. In fact, he had not been able to stop thinking of her. He'd felt so protective of her that Thanksgiving night. Her vulnerability had both saddened him and appealed to him. Her manner, once so friendly and obliging, had changed so completely, and he sympathized with her, for he, too, had lost a lover and had lost a dog.

Here she was now, still vulnerable, still intimidating in her vulnerability, but the week of unreturned phone calls had strengthened his resolve. He sat beside her. He kissed her on the cheek.

"God, it's good to see you," he said.

Jody looked surprised, though pleased.

"I've been thinking about you," he said. "You and Beatrice. Nonstop."

"She died," Jody said.

"I was afraid of that. I mean, when you didn't answer your phone . . ."

I could have been away, Jody thought. On a trip, she added

defiantly. But that was absurd, she knew, and Everett had been thinking of her. Of her and of Beatrice.

"I'm sorry," she said. "I should have called you. It's just . . ."

"I understand," Everett said.

Jody looked at Everett. He wasn't smiling. He wasn't handsome. He wasn't a rose or a god. He was serious, he was tender, he was holding her hand.

"Yes," she said, and again she seemed surprised. "Yes, I think you do."

Epilogue

Jody waited a few weeks before giving Everett the blue sweater she had made for him so many months before. She sometimes suspected that Everett was not as good a person as Simon. He was certainly not as good a lover, but she was in love with him and she realized she didn't really mind. I'm happy to report that they got married in July and adopted a dog, a willowy mutt they named Clio who sleeps on the bed between them. Simon has moved into the lovely cottage with its even lovelier garden in Virginia where he is known as one of the most popular and active members of the hunt. George, you will not be surprised to learn, moved to Brooklyn with Alexandra beneath the benign gaze of the Statue of Liberty. He quit his job at the restaurant, began training dogs full-time, and I hear he is now earning a handsome living. His most important and most time-consuming and most frustrating client continues to be Jolly. Jamie's twins got into the preschool of their choice after a generous contribution. Doris, though, did not win a seat on the City Council. To console her, Harvey bought her another teacup Pomeranian, a male named Franklin, and she decided to breed them, which she did, selling one of the two puppies and keeping the other. Polly recovered from her grief at the loss of Chris, but has not yet, as far as I know, replaced him, though George still fixes her up on blind dates. Polly continues to live in the same apartment, where her friend Laura has taken over George's room and share of the rent, and on almost any morning of any season, you can see the two pretty girls walking their big, dancing dogs through the towering trees of Central Park.

Acknowledgments

I would like to thank my friend and editor Sarah Crichton and my friend and agent Molly Friedrich for their care and skill and sense of fun. I would also like to thank my son Tommy Denby for the title.

A Note About the Author

Cathleen Schine is the author of *The Love Letter* and *Rameau's Niece*, among other novels. She has contributed to *The New Yorker*, *The New York Review of Books*, *The New York Times Magazine*, and *The New York Times Book Review*. She lives in New York City.